Servants of Destiny

First Edition

Tammy Jo Eckhart

Servants of Destiny

First Edition

Published by The Nazca Plains Corporation
Las Vegas, Nevada
2006

ISBN: 978-1-887895-77-4

Published by

The Nazca Plains Corporation ®
4640 Paradise Rd, Suite 141
Las Vegas NV 89109-8000

PUBLISHER'S NOTE
Servants of Destiny is a work of fiction created wholly by *Tammy Jo Eckhart's* imagination. All characters are fictional and any resemblance to any persons living or deceased is purely by accident. No portion of this book reflects any real person or events.

Cover Photos, Blake Stephens
Editor, Blake Stephens

Dedication

This, my first novel, is dedicated to my husband, Tom, who works as my first and primary editor. Thank you for all your help in making my ideas clearer.

Acknowledgements

Besides my husband I want to thank several other people who have helped me with this novel.

First, a hug to my slave, Fox, whose work around my house gives me more time to spend writing and whose encouragement helps me stay focused when I feel down.

A "thank you" to Susan Wright for reading this novel and agreeing to write a blurb for it. I respect your work so much, Susan, and I was thrilled that you took the time out of your busy life to look at mine.

I want to say "thanks" to a few members of my fan site on Yahoo groups who have given me helpful feedback about this novel and other pieces of fiction I am always working on: Peter, May, Janine, John, and Cloudboy.

A "thank you" to my mother who gave me my creative writing talent even if she isn't too sure about the directions it takes me. My parents still love me and find my erotica to be "well-written" even if it isn't their thing.

Servants of Destiny

Tammy Jo Eckhart

Contents

Chapter One:
A New Journey

Marelda nodded at the bulletin posted in the town square. *That's what I need*, she thought, noting that a slave auction was scheduled. She recalled the words spoken to the Hilmer prince on his wedding night to Ariala, Mother of All, "She shall be your life, and you shall be her helper." *Perfect role for a slave, and perhaps this time it will be done correctly. I'd better hurry before the cream is taken.* Winding her way through the crowded city square, she pushed her way close to the auction block, where a young woman had just been sold.

"Argh, the quality of this stuff gets worse each season," an oily-looking yet richly-clothed merchant commented beside her.

The merchant's equally well-dressed and oily companion nodded. "Is your item up soon?" he asked. Marelda noted an evil twinkle in this man's eyes.

"Yes," the merchant replied with a sneer. "You'll teach him to run away from me, won't you, my dear Rozeny?"

"Aye, he'll wish he had stayed in your factory," Rozeny replied.

Marelda turned her attention back to the auction block, keeping her ears tuned to the two merchants so that she could learn more about this recaptured runaway. A live runaway was rare these days, especially in Vanhilmer. "A thief who isn't a thief" was the way the prophecy read.

After two sad-looking twins had been sold to a fat tavern owner, the two merchants beside her stirred and nodded at the block.

Marelda looked and saw the young man they were referring to. He wasn't terribly tall, perhaps an inch or two above her. His curly black hair hung down to his waist and covered his face. His olive skin was just showing recent bruises, and the brand of "thief," a stylized letter T, was clear over his right breast, while the "runaway slave" brand, an R, showed on the left one. Even the illiterate masses would understand the marks and turn a runaway in for a reward. Runaways rarely got the opportunity to escape again, and the penalty was the royal mines, a harsh, brief life. The auctioneer brushed aside the slave's hair and revealed almost-black eyes that glared at the crowd in anger and ill-hidden fear.

Marelda glanced at the bracelet she wore, then back at the slave. She arched her eyebrows in surprise as the bracelet her tutor had given her glowed with a slight white haze. "But his hair and complexion are so dark," she pointed out softly, so the bracelet insisted with a tiny jolt of pain. With a sigh, she paid closer attention to the auctioneer's speech.

"... skilled in gem carving; and gentle on the eyes, eh?" the auctioneer laughed with a nod toward the evil merchant, whose mouth visibly watered at the sight of the slave.

"But he's branded!" a voice from the crowd shouted.

"Yes," the auctioneer stuttered with embarrassment, but quickly thought up a reply. "He was a runaway for five full years, but the army found him and returned him to his owner, Gandler Briehan." At this the auctioneer nodded to the merchant.

"He is as skilled today as he was when he ran away," the merchant declared. "See this ring," he announced, holding up a fat finger with a gaudy band around it. "He crafted this last night, under whip. Imagine what he will do for you after you break him down into his rightful place."

Marelda shook her head both at the obvious lie and in amazement that the crowd seemed to believe it. She turned her eyes back to the sales block and saw that the slave seemed to cast his most hateful glances toward his soon-to-be-former owner. The bracelet gave her another tiny jolt of pain insisting on its correctness.

"Now let's start the bidding on this fine lad, called Dolan. It will start at two hundred coppers!" the auctioneer announced.

Marelda watched and listened as the bidding increased to one silver, then ten silver, then a gold. Finally, only the evil merchant remained in the bidding at one gold and thirty silver. This merchant and the slave's former owner chuckled at their obvious victory.

"One-thirty going once," the auctioneer announced. "One-thirty going...."

"Ten gold!" Marelda called out suddenly.

"What?" the evil merchant squeaked in shock at this turn of

events. "Ten gold? For him?!" he growled at the woman, a forester by her dress, who dared bid against him.

"Are you sure you wish to bid on this?" the auctioneer asked the new bidder while he glanced at the merchants.

"My bid stands," Marelda answered, not returning the stares from the merchants and the crowd, which now tittered with excitement. Foresters were feared, but not so rare as to draw unwanted attention, both things the princess was counting on in her quest.

The auctioneer shrugged and announced the bid. He waited longer than normal, but the only response from the evil merchant was his snort of contempt. "Then we have a bid of ten gold going once, going twice ... sold to the forester-woman for ten gold."

Marelda stepped through the crowd opposite the merchants and signed the documents of sale. She watched the remainder of the auction from the edge of the crowd. Out of the corner of her eye, she saw her new possession watching her from the holding cage by the accountant's desk. *I hope this is right, Sigrid*, she thought with a glance at the bracelet, receiving a warm sensation from it in return. At least from the words used to sell him he fit the prophecy well. His dark hair and eyes even matched the Hilmer prince himself, just as she matched Ariala down to the birthmark on her left calf.

Marelda returned to the accountant's desk after the auction was over. "I've come to claim my property," she stated, handing the woman her copy of the sales contract.

The accountant looked over the contract, handed it back to the forester-woman, and whispered to one of her associates. This man went to the cage with two burly guards and brought forth the slave.

Marelda looked at the naked body, bruised and dirty, likely from a beating and a hard night in the auction pens, and spoke to the accountant. "Doesn't he come with anything?"

The accountant nodded and handed her a blood-stained loincloth.

"Wow, I really get my money's worth," she replied flatly, tossing the cloth to the slave, who caught it in one hand. "Put it on, boy. You're not for sale anymore. No need to display yourself to the entire world," Marelda ordered. She watched as he fastened the material over his groin and noted that his eyes stared back at her from under his bangs.

"You'll want him chained," the accountant stated. At the forester-woman's nod, the two guards chained his wrists so that they could be no more than six inches apart. One then pulled the boy's head upright by his hair while the other placed an iron collar with chain leash around his neck. The slave glared hatefully at the guards and the woman who'd bought him, but held his tongue.

Marelda refrained from smiling at the slave's obvious internal fight. He looked like he would kill any of them given a chance, but was wise enough to know there was no chance out here in public. When the final set of chains fastened his ankles to his wrists, Marelda handed the accountant a generous tip.

"Come on, boy. We have things to do," she instructed with a pull on the chain leash. The slave grunted once but followed at the longest distance the leash allowed.

The first stop was City Hall. Marelda stood in line with the other recent buyers, but when it was her turn at the window, she asked to see the manager in private. After a moment, a portly, richly-dressed man emerged from an office and motioned the forester-woman and her slave inside.

"I hope this is important, woman. I dislike to dirty my hands in such affairs," the manager sniffed as he sat down.

Marelda placed her right hand flat on his desk and smiled.

At the sight of the royal signet ring, the manager's eyes blinked several times. "I'm sorry, my Lady," he began.

"Please, I just need to properly register this slave," Marelda interrupted quickly, her eyes narrowed, an edge to her voice warning against further talk.

The manager nodded. "Yes, of course. I'll do it myself." He rummaged through his desk and found the forms and a pen. "May I ask your full title, Lady?" he whispered only loud enough for only the princess to hear; the slave was staying at the maximum length the leash allowed.

Marelda took the pen and wrote out the information on the forms herself. Then she placed her seal on the bottom of the form with her signet ring by pressing it into the tiny blob of softened red wax the manager supplied. "Where do I go for a brand?" she asked softly, placing a gold piece in his palm.

"The blacksmith can help with that. He is merely a few stores down and across the street; his sign is visible for blocks," the manager replied with a smile.

"You've been very helpful," Marelda said out loud, adding a bow for effect. She led her property out of City Hall and crossed the road to the blacksmith.

"You're in luck," the smith announced when the forester-woman and her slave arrived. "You just missed the big rush." He wiped his hands on his apron and walked over to the slave. "Hold still, boy," he ordered when the slave stepped back and tossed his head.

"Be still," Marelda ordered gently. She looked back into the frightened dark eyes that seemed to be begging her not to let this rough smith touch him. "Relax and accept it," she suggested firmly.

At those words, the slave looked away and seemed to fade into himself.

"So what do you want removed or placed on him?" the blacksmith asked.

"I think we'll leave the cuffs around his wrists, but the metal needs to be replaced. Something strong and rust-resistant," she stated. She suddenly yanked on the lead chain and brought the slave stumbling toward her. "You're not going to be stupid enough to run again, are you, boy?" she asked but only received a dark glare in return. Marelda placed one finger on the large "R" on his left breast. "The next one goes on the left cheek, on your face and you'll die in the mines," she clarified. "So you're not going to run, are you?"

The boy shook his head silently and backed up a step.

"Trusting them is a big mistake," the smith commented as he took the leash from the forester-woman. "Of course, I suppose we'd all do the same in their place," he added with an odd philosophical tone to his words.

Marelda nodded slightly and leaned in closer to the blacksmith. "And a brand on the right butt cheek," Marelda whispered into the smith's ear. When he opened his mouth to protest and likely demand a high price, she flashed her signet ring. "I have my own marker," she added as she patted her pouch.

The smith nodded and led the slave over to his work table. "Lie down on your stomach, lad," he ordered. This elicited a sudden burst of energy from the slave, who pulled on his lead chain and grunted with the effort to free himself.

Marelda stepped back and leaned against the wall of the shop. She watched as the blacksmith took up his short horse whip and the slave fell into a petrified crouch in the dirt after a few lashes. She nodded when the smith looked at her for approval.

The smith pulled the slave up onto the table. He locked the wrist and ankle cuffs to the legs of the table so that the boy was forced to lie stomach down. The slave was now silent and placid. "Now just try to relax, boy. It will be over soon," the smith said in his gentlest voice.

Marelda joined the smith. She handed her branding mark to the smith, who fastened it cunningly onto the end of his stoker. She watched as it was heated in the coals until it glowed bright red.

"You may want to watch him," the smith cautioned under his breath.

Marelda nodded and walked to the other end of the table. She brushed back the slave's bangs to find him staring into space. Even waving her hand in front of his eyes, did not cause a response. She braced her hands on his shoulder blades just in case.

At the application of the brand, the slave bucked and screamed. His eyes rolled in terror, but he found his gaze captured by the forester-woman's own bright green eyes. Soon the pain died down and he felt the branding iron removed.

"That's so no one will get any ideas about either taking you or helping you run off," Marelda stated. She nodded to the smith and returned to wait by the wall.

In about half an hour, the smith and the slave approached the forester-woman. The smith handed back the branding mark and stepped aside as the slave stepped forward. "Turn around, boy, and show her our work," the smith said.

The slave turned around slowly. The ankle cuffs and collar had left only the slightest mark, most likely because of his earlier struggle. The wrist cuffs had been replaced with new ones made of a silvery metal.

"Stop a moment," Marelda said as she placed a hand on the slave's shoulder, getting another fearful toss of his head in response. She walked around him, then knelt down and looked at the brand closely. "A fine job," she told the smith as she rose and took out her money pouch. "How much will that be?"

"Well, now. For the materials and time, that would be," the smith paused to calculate in his head, "ninety-five copper?"

Marelda took out a silver coin from her purse and handed it to him. "Keep the change," she said. Turning to her slave, she looked into his eyes and directed, "Follow me, and don't even think of trying to run."

The slave waited for a second, then followed his new owner out of the blacksmith's shop and down the street. He ran into her when she suddenly stopped in an alleyway.

"Hold out your hands," she ordered. When the slave complied, Marelda took a small packet from her purse. She sprinkled the wrist cuffs with the fine powder inside the packet.

The slave watched closely as the forester-woman now recited several words over his cuffs, surely magic if the rumors of her kind, green-eyed and female, were even slightly true. The odd green light which arose around her hands and the cuffs as she chanted seemed to concur with the rumors, and suddenly a bolt of pure pain shot through his arms, driving him to his knees. He gasped as she pulled his head up by his hair.

"Now those won't come off until you die. And if you ever run off," Marelda continued in an even, calm voice, "I know the spell to cause pain like you just felt, only one hundred times worse. Stand up and follow me," she ordered.

Marelda laughed inside, as she felt the anger mixed with horror radiating from her property as he followed her back to her hotel room. She winked at the clerk, who stared at them as they went upstairs.

Once in the room she took him into the bathroom and turned the faucet on the tub. "Get out of that cloth and into the tub." She took the rag from him and threw it into the trash bin in the corner. "Make sure you scrub yourself well. You don't want me to have to do it," she stated before leaving the room.

"Damn!" the slave muttered as he stepped into the tub of steaming water. He groaned as water covered him, the three brands marking him as slave, runaway, and now someone's property still tender. He turned off the water and picked up the scrub brush. Looking at it for a moment, he decided to place it back on the nearby table and instead took the washcloth along with the ample bar of soap.

The slave scrubbed himself for a few moments, then finally broke down in tears. "Damn fool!" he cursed himself. He went over the entire capture in his mind for the millionth time. At the sound of the forester's voice in the other room, he quickly sniffed back his tears and resumed his cleaning efforts.

"Your hair as well," Marelda stated as she returned to the bathroom. She pulled up a chair and sat by the tub.

The slave glanced at his owner as he rinsed himself off. Then he took the offered bottle from her and poured the yellow liquid into his hair. He wrinkled up his nose at the odd smell the liquid sent forth.

"Work it in good," Marelda instructed him with a chuckle. "It's medicated, so it will kill anything you picked up on the run or in those cages." She stood up when his head was a globe of suds. She filled a glass with water from the tub. "I'm going to dump water over your head, so close your mouth," she said before doing so. She rinsed the suds out of his hair with several more glassfuls, then sat back down.

The slave sat in the water, which had now cooled a great deal, and glanced at his owner. He opened then closed his mouth.

"Now I believe that if you were mute, the auctioneer would have told the crowd." Marelda rested her arms on the back of the chair and relaxed as she spoke. "So I know you must be able to talk, and I suspect from the movement of your mouth a second ago that you want to talk. So go ahead, boy, talk."

The slave mumbled something.

"You have to speak up, boy."

"Do you have any orders?" he said, looking directly at her for a brief second. He placed the washcloth on the side of the tub and the soap in its dish as he spoke, trying to appear calm and fearless.

"Hear that?" she asked no one. "That is a nice voice." She held out a towel. "Let the water out and dry off. I have some people coming to see you. Don't worry," she added as his body went rigid with fright at her words, "they aren't going to do anything painful to you."

The slave stepped out of the tub after his owner exited the room. He released the water from the tub then shook out most of the water in his hair over the tub, before rubbing it with the towel after his body was dried. All the time his ears were straining to keep track of his buyer. He stood up straight and walked into the other room, where his owner stood by the window.

Marelda didn't even turn around when a knock came at the door a few moments later. "Get that, Dolan," she directed.

The slave flinched at the sound of his name. He hadn't been called that while he was running, giving himself different names at different times. It reminded him of his slavery but also surprised him because he expected a new name with a new owner as he heard often happened after a sale. Today's auction had been his first. After a second of shock, he went to the door and opened it.

"Well, that is some greeting," the man who stood there replied with a grin.

The slave stepped back, standing behind the door as he opened it. Dolan felt his face burning in embarrassment. He closed the door but remained by it after the man entered.

The man bowed to the forester-woman, who was still looking out of the window. "You sent for a barber, Ma'am?"

Marelda now turned around; in her hands were a small jar and a piece of paper. "Yes. I was told that you are the best barber in the town."

The man bowed again. "It is kind of people to say so," the barber replied. He stood and contemplated the forester-woman for a moment, then nodded at the hat which covered her head so completely that no hair was visible and sighed. "I can fix even the worst of haircuts, Ma'am."

"I'm sure," Marelda said, handing the barber the paper and jar. "But it is my slave who needs a haircut."

The barber turned back to the naked slave, letting his eyes openly sweep over the naked body. "And what would you like done?"

"The instructions are written there," Marelda indicated the written words on the paper he now held. She reached into her purse as the barber read.

"I cannot do this," he began.

"It is all quite legal, I assure you," Marelda stated.

The barber frowned, "Borderline legal. I take a risk."

Marelda held out a gold coin. "Will this lessen the risk?"

The barber took the coin, more than he could make in two weeks. He looked at the jar. "Let the risk fall on your shoulders, then," he stated.

"Agreed," Marelda informed him. "I know what it does," she added when the barber merely eyed the jar.

"Very well," the barber agreed, stowing the coin in his purse. "We'll start with the body then," he told the slave, as he faced him and grinned.

Dolan looked from the barber to his owner and then back. His right fingers tapped nervously on his thigh as he struggled not to do anything he might later regret. He opened and closed his mouth a few times.

"Lie down on your back, please," the barber directed as he

approached with the straight razor from his bag.

"What are you going do?" Dolan asked as he backed up into the door.

"Shave your entire body," Marelda said as she sat on the edge of the bed so she was nearer the action. "Don't worry, that's legal. Your facial hair will be trimmed as will that on your head. It will make you more attractive," she added with a small smile.

Dolan's face fell as the question of why she had bought him seemed to be answered by this information. His eyes focused on the space directly in front of him and his body moved to lie down where the barber pointed. He lay there under the razor, moving his legs apart as directed, lifting up or parting his genitals and ass, and flipping onto his back on command. He glared at his owner once but when she offered her hand to help him stand, he turned away.

When he stood on command, the contents of the small jar, a sweet smelling lotion, were spread all over his skin where the hair had been trimmed and shaved. After a few seconds a slight tingling sensation filled his body. "Well, no need for you to ever have this experience again," he heard the barber mumble as he finished cutting his bangs.

The barber stepped back and nodded at his work. "Do you approve, Forester?" he asked.

Marelda stood and walked around her property, noting that his eyes followed her every move. "Wonderful. You deserve this," she said, offering the barber a silver coin.

The barber shook his head. "Ah, I would waive any more money for an hour with him," the man grinned as he bargained with lust-inspired words and touched the slave's hip.

Marelda narrowed her eyes at the same time her property did. "Sorry, I just bought him. It would hardly be fair to rent him out before I've had the chance to sample him myself," she explained.

The barber nodded and picked up his equipment. He took the other coin and waved off the slave as he opened the door. "I'd best leave, then. Thank you, Madame Forester."

Marelda shook her head as the door shut and tilted her head to one side. "Come on, let's see what you look like, Dolan," she said, grabbing his limp hand and steering him back into the bathroom, where a large mirror stood.

Dolan looked at his reflection, startled at the smoothness of his tanned olive skin. His body had not been particularly hairy, so the pubic area was the first thing which caught his eyes. When even slightly aroused, he knew that it would be most evident now that he was destined to live most of his life naked in some brothel. That was the only place that made sense now that he'd been reduced to the ideal form for a male sex slave.

He glanced at his owner and wondered just who she worked for. He turned his attention back to the mirror and examined his face. The tiny bit of black hair left on his chin and right above his lip by the barber was only the amount that had grown back during his few days in captivity. The facial hair, the sign of slavery for men, had been the first thing he'd gotten rid of after running away. Even the small amount there made his stomach tighten at his hated servitude. His bangs had been trimmed and the rest of his wild curls cut back to only shoulder length.

"I think you look very nice," Marelda commented. "Not having to worry about removing all that hair will save you lots of time," she stated. "Ah," she sighed and turned to the main room as another knock sounded at the door, "the tailor must be here."

Dolan stood in the door between both rooms and watched as the forester-woman let in the town's finest tailor and her slave girl. He almost placed his hands in front of himself to hide his cock, then decided to cross his arms over his chest. If this was to be his new lot in life, then why fight it? However, he couldn't look directly at the other slave, who was staring openly at him. The girl fingered her short hair, the sign of slavery for women, nervously as she glanced down at her own feet.

"You sent for me, Ma'am?" the tailor asked as politely as she could.

"Yes," Marelda motioned to her slave, and he joined them. "I just bought him, so he needs some clothes."

The tailor sniffed. "What you want is a common clothing store, Forester," she said.

"No," Marelda took out a gold coin and held it up. "I want clothes to my specifications, and I want them immediately. Can't you do that?" she challenged tossing the coin into the slave girl's hands.

The tailor looked at her slave, who after a bite on the coin nodded its authenticity. "I can do what you ask." The tailor now looked more closely at the slave and smiled. "I can see that you need — special clothing for this one."

"Good," Marelda said. She handed the tailor a piece of paper and another gold coin. "I want two pairs riding pants, one riding vest, two work shirts, one all-weather jacket, and the hardest pair of boots you have."

The tailor nodded as she took out a pen. She motioned to her slave, and the girl bent over so that her mistress could use her back to write on. "Did you have specific colors for these?" the tailor asked.

"No, I don't care about colors for these items; however, the next items I'd like your advice on, please," Marelda flattered the woman with both her words and a smile which she learned at court could bend even the most crusty old administrator to her whim without him being aware of it.

"Yes, Ann can take his measurements while we discuss these other items," the tailor agreed. She handed her slave a tape measure and a working pad and pencil. "Now for his coloring I'd suggest very basic tones," the tailor said.

"I want some color," Marelda stated; she glanced to find her slave moving obediently under the other's direction as he was carefully measured. "How about a green? That's my favorite color."

The tailor shook her head. "Well it may look good on you, Madame, but it will make him look sickly." She placed her hand on her chin and thought for a moment. "Red might add some fire to him."

Marelda blinked at the suggestion, which fit so well with the old religion of the prince of Hilmer, then slowly nodded. "All right. I can live with red," she said with a tight smile. "So the shirt is to be red, of your finest material."

"Of course. And the pants and vest a soft black leather?" the tailor asked, her pen poised over the list.

Marelda nodded. "And the boots? I hear that color there is all the rage in the big cities," she commented, thinking of the highest-level slaves in the palace.

"Yes," the tailor replied as she scribbled on the list. "Is that where he'll be working?"

"A very upper-class establishment," Marelda simply replied. "Red as well, then?"

"Yes, and," the tailor paused and prompted both with her voice and a shake of her head as her slave now measured the boy's groin area. The tailor frowned, because usually her girl was gifted at getting some reaction from male clients, but this slave reacted like a eunuch.

"Underthings?"

"Just whatever for the traveling clothes, but something, ah, interesting for the others. Whatever you think is best," Marelda added with a smile.

The tailor nodded. She took the work pad from her slave, who had returned. "Ann, go and get any items on this list that we have in stock. Bring them back here immediately," she ordered.

The slave girl bowed and hurried from the room.

"How much will this cost?" Marelda asked, watching the tailor circle Dolan slowly.

"Oh, I believe that two and half gold will cover all materials and work. The common items will be delivered to you as soon as possible. The custom-made ones should be ready in a few hours, and those can also be delivered to you, of course," the tailor added, walking around the male slave. As she paused to examine the slave's ass better, she felt the customer's hand around her arm.

"You've been most helpful," Marelda insisted, "but I don't want to keep you from your work. I have a busy schedule to keep. Thank you," she added, pushing the tailor out the door with one more gold coin in her hand. "Keep the change," she called back through the door. She found her slave looking at her with a sad resentment drawn in every part of his face.

Dolan looked at himself in the mirror again, wondering if he'd fit in with the high-class whores she'd referred to earlier. He was trying not to stare at his owner, who was taking a bath in the same room. The green eyes were beautiful and bright, but since most free folk had light hair and eyes, it merely reinforced her natural status above him. Her hair, well, that had been a shock to say the least. The auburn curls had tumbled out after she had removed her hat. He would have bolted for the door at that moment, thinking it his best opportunity to run, but the hair had raised many questions. Red hair was very rare, usually only found among the highest of the aristocracy. But that didn't fit with his conclusions about working for a brothel, so he forced that fact to the back of his mind. Since she asked him to get dressed while she washed and didn't object to his presence in the same room, he had taken the time to observe her more closely.

"Do those clothes fit well?" Marelda asked as she soaked in the warm water. After hiding her identity from everyone she could, she had decided to at least give her property a hint. But the hair was as much information as he was getting without direct questions.

"Yes, they fit well," Dolan replied stiffly, looking at the brown leather riding pants and vest, the hard boots, and the cream cotton shirt. The underwear felt uncomfortable, since he had never bothered to steal such items while on the run and had certainly never had any in the factory where he had been raised. The clothes were better than anything he had ever taken from some hapless person's clothesline. But clothing didn't change who he'd become again when everything else about him screamed out "slave" and "whore."

"Good," Marelda stated. She stood up and wrapped a towel around herself. She opened the tub drain and dried her own shoulder-length curls with another towel.

"What should I call you?" the slave suddenly asked.

"Well, my name is Mar...y. It's Mary," she quickly amended. "So as long as you do as you're told, I don't mind if you call me that."

"OK," Dolan replied, nodding as if this confirmed his conclusions. "May I ask where you're taking me, Mary?"

"You've gotten your voice back, I hear," Marelda commented as she went into the main room. She picked up another piece of paper and handed it to him with a gold coin. "Take these to the blacksmith and bring back the package that I ordered earlier. Then go to the general store and get yourself a backpack and a bedroll. I expect you to be back in no more than a half an hour," she added.

Dolan looked at the money and paper. "You trust me to do this, Mary?" His voice sounded both awed and suspicious.

"I told you that those cuffs will guarantee your obedience," she reminded him. "I trust the cuffs, and I trust my magic. I'll trust that you aren't stupid."

Dolan nodded and left the hotel room. Once outside, he walked through the crowd in the cautious, hunched manner he was used to as a slave and then as a runaway. He went to the general store first and bought the cheapest bedroll and largest backpack he could find. Taking the change, he cut across town through the alleys and waited in the entrance of the blacksmith shop, watching the man at work.

After a few moments the smith glanced at the slave and grunted, "You certainly look different, boy. You've come to pick up the package?"

Dolan nodded and stepped into the shop. He held out the paper and the remainder of the coins.

The smith took a small bundle wrapped in oiled leather from a shelf and handed back a few coppers of change. "You're very rude, boy," the smith stated as the slave took the items silently, still looking him in the eyes.

Dolan lowered his eyes and started a calculated apology. "I'm sorry, Sir. I did not mean to offend you."

The smith looked the boy over closely and snorted in approval of his looks, now clearly visible after his bath. The slave was now a temptation, but that brand he'd placed on him was a clear "do not touch" sign, so he simply returned to his anvil.

Dolan stepped a little closer and asked quietly, "Sir, is the package to her specifications? I do not mean to imply that you would not do an excellent job," the slave added when the smith glared back at him, the hammer poised over a piece of hot metal. "Only, such an important person might get very angry if something were wrong," he suggested, hoping for information.

The smith's eyes blurred with fear for a moment, then he nodded. "Don't worry, boy. It's done perfectly. I wouldn't risk the wrath of one of them," he added, then started pounding on the hot metal with his hammer.

Dolan bit his tongue and went back outside. He counted the coins in his hand, and headed toward a food cart just a bit down the street. Around the corner of the smith's shop, a voice called to him. He turned to find the blacksmith's apprentice whispering to him. The slave moved in closer, not even slightly surprised that a free man would want to do business with him. Being a slave hardly mattered when coins were in your hand.

"Hey, boy," the apprentice whispered. "For just a few coins, I can get those off for you."

Dolan let his eyes glance across the cuffs, which the shirt left just visible to public view. "Why would you do that?"

"Let's just say that I got a soft spot in my heart for freedom," the apprentice said. He held up the metal clippers.

"How much would it cost?" Dolan asked, allowing the coins to be visible enough for the apprentice to count them.

"Why I would do it for a mere seventeen coppers," the apprentice named the exact amount in the slave's hand. "And I'll throw in getting rid of the beard, too," he added when the slave turned away slightly.

Dolan thought about the threat Mary had made. He considered it carefully, then handed the apprentice the coins. "Do it. What have I got to lose?"

Dolan sat down on a tree stump and held out his hands. The cuffs weren't tight and the metal cutter slipped under them easily. But as soon as they closed on the cuffs, the slave's body convulsed with the pain he had felt earlier, only a hundred times stronger, shooting through his entire body.

"Oh, Lady and the Lord too!" the apprentice yelled as he jumped back, letting the metal cutter fall to the dirt. The slave slumped onto the ground and jerked a few times before he moaned and struggled to his feet. "You get away from here!" the apprentice yelled, tossing the coins into the dirt and running into the shop.

Dolan knelt down in the dirt, trying to catch his breath as he retrieved the coins. After a minute, he rose to his feet and shook his head to clear it. "I guess I'm stuck," he whispered to himself. He walked very slowly back to the hotel, the full amount of change in his pockets.

As soon as he entered the hotel, strong arms grabbed him. The cuffs had drained him of fight, so he just let the two men, slaves of the inn most likely, drag him through the hotel and out to the stable, where the forester-woman and a large man, a professional slave beater by the look of his clothes, waited with a horse whip.

"Take the clothes off!" Marelda ordered.

Dolan felt the two men remove his clothes quickly but carefully. Then he was pushed against a pole at the center of the court. His hands were tied tightly above his head, making him arch up onto his toes. He pressed his body against the wood; the previous day's lesson at the jeweler's factory had taught him to use it as a brace. She knew. It couldn't be because he was a few minutes late. No, she knew that he had tried to remove the cuffs. "I'm sorry, Mary," he said when she walked up to him. His head smashed into the pole from the force of her slap against the back of his head.

"You've lost that privilege," Marelda snarled. She gripped his curls and yanked his head back. "If you have a question about me, you ask me, not anyone else," she growled softly so that the others wouldn't hear.

The slave looked at her in surprise. Before he could answer, she stepped back and the crack of the whip sounded. His body arched with the pain. He tried to move with the lash, but his body rebelled and pulled away from the pole, trying to free itself.

"Count it!" Marelda ordered with a stomp of one foot for emphasis.

"One," the slave stated and took one quick breath before the next stroke hit. "Two!" he squeaked.

At the fifteenth Marelda held up her hand, and the whipping stopped. She moved to the pole and touched the slave's head, eliciting a weak attempt to flinch out of reach if possible. "I didn't hear that last number very clearly," she stated.

"Fifteen," he repeated. He had taken double that amount of punishment the day before, but the bruises and scars were fresh, so these strokes seemed twice as hard. "I'm sorry, Lady," he said and groaned when she pulled his head back by his hair again.

"That's not a proper title for a common woman to aspire to," she told him after a pause to remind herself of her mission. "Try again."

Dolan licked his lips and said the female equivalent to the word that even the severest punishment at the jeweler's shop had not been able to rip from him. "I'm sorry, Mistress. I'm very sorry," he sobbed.

Marelda stepped back and said, "He's had enough for now." The two men who had dragged him there now released his hands, then half-carried, half-dragged him back up to her room, where they laid him on the wooden floor. She handed them their fee, which they would split with the innkeeper, and locked the door behind her. "Damn fool!" she cursed him as she threw his clothing and the packages he had purchased onto the bed.

She took a switch she had cut outside and tapped it on the floor in front of the slave's face. "That was for trying to remove the cuffs and for asking the smith leading questions about me. This is for the thought of running away," Marelda explained as she walked to the other end of him.

The slave screamed when the switch landed on the bottoms of his feet. He scrambled away as best he could, but the beating continued until he was backed into a corner, his feet tucked under him. Dolan whimpered as he panted and eyed the switch.

The forester-woman bent down, her hands poised on her knees, a look of wonder in her eyes. "That's never happened to you before," she guessed. "It's a very common punishment where I'm from," Marelda commented as she stood, picked up her own backpack then returned and knelt next to him. After a few seconds she found the small jar she wanted. "On your stomach," she ordered when he tried to crawl away.

When the slave was lying flat again, she rubbed the ointment into the bleeding cuts on his back and the stinging welts on his feet. "I wanted to leave here tomorrow, and now we may have to wait a day thanks to you!"

"I'll do what you command, Mistress," Dolan promised, clenching his teeth as the ointment seemingly burned into his flesh.

"You're damn right you will," Marelda emphasized. When she had finished with his wounds, she wiped off her hands on his legs and stood up. "I was going to take you downstairs to eat with me, but you're in no shape now."

Dolan watched her boots walk to the door as she went to leave the room. He heard her lock it behind her. Going without food was something he was used to, especially on the run. Sleep was a rarer commodity. He closed his eyes and tried to block the burning pain on his back and feet from his mind.

The slave slowly opened his eyes in the morning sunlight, somehow filtered instead of the direct rays he had awakened to while on the run. He blinked a few times, trying to remember where he was. The ground beneath him was not earth, his eyes and body informed him, but wooden planks. The hotel. He saw the forester's boots and pushed himself up to his elbows slowly, letting his eyes glance up at her frowning face, then back to the floor.

"So, you can move. Can you get up and get dressed?" Marelda asked coldly, tapping one foot impatiently.

Dolan pressed himself back onto his knees and took a deep breath. "Yes, Mistress," he replied; an angry edge to his voice betraying his disgust at using the title.

The forester-woman placed her hands on her hips for a moment then grabbed his clothes from the bed. These she tossed down to the floor in front of him. "Put them on, then, and bring your backpack and bedroll down to the lobby with you."

Dolan nodded as he watched her leave. Carefully he stood up and went into the bathroom. He looked at his face in the mirror and decided to risk taking the time to wash up a little. After washing off his body with a cloth, he relieved himself and double-checked his face. True to her word, the areas which had been shaved the previous day showed no signs of hair growth. *And she was right about you as well,* he thought as he looked at his wrist cuffs.

He returned to the main room and pulled on the underpants and shirt. His back was stiff, and the material of the shirt irritated his skin. Next he pulled the outer shirt over his head and tied the lacings. The pants required him to balance awkwardly on one sore foot at a time, but he managed to get them on. He sat on the bed and lifted each leg up to put the boots on. Finally, he swung into the vest. The coat he draped over one arm; the bedroll was already fastened to the bottom of the backpack, which he found contained other clothes, a lantern, some oil, and food he had not purchased. High-quality traveling supplies, he guessed. Wherever he was going, they would apparently take good care of his physical needs.

He groaned slightly as he walked down the stairs, the pack heavy on his tender back and feet. He feared that he'd be glad to be on his back in a brothel by the time this journey was over. The forester-woman waited for him by the reception desk. He paused at the bottom of the stairs until she nodded for him to approach.

"Ready to eat?" Marelda asked her slave.

"Yeah," he confirmed quietly. She took the backpack and coat from him and gave them to the desk clerk, who stowed them behind the desk. Her friendly smack on his back drew out a hiss of pain, but she only told him to move it.

The forester-woman and her slave went to a table in the corner. After a few words, the slave sat down also but didn't touch his menu. Frankly, he doubted he was supposed to, and his reading skills were minimal at best. The waitress came, and the forester-woman ordered for both of them.

"So," the forester said as she turned to her slave with a calm smile after the waitress left, "how long has it been since you ate?"

"About two and half days," Dolan replied. He felt very uncomfortable sitting at the table with her, this woman who could hurt him from miles away and seemed to know his every thought, this woman with mysterious red hair and an air of authority that made people obey. Back at the jeweler's all the slave children had eaten whatever they could grab from the kitchen as they were herded back to their cells at night. The rumor was that the adults actually got to sit down to one meal per day, but by the time he was sixteen his resentment had grown so strong that not even that promise could keep him from running off.

"Boy!" Marelda snapped her fingers in front of the slave's face, and he jumped back in his chair. "I asked you a question."

"I'm sorry. Would you repeat it, Mistress?" he pleaded flatly, cursing himself internally for letting his concentration waver. That was how slaves died; not being aware of everything and everyone around them and thus making mistakes. Owners were rarely tolerate of multiple mistakes, and he'd already made some big ones.

Marelda leaned back in her chair and repeated herself, "I was wondering if you really did work in a jewelry shop, or if that was a scam? Did you hear me this time?"

Dolan tapped his fingers once, not taking the bait. "Yes, I did work in a jewelry shop. It's been a long time, so I don't know how good I am anymore. I didn't make that ring he was showing off," he added.

"I figured that," the forester-woman replied. "How long were you on the run?"

The slave looked directly at her for a moment, then smiled, pride shining from his eyes. "Five years."

"And you stole to survive during that time?"

"Yeah," he replied and nodded over and over as he counted on his fingers as he explained further, "clothes, food, a place to stay. Even with a clean shave, everyone seems to know you're a slave, because we're darker than most free folk. So you keep running and taking what you need to live."

"Five years is a long time." She spoke as though she were familiar with runaways, or at least the laws concerning them. "So how'd you get recaptured?"

Dolan squirmed under the forester's gaze. "This serving girl told me that I could come to her diner for a free meal if I helped her carry out the garbage. Like a fool, I did. It was a set-up, but at least they waited until after I ate before they dragged me away."

Marelda smiled and was about to speak when the waitress brought their food. "Eat what you can, Dolan," she ordered, digging into her fried potatoes first.

The slave looked at his own potatoes, the single fried egg, the slices of warm bread and ham. A glass of some type of fruit juice was placed before him. He looked at the forester's meal and saw with amazement that it was the same thing. With determination he wolfed down the food and finished before she did.

"If you get sick from eating that fast, you'll have to suffer the consequences," Marelda pointed out to him as she continued eating.

After a few minutes of silence, the slave ventured to pose an inquiry. "Where are we going? I mean," he clarified at her arched eyebrows, "where does your client live?"

"My client?" The forester-woman chuckled at the question.

"The person you bought me for," Dolan said.

Marelda pointed her fork at herself. "You're looking at her."

"You own a brothel?" he asked without thinking.

The forester-woman spit out her food in the fit of coughing this idea brought on. "A brothel? Why the hell would you think I owned a brothel, boy?"

The slave shrugged his shoulders several times as he tried to talk. "Well, the nice clothes, and the shaving, and I don't know why you'd possibly need me. I always hid in towns, not the wilds." The thoughts came forth in a rush.

The forester-woman laughed out loud for a few seconds. "Oh, no, boy. I don't own a brothel. I just like less hair on my men."

"Oh," Dolan sighed with relief. "Then it will be a jewelry store or a restaurant that you own. No," he verbalized the shake of her head. He sat silently for a moment until she finished her meal and pushed her plate back. "Then why did you buy me, Mistress?" he asked very pointedly.

"Well, I heard your former owner talking with his sleazy friend. You should thank me, by the way," she added; "they sound like they had an evil life lined up for you."

The slave blinked for a couple of seconds, then lowered his gaze in sincerity. He knew which friend she was referring to; he'd serviced him a few times before he'd run. "I do thank you for not letting that man buy me."

Marelda sat back in her chair, shocked by his attitude. "Well, I do have another reason for buying you. I need a good thief."

Dolan now sat back in his chair, shocked at her words. "You need a thief?" At her nod, he laughed slightly. "You didn't pick a very good one. I got recaptured, remember."

"Yes, but after five years. That's the longest time on the run for a slave that I've ever heard," she told him, emphasizing that this was important.

Dolan let this comment pass and asked another question. "How'd you know my name?"

"The auctioneer announced it," the forester-woman replied as she laid several coppers on the table. "Remember?"

"Yes, I do, now that you mention it," Dolan muttered, "though I tried not to be there for the bidding." Then he frowned at her again. "Am I getting a new name, Mistress?"

"I see no reason for a new name. Let's go," she said, standing up.

The slave stood also, biting back other questions, and followed her back out to the reception desk, where they retrieved their coats and packs. The forester-woman paid the bill out of the seemingly inexhaustible purse which hung from her waist. Marelda motioned to a dark black horse standing right outside the inn where they could see here. "This is my mare, Magefinder, and this is Sugar, her mother, whom you will ride," she told him as she patted the gray mare. They mounted the horses, Dolan clinging for his life for the first few miles, and headed west out of town.

When they reached the edge of a woods about forty miles from the hotel, Marelda reined her horse in and dismounted. She looked up at the slave as he eyed the road, then her. Slowly Dolan dismounted and took the black mare's reins from her hands. "Tie them to the tree on the right," she instructed, pointing to two fairly close trees a short distance from the road.

The slave gingerly walked to the trees. He tested his feet as he tied the reins up. After one glance back at the forester-woman, who was unpacking one of the backpacks, he bolted for the deep woods.

Marelda just shook her head as she laid the backpacks in a pile and unsheathed her sword.

Dolan ran through the trees and low bushes without pausing for a good half mile. Then, his feet burning, his back aching and his lungs throbbing, he stopped and turned back toward the direction of the clearing where he had left the forester-woman and the horses. He lifted up one sleeve of his coat, which had slipped down, and laughed at the metal cuffs. Nothing, not a thing.

He walked at a leisurely pace as he thought about the bolt of pain that had stopped his first attempt to run. "Suggestion," he muttered to himself. "It was a weak spell, meant to scare me. I don't scare that easily," he chuckled out loud.

"That's too bad." The forester's voice made the slave jump and turn in mid-air. Marelda placed the tip of her blade to his neck. "No running now; I don't want to accidentally decapitate you on our way back to camp."

"Fuck," Dolan muttered as he walked ahead of the forester-woman. He looked around, desperate for anything that offered hope. His wrists tingled, then burst with the same pain he had felt the day before.

The forester-woman waited as the slave fell to one knee and shook his hands in an attempt to drive the pain away. When the pain stopped she heard a groan, half of pain and half of anger, escape his lips. "See, they do work," the forester-woman said as she tapped his shoulder with the flat of her blade.

"What are you going to do with me?" the slave asked as he glanced back over his shoulder, his dark eyes blazing with terror.

"Unfortunately, I'll have to punish you," Marelda sighed. "I was really hoping you had learned your lesson. Now get up and start walking," she added harshly with an extra push.

Dolan blinked and stopped when they reached the edge of the clearing. The backpacks were stacked together, and a fire circle of rocks had been set up. "But how did you catch up with me?" he asked.

"Between the two trees," Marelda ordered, ignoring his question. "Face the camp. Now take off your clothes."

The slave clenched his fists and held them firmly at his sides.

"Take them off or I will cut them off," Marelda threatened as she moved and placed the tip of her sword at his throat.

His black eyes narrowed. "Your money," he replied. The slave gasped and doubled over as the blade cut through his shirt, his vest, and a bit of his flesh. The line of blood stung as it trickled down his chest. He placed his hands on the blade as it paused at his waistband. "I'll take them off," he quickly promised.

Marelda used the blade's tip to tilt his head up. "There's a title of respect missing, slave," she stated.

Dolan swallowed and tilted his head back further as the blade grazed his skin. "Mistress. I'll remove the clothes, Mistress," he agreed. His body shook as he slipped the remains of the shirt and vest off.

"Fold them," Marelda ordered as she squatted in the grass in front of him, her blade now leveled at his groin, but a foot away.

The slave blinked but picked up the clothes when the blade moved. After folding them, he laid the shirt and vest right under her blade. His boots he placed next to these. He also removed and folded his pants and underclothes to buy some time.

Marelda stood up, the slave straightening as she rose. A glance at his limpness elicited a shrug from her. At the castle a slave of his looks would be hard as a rock by now from years of training and conditioning, but then he wasn't a royal slut, just a recaptured runaway. "Place one hand on each tree," she instructed.

The slave had to stretch out to accomplish this. When she ordered him to raise his hands, he felt a click and heard the tap of metal. Quickly the forester-woman had attached his cuffs to matching rings in the tree. "Where?" he began.

"I prefer to be prepared," Marelda answered as she kicked his legs apart.

Dolan groaned as this shifted his weight to his wrists. "I won't kick, Mistress," he promised as she tied one ankle to the tree as well.

Marelda stood in front of him, another thin leather strip in her hand. "You don't really think I'm going to trust you on that, do you?"

Dolan started to bow his head so he could watch her tie him but then pursed his lips and focused on the fire circle at the camp.

"I don't carry a whip around with me," Marelda said as she picked up a freshly cut switch from the ground next to her mare. "I was hoping I wouldn't need such devices, at least not for correction. Well, I suspect there won't be a shortage of other items to use out here in the wild." She brought the switch down across the cut on his chest left there from her knife.

Dolan sucked in his breath but remained still. He glanced down with his eyes only as a cold hard object touched his chest. In her hand, the forester-woman had a tiny vial and was catching the blood as it dripped from the wounds.

"Now, since your little stunt took up about an hour of my time, you'll be beaten for an hour," Marelda explained as she walked around the trees to his back.

Dolan turned his head as far as he could to watch the forester-woman. "An hour?" he repeated. His head spun as he remembered his beatings these past few days. "I won't last, Mistress," he informed her. "You've spent a goodly amount of money on me. Surely you don't want your property destroyed, Mistress," he pleaded, cursing internally that his wretched life meant so much to him.

"You'll not be destroyed, at least not physically," Marelda assured him.

The first stroke cut across both shoulders. Dolan braced

immediately for the next. Several seconds passed and nothing happened. The place were the switch had struck now burned and he felt a swelling there. He looked back at the forester-woman and saw her standing still, her hands on the switch and her eyes closed. "What are you waiting for?" he demanded loudly.

The forester-woman opened her eyes. "You'll be here a long time, slave. You just relax and let me go at my own pace."

The slave shook his head and cursed under his breath. His skin seemed to tingle everywhere; his toes and fingers twitched as time passed. The next stroke landed on his calves and forced a loud gasp from his lungs. Then silence as the air around him teased the new welt. His skin itched in anticipation.

Marelda smiled as she counted off a full minute between each lash. Her instruction at the castle under the tutelage of the chief advisor, Alroy, had instilled in her the need for patience and control. It was a fact that a beating done under this method was more of a punishment for the slave then one done violently and quickly. Each minute that passed should be forcing the boy to admit that she had the power. Each minute then would make him more gentle and obedient. At least that's what she had been taught. The next lash landed on her brand on his ass cheek.

"Sixty," Dolan whispered when the forester-woman stood in front of him and tilted his head up by his chin. "Sixty," he repeated, his eyes seemed far away.

"That is correct. It's good you keep track even when not ordered," Marelda told him. She tossed the switch away as she walked to her backpack. She came back with a blanket and her jacket. "I really wish you hadn't run," she told him with a sigh as she reached into her jacket.

"Me, too," Dolan murmured. He flinched as she touched one of his nipples. Something cold and wet was being placed on each nipple. He opened his eyes and bucked as far as his bonds allowed as his eyes focused to see two silver rings in her hands.

"I need to do this tonight. You could have been lying down for it; it would have been easier," Marelda told him as she opened one silver ring.

"You said no brothel," Dolan reminded her as loudly as fear and exhaustion allowed.

"There is no brothel," Marelda assured him as she knelt in the grass. She laid out a white cloth and laid both rings and a vial of yellow liquid on it.

Dolan searched his mind. Yes, he was sure that in the auction cages only the slave prostitutes had their nipples pierced. He licked his dry lips and ventured a more polite question. "Mistress, are not those types of rings a sign of sexual use?"

Marelda nodded as she poured the vial's contents into an ornate bowl she had just taken from her backpack. "Yes, but I suspect you know that not having them doesn't mean you won't be used by your owner," she said with a glance at him.

Dolan clenched his fists and shook them as much as he could. "I thought you needed a thief!"

"I do, in part," Marelda agreed as she stood in front of him, holding the bowl just in front of his face. "Breathe this in. It will help with the pain."

The slave swallowed once then focused his eyes over her shoulder and on the fire circle. Each deep breath made him feel a little more light-headed. The following piercings caused him only groggy moans and vague feelings of pain. Whatever had been in the bowl seemed to have dulled his mind until everything turned black.

Dolan lifted his head and slowly opened his eyes to the sunlight. He moved his legs up to his chest. His sudden attempt to sit up, however, was unsuccessful, since his hands were tied to the tree behind him. Somehow he had been cut down and retied, and a blanket tossed over him. He didn't remember any of it until the blanket slipped down and pulled on the nipple rings.

He bit back his scream as the memories of the previous night returned. In the past four days he'd been beaten more than he could remember in such a short period of time. The jeweler had used beatings less often than other forms of punishment, often tied to humiliations that few free people could comprehend, because he needed your hands to create his rings and things to sell but your mind and soul were irrelevant. Dolan tilted his head back against the tree and tried to calm down so he could think. After a few moments the pain in his nipples subsided, so he ventured moving and looking around. The horses were gone! By the camp the forester-woman remained, obviously doing some type of weapons exercise, so robbers were not to blame for the missing mares.

The forester-woman was dressed in only her riding pants, a loose shirt and her boots. Her red hair hung free, blown by the slight breeze as she moved her sword in a series of patterns. She ended her exercise by bringing the sword around her body and over her head in a full arc and impaling it into the earth.

Marelda wiped her face with a cloth, then tied her hair back at the nape of her neck with a leather thong. She glanced at the slave as she pulled her sword from the earth and smiled when he tilted his head back against the tree and closed his eyes. Sheathing her sword, she approached him and tapped him with her foot. "You ready to get up?"

Dolan glared at the forester-woman as she cut the leather binding him to the tree. She took the blanket from him and stood up.

"Come on now; eat something and get dressed, boy," the forester-woman ordered. She waited for him to walk before her.

Dolan pulled on the same garments he had worn the day before, or so she told him. An examination of the shirt and vest confirmed she had sewn them. He suspiciously eyed the large piece of bread she handed him but took it and ate it slowly.

Marelda finished dressing and collected all of their belongings. She took a silver whistle on a chain around her neck out from under her shirt and blew on it three times. Dolan stood up and looked around, wondering what the forester-woman was up to, but she simply double-checked the ashes to make sure the fire was out.

A few minutes later both horses returned. Marelda patted each and accepted their nuzzles with a happy sigh. "Treat them well and they will always be faithful to you," she said.

"Ever think of treating the rest of your property that way?" Dolan muttered slowly. He cursed when the point of her blade, this time a dagger, was once more at his throat.

"I've fed you and I've clothed you. Both, I suspect, far better than you have ever had in your life. I've even allowed you to be without chains and to ride instead of being dragged behind my horse!" Marelda's eyes flashed angrily as she moved closer to him. "I offered you trust, and you have repaid me each time by trying to run away."

Dolan backed away and was surprised that the blade didn't follow him. "I thanked you for saving me from Rozeny. But how can I possibly thank you for enslaving me?"

"I only bought you; I didn't enslave you," Marelda pointed out as she returned her dagger to its hilt. "Just show me the respect your lot has ordained for you. All of us have things we must do. It is our destiny." Marelda tossed him the reins to his mount. "I certainly didn't buy you for your charming personality," she commented as she mounted her mare. "Fetch the bags and mount up."

Dolan frowned but followed the forester's orders. As he swung his leg up over the saddle he noted that his body didn't ache as much as he thought it should. He wanted to ask her what ointment she had used on him while he was unconscious, but he suspected no question would be answered until he apologized. Threats could pull such words from him, but her silence couldn't; of that he was certain. She'd tell him what to do, then he'd obey because he had to. Like she said, she didn't buy him for his personality, so why be anything other than the tool she needed?

In silence the two travelers continued west.

Chapter Two:
Holy Ground

They ate lunch in the saddle, which was awkward for Dolan, but he managed, and by the time the sun was getting low in the sky they had traveled over sixty more miles. The clearing where they ended their day's journey was near a very old church. The size of the ruins indicated that once it had been mighty and important, but now its congregation seemed more likely to consist of small animals and robbers lying in wait for foolish travelers.

The slave, more reconciled to his lot by both his punishments and the forester's silence during their march, tied their horses to a nearby tree as directed and slowly went back to the forester-woman, who stood gazing at the church. He cleared his throat once.

"Yes?" The forester-woman said as she looked through a gold-trimmed book with three thin strips of colored fabric, green, red, and white, dangling from the binding, which she had removed from her pack.

"Do you have any instructions for me, Mistress?" Dolan asked, hoping it would be to get the horses ready so they could travel further. His nipples and back hurt from being bounced around on the gray mare, but he feared there might be something lurking in those ruins that could kill him.

"Yeah, go get some firewood and make a fire. Then start supper." Marelda replaced the book and unsheathed her sword. "Do I have to shackle you?"

Dolan's face reddened slightly as he shook his head. "No, Mistress. I'll do as instructed; I'll be a good ... slave," he added the last word with a bit of defiance, watching the forester's response closely.

Marelda simply shook her head and gave a tight chuckle. "I'll be back by the time you're done, boy."

Dolan watched as she walked into the ruins and out of sight.

"Shit," he muttered softly. With a shake of his head he set off into the nearby woods and collected an armful of stones. When he returned to the woods for the firewood he looked at the trees carefully. His feet itched to run, but his sore back and chest told him not to. When he had built up a ring of stones and placed the wood inside, he fumbled through his pack and found flint in one of the outer pockets. He noticed the sun was substantially lower now.

"OK, priest!" Marelda called as she entered the nave of the church. "Come out and answer my questions, and I'll leave you alone." She moved cautiously, her eyes watching each elongated shadow that the setting sun cast through the broken stained-glass windows.

She spun around at the sound behind her and sighed when a rat showed itself. When she turned back toward the altar, a tiny old man was standing there examining her closely. "I haven't come to harm you," she tried to reassure him as she moved closer.

"Is that why you carry your sword unsheathed?" the priest asked bitterly. "What do you want here, warrior?" he demanded, moving one hand slightly.

Marelda sidestepped the fireball easily. The sphere sizzled and smoked where it landed; the rat she'd seen earlier screamed before falling silent.

"Ah, not a warrior then," the priest said. "A forester-woman. You fight and know magic too, eh?"

"Yes," Marelda said. "So, let's just talk, and we can both spend a quiet night alive."

"What do you wish to talk about?" The priest calmly invited her to join him down on the steps to the altar. "As you wish," he said with a bow when she rejected his offer with a firm "no".

"I need a book from you, priest," Marelda said.

"A book. What book?" The priest peered at her from milky irises, which the forester-woman figured were just a trick to trap her.

"The book of maps which will take me to the three sacred treasures of Vanhilmer," Marelda explained.

"Bah!" the priest spat at her, and the spittle burned the stones of the floor. "Only a member of the Vanhilmer clan may seek these treasures!"

The forester-woman removed her hat so that her auburn hair fell down into view. "I am she," came her declaration.

The priest sucked in his breath but then snorted, "You could have dyed it! I'm not such an old man as to have lost my mind."

"Then my signet ring should be the proof you need," she said, holding her hand out. "Since you are obviously not as blind as you wish to appear," she added with a chuckle when his eyes glowed red, the color of the ancient fire god of the Hilmer, he who dealt in blood and war.

The priest sprang forth and grabbed her hand. He examined the ring closely. "Could have been stolen."

"Then you have lost your mind, old priest. Anyone not of royal blood would perish in flames if she but slipped this around the top of one finger," she reminded him. "That was your god's doing," she added.

"It is not time," the priest suddenly said as he released her hand. "It is not time."

Marelda followed him as he walked away. "The stars say that it is time; the scriptures declare it is time. And I am the only one in my family who cares about the prophecy anymore, just as they foretold."

The priest ignored her and walked away mumbling, "It is not time," over and over.

Marelda found herself face to face with a very solid door. "Damn it! Open up, you bastard!" she swore, pounding on the door.

Dolan had just decided that the stew he had thrown together from the rations in their packs was done when the forester-woman returned to the clearing. He didn't say a word as she sat down and handed him her plate. After filling her plate with more than half the stew, he ate the rest out of the cooking pot. "Do you want wine, Mistress?" he asked after they had finished the stew. "I found some in your pack."

The forester-woman glared at him. "Did I tell you that you could go nosing around in my pack, boy?"

The slave set the pot down with his spoon in it. "No, Mistress. I'm sorry, I was checking the food supply and found it. It was the only food in your pack, so I assumed it was for you alone."

The forester-woman nodded, then handed him her plate. "No, the wine is not to drink casually. Go wash these in the stream," she ordered, indicating the thin stream nearby.

Dolan did as he was bid and cleaned up the camp, adding another log to the fire. He stood across the fire from her and waited silently.

"Come here, boy," the forester-woman commanded as she pulled her backpack onto her lap. The slave knelt in front of her where she ordered, watching her closely. She took out the package that he had retrieved from the blacksmith and handed it to him. "I hope you know how to use one. You're going to need it."

Dolan looked at his owner for a second then opened the oily leather wrappings. Inside was a dagger of strong metal. He left it in his lap and looked back at the forester-woman. "You trust me to carry a weapon?" he asked, his mind spinning with questions and confusion.

"Yes, unless you have a moral problem with it," Marelda told him with a twinkle in her eye.

"No; if you want me to carry it, I will," he said, looking at it again. Slaves very rarely got to even touch weapons, let alone carry them. Closer examination revealed that the metal was engraved with odd symbols and signs.

"If you look at your cuffs, you'll see similar markings," the forester-woman suggested.

Sure enough, when he compared the metal of the cuffs to the dagger, many of the same symbols were repeated. "What do they mean?"

"Well, as you've learned, I hope, the cuffs can't be removed. Also, they let me know what you've done, and I can punish you for running off from far away. The symbols are the spells that enchant them. Likewise, this dagger will return to you upon recitation of a certain phrase if you lose it, and if you ever," she now grabbed his shirt collar and pulled him close to her, "ever try to use it on me, it will envelop you in flames and burn you to death. A very, very painful way to die." She paused, then added, "You don't need to try that to find out if I'm telling the truth, do you?"

"No, Mistress!" he declared. "I'll believe everything that you say to me from now on."

"Good; I'm not in the habit of lying," Marelda replied as she looked back at the church ruins. "So, do you know how to use it?"

"Yes, I had one when I was running," he said. "It's easier to hide than almost any other weapon." He felt the weight of the dagger in his hand and looked at it more closely. "What is the phrase to recall it?"

"It's very simple, so you shouldn't forget it," Marelda began. "You say, in a very serious voice, 'Unto me return, O dagger.' Easy, huh?"

The slave nodded. "It's a little awkward, but I'm sure I can remember it." He stood up and placed the dagger in his belt where it could be easily reached but would not interfere in daily activities. He stood still as she rose to her feet as well. Her scent, similar yet enticingly different from either his or the horses', made his face redden. "Do you have any orders?" he asked, his voice husky with desire, his pants betraying a slight stirring in his groin. He hated her, he hated anyone who owned him, that had been his solemn vow from the day he ran, so his physical reaction only made his blush deepen.

Marelda nodded sadly. "Aye. I need you to steal a book for me."

"Steal a book?" he asked, walking with her as she placed one arm around him and pulled him along with her.

"Yes; the priest wouldn't give it to me, so you'll have to steal it," she said.

"Oh." He stopped and looked up at the church's crumbling exterior. "Is there any special reason why I have to steal it?"

"Other than the fact that I'm ordering you to do it, you mean?" Marelda asked with a grin.

"I'll do it on your word, obviously, Mistress," he hastened to assure her. "But if I know what type of protection the book has, I'll be better equipped to get it for you."

"Well, I imagine that it isn't locked up or anything. It just has a crazy priest guarding it. So, while you get the book, I'll kill the priest," she stated, releasing his shoulders and opening the church door.

"That might bring the wrath of the gods on us," Dolan pointed out.

Marelda tilted her head as though thinking, then shook it. "I don't think so. Not this particular priest."

They walked through the chapel unchallenged. The door behind which the priest had vanished was still locked. "Can you pick it?" she asked softly.

The slave nodded and crouched down. He took out a small pick that he had also found in the front pocket of his backpack; clearly she knew which tools a thief needed just as he had learned to use them on the run. After a few seconds the door swung open.

They entered the dark room and saw an old book, not much smaller than the one she already carried in her pack, sitting on a bookstand at the center of the room.

"Go away!" the priest ordered as he suddenly appeared out of thin air in front of them. He looked younger and more powerful than he had before. Her guess had been correct, because he now wore the military robes of the ancient Hilmer god.

"Just give me the book as is my due, and we will leave you in peace," Marelda promised.

"It is not time!" the priest howled and threw a fireball which grazed the slave's leg.

Marelda pushed the slave toward the book and in the same motion pushed the priest back. "Get the book!" she ordered, her sword at the priest's throat.

The priest's eyes glowed red as he murmured words and waved his hands toward the forester-woman. Marelda seized the priest's hand and forced his second fireball to miss her slave so that it flew sizzling and smoking into a wall. The wall swayed, and dust fell from the ceiling.

"Crazy fool!" Marelda snarled as she shoved the priest away and threatened him with her sword.

"I have it!" Dolan announced, holding onto the book with both hands. His eyes widened as the priest lunged at him, then stopped, the blade of the forester's sword protruding from his chest, the blood bursting out with the final pump of his heart.

"Hurry!" Marelda yelled as she pushed the priest off of her sword with her foot. She led the way out of the crumbling church. No sooner had they cleared the door of the church than the roof creaked and fell in.

The slave threw himself on the ground, the book pinned beneath him. The bricks and wood from the church rained down on them. Dolan held his breath until the falling materials ceased. He coughed and pushed himself up. The forester-woman was lying next to him laughing softly. "Are you OK?" he asked as he checked his own body out with one quick look.

"Yes, I'm fine," Marelda replied. She stood up and dusted herself off, then offered her hand to the slave.

Dolan handed the book to his owner but refused her hand as he stood up, dusting off his clothes as well. "Is this the book you wanted?"

Marelda looked at the book's cover, then thumbed through it. "Yes ... it is ... my destiny," she replied between breaths as she tried to stop laughing and crying at the same time. She picked up a brick and threw it toward the pile of rubble where the church had stood. "Damn you, priest!"

Without another word, the forester-woman turned around and went back to their camp. There she sat by the fire and started to read the stolen book.

Dolan stood for a few seconds looking at the ruins, then at the forester-woman. After reassuring himself that she would not be needing him for a while, he went back into the ruins.

Carefully he waded through the fallen bricks. Whenever he spotted something shining in the rubble, he dug down and picked it up. Most items he discarded, but he kept two candlesticks and several copper coins he found. He also retrieved three other books which had not been pummeled to pieces by the collapse.

The stars were starting to shine in the night sky when Dolan returned to the fire. He placed the items he had found on the ground in front of the forester-woman.

Marelda looked over the book then frowned. "Why did you steal these things?"

The slave crouched down and wrinkled up his brow in bewilderment. "The church is no more, so I thought *you* might profit from them."

"This is a quest, not a treasure hunt, Dolan." She placed her new book to one side and looked at the items. "Take these back," she instructed him, handing him the candlesticks. "And these," she continued, picking up the books, "are just hymnals. Not useful unless you want to sing."

Dolan took these books also, with a sigh.

"We can keep the coins; they belong not to gods, but to people," she reasoned out loud. "Return the other things now," she ordered and resumed her reading.

Dolan went back to the ruins and found the spots he had retrieved the items from. He replaced each of them carefully, then froze at a sound near his feet. He swallowed as a fat rat ran by his boots.

The slave returned to the fire and stood on the opposite side from the forester-woman. He added another log to the fire, then moved around closer to her. He watched the fire, poking it with a stick, sending sparks flying into the night air.

Marelda laid the book inside her pack and watched the slave play with the fire. The flames' light bounced off his lean face, highlighting his beard and mustache. His curly hair was tucked behind one ear on the side nearest her. After a while, he turned and looked back at her for a moment. "You did a good job tonight, thief," she said, using the word as a compliment.

"I'm sorry about the other things I stole," he apologized, uneasy under her gaze and cursing himself for doing something he'd sworn he'd never do, caring about what a free person might think. He heard her stand up. Out of the corner of his eye he saw her take out her bedroll and lay it near the fire where she had been sitting.

"It's time we hit the sack," Marelda announced. She watched her slave nodding as he tossed his stick into the fire. Then he got his own bedroll and started to lay it down. "Closer to mine," she said, catching a corner of it as he flipped it out. She helped him spread it out right alongside of hers, her body closer to the fire.

Dolan suddenly felt his heart pounding as his lungs struggled to take in air as he watched her take off her coat and loosen her hair. She sat down and started to remove her boots. Feeling a knot in his stomach, he knelt and grasped her boot. "May I?" he asked softly, a frown betraying his internal confusion.

"Please do," Marelda agreed with a smile, the light of the fire showing him how much this pleased her by the smile on her face. She let him remove her boots, then watched as he removed his own. She placed her hands over his as he started to slide his vest off. "Be still, and move only on my command," she whispered.

Dolan had been with many women while on the run. All had been peasants or slaves with whom he had shared only a few minutes. These quickies and the rapes he had endured while at the jeweler's had been his only sexual encounters, so the feelings of desire he now felt confused him greatly. He made himself concentrate on her touch and her words, determined to learn and afraid of displeasing her in any manner, lest her magic shrivel up his cock permanently.

Marelda slid the vest off his body and let it fall. Next she unlaced his shirt and helped him lift it and the undershirt over his head. "This is healing well," she commented as she touched the scar on his chest which her sword had made earlier, but not commenting on the marks from his beatings. The newly pierced nipples she ignored. She told him to stand, then unlaced his riding pants and slipped them to his ankles where he stepped out of them. She could see that he was aroused, but his skin also felt clammy from fear. She opened his bedroll and let him crawl inside. Sitting there, fully clothed still, she ran her fingers through his hair, pulling a curl and letting it bounce back. "Have you been with a woman before, Dolan?"

He nodded and swallowed once before answering. "Just peasants and slaves whom I met while on the run, and the jeweler's friends and family would amuse themselves with me on occasion," he added in explanation, though his blush indicated it embarrassed him to say so.

"So you know how to please a woman?" Marelda pressed, giggling as the handful of his dark curls bounced back.

"Probably not," he said, then whispered, "There was never much time. A quick fondle, sometimes a fast in-out with girls. I never did more than what I was ordered to do with a free person." He shuddered as though expecting a slap, then turned his head away and continued, "Hope that doesn't offend you, Mistress. I'm not trained for this sort of thing."

"No; it's been your life, Dolan." She bent nearer and gently kissed his forehead. "I'd like to teach you how to please me, Dolan. I think you are a very attractive man."

He turned his face up toward hers, his breath ragged with a mixture of feelings. "I'm very willing to learn," he admitted, his voice low and hoarse. He felt and saw the forester-woman stand up. She slid out of her pants and kicked them aside. She unbuttoned her shirt and let it fall also. She untied his bedroll and told him to get up. He stood up and watched her join the two bedrolls together into one large one. The fire played with the curves of her hips and breasts outlined in a cream-colored fabric which he didn't recognize on sight. Her body shape was slightly unfamiliar to him. All the peasants and slaves had either been very plump or very thin. The free friends of the jeweler were invariably fat and over decorated. The forester-woman was curvaceous but solid, well-tanned and muscled. He reached out and touched her shoulder, then jumped back as though fire had shot from her, a fire which a wise man would avoid and a foolish man would run to. Dolan swallowed again knowing that he could lay claim to neither term as long as her cuffs marked him.

Marelda smiled up at the slave and motioned him to return to the bedrolls. Once he was lying on his back, she crawled in and lay on her stomach, half on top of him, leaning over him on her elbows.

She looked into his face, afire from the fear and arousal he clearly felt. Already there were sparks along their skin, teasing them and warning them of necessity. "Take off your underclothes," she ordered huskily as she sat up.

Dolan arched his hips and pulled the pants off. He laid the clothes to the side opposite her. He looked at her arms poised over him as she leaned back down. Licking his lips, he reached out to them with his hands.

"No," Marelda replied softly. The slave froze, his hands still raised. "A slave should follow directions, not move of his own will until he has learned how to pleasure his owner. Do you want to learn how to please me or not?"

Dolan lowered his hands to his sides slowly. "Yes, Mistress." Her hands started to roam over his body. First, she traced each of his fingers, felt the lines on his palms and kissed them gently. Now her hands traveled over his jaw and familiarized themselves with every inch of his face. His breathing increased as her hands journeyed down his neck.

Marelda squeezed his firm chest muscles once, then let her fingers flick each of his nipple rings. His cries brought a smile to her face.

"They're for you, then?" he asked as his nipples throbbed.

"In time, I think you'll learn to appreciate them too," she replied as she gently kissed each nub. Marelda now turned her attention to the two brands, frowning for a second at the crude work. She traced his ribs and made a mental note that he needed a little fattening up.

Dolan felt himself drift away as her hands caressed his balls. His cock responded to her caresses, but his mind had now placed him safely away. He barely heard her words, but he arched his legs up so his ass was lifted up under her hands. Though he tried not to feel anything nor to resist, still his ass tightened as she pushed one finger inside. The jolts of pleasure and terror he felt earlier seemed to have strengthened.

"I can't," Dolan whimpered, drawing his knees up to his chest and rolling to his side. When her hand rested on the small of his back he yelled, "No!" and leapt from the bedroll and dashed away.

Marelda sat up and watched her slave run a short distance away, then fall to his knees in the short grass. For a few minutes she weighed her options, then picked up his underclothing and walked to him. "Here are your clothes," she said, dropping them in front of him.

"I'm sorry," Dolan said when she crouched in front of him. He felt the blood of his past shame crawl to the surface of his skin.

"Hey," the forester-woman shrugged and tried to sound calm but not insulted, "if you don't find me attractive, I'm not going to force you. At least not right now. I have a little time to give you for that."

When she stood up and turned away, Dolan grabbed her ankle. "Please," he pleaded when she glared down at him. He released her ankle and stood up. "I think you are the most beautiful woman I've ever seen."

"Beauty is obviously not enough," Marelda stated and headed back toward the campfire.

Dolan scooped up his clothes and walked after her. He stopped by the bedroll where she lay and knelt down. "Mistress?" he asked softly.

Marelda rolled over and looked at him, her face softening when she saw the tears in his eyes.

"Take me," Dolan stated but did not move.

"I don't think you want me to," the forester-woman replied. She sat up and touched his cheek. "What's going on with you, boy? You seemed so far away before you bolted."

Dolan sighed and pulled himself up straight. "It's been a long time since I was used for an owner's pleasure," he lied because the jeweler had beaten and raped him repeatedly before the auction. "But," he continued as he bent down and slipped under the top part of the bedroll, "I'm ready for you now." He bent his knees so that his feet were closer to his butt and the bedroll was lifted up by his parted knees. When she did not touch him, he looked at her as she sat watching him silently.

"It was when I penetrated you that you panicked," she whispered, more to herself than to him. Now she touched his nearest knee and nodded when his body tensed reflexively. "I think that your former owners used you harshly from quite an early age. Am I correct, boy?"

Dolan looked at her in complete confusion. Why was he letting her even put him in this position? Why wasn't he fighting like he had before? He shut his mind to the memories that flooded him suddenly. Arching his hips, he moaned and begged, "Please, Mistress. Claim me now. Before I lose my nerve."

Marelda pushed his one knee down so that his leg was lying

flat. "Not tonight. Another lesson for tonight," she whispered, her voice husky. "Sit up and give me your hands."

Dolan sat up slowly, stunned that she refused to do what the jeweler and his friends had done to him over and over. He held out his hands, palms up. She took his hands and moved them behind her back.

"Unfasten my breast wrap," Marelda ordered as she placed his hands on the hook-and-eye closure. When he hesitated, she smiled and observed, "Those short encounters never involved more than a flipped up skirt, did they? And I bet the free women never let you see them completely naked, did they?"

"No," he admitted as he fumbled with the ties.

"Did the jeweler have a wife?" the forester-woman asked, smiling as he managed to undo the first tie.

"Yes," Dolan sighed and felt the wrap come loose in his hands. He waited breathlessly for her next command.

"You were a young man before you ran off." Marelda pushed him gently away and took hold of the wrap. "Didn't she ever enjoy you?"

"She usually only watched her husband, but she did have occasional tea parties," he heard himself say. His mind marveled at the way she was getting him to talk. He watched as she removed the wrap revealing her moderately sized breasts. "What should I do?" he begged, his body crying out to her of its own accord.

"Just touch them gently," Marelda instructed him. She sighed as he tentatively ran his fingers over their fullness and across the nipples. After several moments, she felt a moan build in her throat. "Stop," she huskily ordered.

Immediately, the slave drew back, placing his hands on his thighs.

"That's enough for tonight, boy," she said, her tone the same as when she had ordered him to get firewood. She took a plain cotton shirt she had stashed in her bedroll and pulled it over her head. She smiled weakly at him, sorry that it was best to end their encounter for the evening. "Put your underclothes back on, and let's get some sleep."

"What?" Dolan gasped out loud. Her stern glare, however, silenced him. He put on his clothes as quickly as his arching cock allowed. He lay down on his back, too aware of her body next to his. She rolled over onto her side, facing him, and moved very close.

"Good night, Dolan," Marelda whispered, placing one arm over him and resting her head on his upper arm. She didn't tell him to move or pull away when he placed his hand over hers, which lay on top of the "R" on his chest. For a brief moment as sleep overtook him, he considered just how far away he might get if she were soundly asleep.

The slave woke with a start and looked wildly around him, wondering how many seconds he had before the cell door was flung open and he was herded upstairs to work. Then he felt the material on top of him and cursed himself for being a fool. He sat up, shaking his head lazily to clear his mind. This was a luxury only freedom gave. He ran his hands down his arms, feeling the goose bumps from the chilly morning air. No, his hands informed him of his true status when they reached his wrist cuffs.

Dolan stood up and looked around the camp. Marelda's sword, bow and quiver lay where she had placed them last night, but the forester-woman was nowhere to be seen. Her backpack was missing. The slave glanced back at the ruins of the church and looked over the surrounding terrain, then simply shrugged.

Once his pants and boots were on, he headed toward the area she had designated as their toilet. As he relieved himself he heard the clear sound of water splashing. He laced up his pants and headed toward the sound. As he got closer he heard the forester's voice and another woman's. Through a tiny hole in a bush he watched the two women in the water. The other woman was older, not fat but more buxom than the forester-woman; her golden hair fell over her naked shoulders.

"It is sorrowful to hear that the priest had to be killed," the older woman said as she rubbed the hair of the forester-woman into a soapy foam.

"He claimed it wasn't time," Marelda replied. "You are sure, Sigrid?" she asked, glancing over her shoulder.

"Positive," the other replied, then gently pushed the forester-woman under the water several times until her hair was soap-free. "Besides, he worked for the old god of war, Mir, not the Divine Couple where unity, strength and your future lie. My teacher before me, and the one before that, and the ones in several past generations have studied and worked hard on understanding the sacred text. All the signs are here; your own power was the last one to be fulfilled. But tell me more about the slave?" she asked with a playful splash at her pupil.

"Nothing more to tell," Marelda stated.

"Haven't you performed any of the rituals?" the blond asked with a frown.

"I've done the piercings and given him the dagger. Both charged with our mixed blood," Marelda responded.

"Blood," Dolan whispered, then shrunk back when the older woman turned toward his direction.

"Didn't you place your mark in him last night?" The mage sounded slightly concerned.

"He wasn't ready." Marelda felt her face redden at the other woman's frown. "It is important to me that he is ready for it. He's had a harder life than I could have imagined; he has to trust me if I'm going to trust him. If I can't trust him, I'll be dead before we exit the first gate," she added.

Sigrid rolled her eyes at the idealism of youth. "Don't want too long," the mage cautioned. "It may prove more fatal than distrust."

Dolan jumped back as the eyes of the blonde woman seemed to focus on him again. He ran back to camp as quietly as he could. He had just finished separating and rolling up the beds when the forester-woman returned, clothed for the day's journey.

"You're awake," Marelda said, not giving any indication whether she knew he had been spying on her or not. She handed him a handkerchief. "Breakfast," she told him.

Dolan opened it to find wild strawberries. "Thank you, Mistress," he said, determined to be very polite and humble before this obviously powerful and dangerous woman, a forester perhaps but likely something more. As he ate he watched her read the book he had stolen. What had that other woman meant about marking him? He already bore her brand. The penetration, that had to be it. There must be some ritual that she needed to perform while using him. He cleared his throat after he finished the fruit.

"Ready to go?" the forester-woman asked, looking up over the book.

"Yes, Mistress," Dolan replied as he stood up. He held out the handkerchief, and she took it from him and stuffed it into her vest pocket.

"Get your gear on Sugar then, and let's move out," Marelda ordered. They readied their animals silently. The forester-woman raked the black remains of the fire to make sure it was out. Finally, with a glance at her wrist she mounted her horse. "Looks like we are on track," she said with a smile.

Dolan followed her down the road, riding just slightly behind and to her left. His mind whirled with the questions he wanted to ask – marking, the blonde woman, that strange band on her wrist she seemed to talk to a moment ago, old books and evil priests. So why didn't he ask? What was the worst she could do? Kill him? She'd paid a lot for him, but then again she'd been throwing around money like there was no tomorrow, and that certainly hadn't saved him before from the thrashing of his life. Whenever she glanced back at him, her frown deepening every time, he shifted uncomfortably in the saddle. Could she read his mind too?

When the sun reached its zenith, Marelda guided her horse to the side of the road and turned to face her slave. "I thought we'd reached a comfortable level of interaction last night. So what's on your mind that makes you look at me like I'm the devil?"

Dolan shrugged and looked down the road. "Just wondering if you were angry about last night," he finally said.

Marelda cocked one eye, then chuckled. "No, you'll give in when the time is right." She turned her horse toward a nearby meadow, then got down when her slave followed her. "Let's eat here and rest a minute."

Dolan sat down across from the forester-woman and ate the bread, meat, and cheese she offered him. They didn't talk, because she had those two books open and sitting on the ground in front of her, and she was reading them intently. The questions whirled in his mind as the surprisingly good food filled his stomach but didn't curb other hungers.

"You mentioned that this was a quest, back at the church," Dolan suddenly said. Marelda looked up at him silently. "Can I know what you meant by that?" he asked.

Marelda turned the first book to him. "You can't read, can you?" she asked as he just nodded at it. "So I'll explain briefly all you need to know. This book has been in my family for centuries. There are treasures that we lost that I must find. The first book describes the treasures and the rituals to be performed with them when I return home. The book you stole last night tells me where they are, how to get there, and who guards them."

"So where are we going?"

"Each treasure is hidden behind a magical gate and guarded by a sorcerer. Each of them is dangerous, the danger increasing with each one we claim." She placed the first book in her lap. "But with your help, we will get through them safely."

"I'm just a slave," Dolan snorted slightly in disbelief at her tale and partly from knowing what he truly was.

"You're a little more than that," Marelda replied thinking about the description of the bridegroom of Ariala, the Mother of All, the first of her own line. She closed her books and replaced them in her backpack. "Let's go."

Chapter Three:
The First Gate

That night their camp was by an old well with sweet-tasting water. Dolan was once again in charge of setting up camp while the forester-woman went out and looked around their area.

"This is the place," Marelda announced when she returned.

"The place?" Dolan asked as he stirred the stew he was cooking.

"The first gate is here," Marelda simply said.

Dolan looked around him but saw nothing. "What am I missing?" he asked as he tasted the stew.

"You'll see in a few days." Marelda held out her plate. "So, we have some time to get to know each other and rest before the battle starts."

The slave's eyes shot up at the sentence. "Battle? I'm not a soldier," he protested weakly.

"Battles come in many forms," Marelda informed him. "Now eat up. This is good stuff. Don't want my good money going to waste."

Dolan tried to smile at what was meant as a compliment, but the idea of some magical gate with a sorcerer left him feeling very unsure.

After the meal, Marelda sat for several minutes watching her slave clean up. She waited until he was seated again before moving toward him. He was perfectly still as she sat next to him, even more motionless as she placed one hand on his thigh. "How are you feeling this evening?" she asked in a slightly husky voice.

Dolan looked down at her hand then up at her face; his eyes seemed wider and his voice softer. "I'm fine, Mistress."

The forester-woman smiled and removed her hand. Her smile widened when this movement caused him to moan slightly. She removed her jacket, then her shirt, and finally her breast wrap, leaving her as bare as she had been last night. "Take off my boots," she ordered.

Dolan quickly obeyed, letting his eyes occasionally move up to her well-formed breasts. When he finished, he massaged her feet for a moment.

"That's nice, but not what I want tonight," Marelda interrupted. She stood up and poked him with one of her feet. "Take off your clothes."

Dolan stood up slowly. Last night she had been slower, nicer. What had that other woman said? His mistress needed to mark him, to perform some rituals. That didn't sound good. He slowly removed his own clothes, noting that she did not move until he was naked.

"Lay out the bedding," Marelda told him as she unbuttoned her pants. She watched him as he laid out the sleeping bags next to each other. He was careful to kneel but not to bend over, as though it might hurt him or perhaps it made him feel like a target. She walked up behind him and felt him freeze in position. "You didn't think I spent all that money on you just to have you steal things for me, did you?"

"No, Mistress," Dolan replied as thoughts of a private harem somewhere now raced through his mind. She had powerful magic, and didn't powerful people often have large estates and many slaves? Regardless, he'd already tasted pain from her magic and her hands, so he did as he was bid. She had also fed him, clothed him, and treated him better than his original master, as she herself had reminded him. He glanced over his shoulder and pushed back one black curl, then turned back to the bedding. "How do you want me?" he forced himself to whisper.

"On your back." When he was in position she lay down on top of him, letting him get used to the feeling of her naked flesh against his. "Just relax," she cooed into his ear. After a few minutes she felt his cock harden against her leg as it responded to the feeling of her body.

She ran her hands over his body as she sat up and saddled his groin. His skin was hot under her fingers, and it marked nicely as she gently scratched him with her nails. He moaned as she flicked each nipple ring up, then down. "Beautiful," she whispered as she slid down further on his legs, then off him completely. Her hands now simply caressed him as she knelt next to him and appreciated his entire body. A lifetime of slavery and living on the run had left him with little body fat but had allowed his muscles to develop slightly so that he was firm and sturdy. The ribs she could make out would easily be hidden once he was eating better and regularly.

Dolan sat up on his elbows and looked at his owner, who seemed to enjoy just touching him. *What's the game? Who's she trying to fool? I know she can't care.* "Why don't you just do it?" he asked suddenly, his voice defensive with fear.

Marelda stopped and looked at him. She sat back on her heels and silently continued to gaze at him. He looked back, pulling his knees up to his chest and separating his thighs as far as he could. She noted with sudden anger that his cock was going soft as well. "If that is the way you want it," Marelda stated as she reached over him and grabbed her pack. She let it bump into his legs as she pulled it over.

Dolan tried to stay focused and aware during what seemed like hours. He heard her open her pack and remove something. Her words sounded strange and frightening; they continued through what he correctly assumed was a ritual. His body was suddenly filled with pressure, but not the pain he had expected, as she pushed something hard inside his ass. After a few moments a sharp pain on his inner thigh brought him back to the present.

"Repeat the words I just said," Marelda repeated, but received a blank stare in reply. She stated the phrase more slowly.

Dolan repeated her words with a concerned frown. He blinked several times as her face disappeared behind his legs and her voiced chanted more strange words.

"Now relax," Marelda said softly. "If you can relax this won't hurt so much," she added, then carefully and slowly turned the dildo a quarter turn and chanted a few more words.

"Oh, Lady and Lord!" Dolan screamed as the nipple rings and wrist cuffs burned him and glowed with a strong eerie green light. He tried to move but found his body too heavy.

"Don't move!" Marelda ordered, then turned the dildo another quarter turn and repeated the magical words. This was done twice more, and each time the metal on her slave burned and glowed.

Marelda finished the ritual and felt a drop of sweat fall from her forehead. She placed her hands on his inner thighs and considered whether to touch him more and calm him in some manner, but she remembered his attitude of just an hour earlier. Looking up at the stars, which were now appearing in the sky, she took hold of the base of the dildo. "I'm going to take it out now, Dolan," she told him as she removed it.

Dolan gasped as he felt the object leave and a sudden surprising emptiness take its place. He lay there for a few minutes, just watching her stand up and put her backpack away. Her body glistened in the firelight, making him realize she was covered in perspiration. He sat up as she walked toward the well. By the time she returned, her body dripping with the bucketful of water she had tossed over herself, he was looking into the fire and wondering what had happened or if any comment would be appropriate.

Marelda gathered up her underpants and her shirt. As she put them back on she heard him speak very softly. "What did you say, boy?" she asked as she sat down on her half of the bedding.

"Thank you, Mistress," Dolan repeated with a quick glance at his owner.

"For what?" she said as she crawled inside her sleeping bag.

"For waiting a couple of days before you did that," he told her. "Am I right in guessing that it's a magic ritual you needed to perform?"

Marelda paused as though surprised by the question. "Yes, it is a protective spell which ties you to me," Marelda stated.

Dolan turned around and looked straight at her. "If it's to protect me, why did it burn me?"

Marelda cocked one eye and sat up on one elbow. "Why did you have to move it along so fast and so impersonally?"

The slave just stared at her for a moment then looked away. Without a word he gathered his own clothes and headed to the well. Dolan looked over his shoulder after he finished rinsing off and dressing. *Who is she? What does she want? Why does she want it? Quest to reclaim family trinkets? Give me a break. There must be more to this than she's told me.* He looked closely at the cuffs around his wrists and blinked at the obviously burned hair near them, yet they didn't hurt now. Neither did his ass, but still it felt open and odd, as though he'd been fucked for several days, an image too based in reality to make him do anything but shudder.

When he returned to the bedding he found her asleep. He looked at her for a long moment, then lay down on his back beside her. He'd heard rumors that lovers sometimes held each other at night. Fighting back a few tears, he turned to his side, facing away from her. He'd never be her lover now that he'd rejected her offer of comfort earlier; why torture himself with such foolishness?

Dolan felt his legs aching as he ran across the field. He could almost feel the sheriff's horse's breath on his neck. The laughter from the men chasing him rang in his ears. His chest felt as if it would explode as he broke through into a forest. The trees and plants seemed to jump into his path as he tried desperately to stay one step ahead of his pursuers. In the distance there was a green light. A warm pulsing heat seemed to issue forth from it. As he neared it, he was able to look into the center. There stood a woman, dressed in a pale green gown, her red hair falling in long curls around her. She motioned to him. He approached quickly, then stopped just inches from her outstretched hands. "Why don't you just do it?" he suddenly yelled at her.

The slave woke up immediately and looked over at his owner, whose open eyes stared into his. "It will be okay," Marelda whispered and placed her hand over his. Dolan looked down at her wrist, and for the first time noticed that the metal band on her wrist, the one she kept looking at, was covered with symbols similar to those on his cuffs. The magic tied them together; it wasn't just her controlling him.

The next day she barely spoke a word to him as she sat and read the two books and made notes on a scroll of parchment. Dolan went into the woods and set a few primitive traps he'd figured out how to make during his five years on the run; even a city slave had to venture occasionally into the wilds. They captured a nice dinner for them. He also found some wild berries that he had discovered were edible while on the run.

At dinner, which he had prepared without being ordered, he handed her a plate and made sure his fingers touched hers briefly. She glanced up at him, half closed her eyes and took the plate. Dolan sat down next to her, closer than he had the previous evenings.

"Mistress?" he began before he started eating. When she didn't reply but simply looked at him, he continued. "You said we could use this time to get better acquainted. I'd like that."

"Would you?" Marelda asked as she picked up the rabbit and tasted it gingerly. "Good job," she said through a full mouth.

"Thanks," he mumbled as he picked up his own meal. After a few minutes, he set his plate down on the ground and looked directly at her. "May I ask you some questions?"

"Go ahead. It rarely hurts to ask," the forester-woman added with a hint of mischief in her voice.

"You have red hair."

"Is that a question?" Marelda replied with a grin as she hungrily finished off her half of the rabbit.

"No," Dolan admitted with a smile. "But I thought only the aristocratic families had red hair?"

"Yes; I told you that we are on a quest for a treasure my family lost." Marelda washed down her food with a swig of water. Her slave continued to look at her with interest. "You want to know who my family is? Are you sure? You might be safer not knowing."

Dolan nodded, then shook his head. "What you did to me last night with those powers of yours have locked me into your service, Mistress," he said, adding a small bow for emphasis. "I'd rather know who I'm serving so I can do a good job of it with less risk of a beating. At the very least, it might help me trust you more," he added boldly.

"Can't you just do what you're told?" Marelda pointed out.

"I've never been good at that," the slave replied with a dry chuckle. "But it really bothered me that you didn't talk to me much today," he admitted. "I don't know why, but I'd feel better if we felt more comfortable around each other."

Marelda stood up and walked to the well. Once there, a glance back at the fire confirmed that he was sincere, since he sat there, his head held in his hands. She looked at her bracelet and concentrated. *Sigrid. Sigrid. Give me a sign. Do I tell him?* After a few moments a light green glow and a gentle warmth flooded her wrist.

"Fine, I'll tell you everything I think you need to know," she announced when she returned to the fire. She sat down and looked at her slave for a moment. "You better eat. It's not much good cold."

"I'll eat while you talk," Dolan offered as he picked up his plate. In the firelight it was hard to tell if he had been crying, but his voice was shaky.

Marelda took a deep breath. "Now don't overreact to the things I'm going to tell you. You just do what I say, and we will both get home in one piece." She held out her hand so he could clearly see her signet ring. "My family is the royal family of Vanhilmer."

Dolan stopped eating and looked up for a moment. Then he grinned and chuckled. "So basically, you owned me before you even bought me," he stated and nodded as though greatly amused. "Well, I'm honored then. If I gotta be a slave, guess I can't get much higher than this."

"You're a little higher. My name isn't Mary, it's Marelda. I'm the youngest of my siblings," Marelda added.

"The heir," Dolan stated as he felt a warmth in his stomach that was an odd feeling of pride. The sensation made him angry; it went against everything he'd ever felt before, and it made him feel like more of a fool for ever trying to run, because it hinted that there was a way to be content in chains. His mind refused to deal with that possibility. He fell silent but continued eating as she spoke, his eyes and ears tuned to her more sharply then ever before.

"Yes. Well, you may have heard legends about how my family once controlled several realms, not just Vanhilmer. It isn't a tale; it's history." She picked up one of her books. "At first, the land was ruled well by a Queen and her Consort, who followed the new law of the Divine Couple, correcting the ancient divisions of wealth, sex, and religion. But they fell into their old ways, teaching their sons and daughters different things, rebuilding old barriers." Marelda sighed, then continued, "Perhaps equality was too risky," she mused.

Sounds like upper-class bullshit to me, Dolan thought silently, but he just nodded wisely and set his empty plate down.

"Three sorcerers stole the sacred crown, ring and necklace during a time of crisis, and were then able to cast a spell on my ancestors," Marelda said, trying to summarize hundreds of years of history. "We lost most of our land. But I can get it back. In fact," she said as she opened the book, "there is a prophecy that says I must get back those treasures and destroy the sorcerers. Not to do so will lead to the end of life as we know it," she added mysteriously.

"I see." Dolan looked at her under lowered eyelids as he set his now-empty mug aside. "I understand, or accept at least, what you are telling me, except why you need me. I'm just a recaptured slave; I'm not some warrior or a scholar or a mage."

"You can offer me unique help," Marelda replied.

Dolan sighed as she turned aside his first objection. "But couldn't you just do some magic and get the stuff you need?" he inquired matter-of-factly.

"No; magic is not always the best weapon against magic. And," she added, pausing to look at his body very carefully and licked her lips lightly, "I need some other help as well."

Dolan felt a shudder run through him as her eyes seemed to drill holes into him. "What do you mean?"

Marelda reached out and placed her hand on top of his. "Just relax this time and enjoy it. I think you could enjoy it more than you dream.

Dolan took a slow deep breath as her hand lifted his up to her lips. His skin tingled as her lips brushed against the back of his hand. "Mistress," he whispered as she moved right up next to him. Her chest was in front of his face; her scent, mixed with that of her clothing, filled his nostrils.

Marelda grabbed his face in her hands and forced him to look directly into her face. "Please do this for me tonight. Please try not to make me angry."

Without thinking and quaking with fear, Dolan placed his mouth on hers and felt her respond as one of the dairy maids he had kissed once did. Encouraged, he opened his mouth, and their tongues met and licked and probed each other.

The fear and horror that had overcome him each night before seemed to melt as her arms tugged at his jacket. He released her long enough for her to remove his jacket and shirt. His own arms settled back onto her shoulder blades, where he caressed them while she undid his pants.

The next step required that they break contact while each removed their own shoes. When she reached for her own pants, his fingers touched her own. "Show me more about pleasing you, Mistress," he demanded softly. His eyes blazed with unfamiliar desire. This was not the animal rutting he had experienced before nor the brutal use he'd fled from; he wanted it to last, and as much as that surprised him he felt compelled to follow his new desire.

"Do exactly as I say. Follow my hands," Marelda commanded.

He followed her hands and slowly undid her pants and shirt. Carefully, almost with a feeling of reverence, he slid them off her. He next lay down beside her and let one hand roam over her body as she directed. She relaxed and closed her eyes.

Dolan felt her skin, so smooth, unblemished, and firm, unlike the other women he had touched before. Her breasts rose and fell in a steady rhythm as his fingertips traced her body's shape slowly. He paused when he reached the soft curly red hair of her pubic mound.

Marelda placed her hand on his and led it back up to her nipple. "Touch these first, and taste them with your lips and tongue, but no teeth," she instructed him.

Dolan nodded as he let his fingers gently circle each nipple. Next he leaned down and kissed each one. After a few kisses, he opened his mouth and took a nipple into his mouth. Her body seemed to relax as his tongue moved almost by instinct. The rosy bud responded and hardened in his mouth, causing him to pull back slightly, his eyes wide in worry.

"That's a good sign," Marelda told him with a hint of amusement in her voice.

"Oh," the slave replied and leaned over further to give equal attention to the other nipple. After each nipple stood straight up in the air and the area around them was flushed dark reddish brown, he continued licking and flicking each with his tongue and fingers in turn. The forester-woman arched her back slightly, thus encouraging his actions further.

After several minutes, Dolan felt her move her legs apart so that he could now see her mound part and another smile which matched that on her face appear. "Mistress?" he asked as he removed his hands from her.

"Mmmm?" Marelda replied as she opened her eyes and focused on him. It took a moment for her to remember that he was not one of the palace sluts who used regularly back home. "Yes, now you turn your attentions down there. Do the same as you did to my nipples. I'll let you know if you make a mistake."

Dolan shifted his weight and moved between her legs. He looked at her sex closely. He had never seen the female body this closely before, all his other encounters being accomplished under skirts and through opened trousers or with his eyes closed tight as his head was shoved between demanding thighs. He lowered himself to his stomach and breathed in her musky scent; in spite of their riding she smelled far better than any of the jeweler's friends. His head spun as he gingerly touched the folds with a fingertip.

Marelda lifted her hips up to entice him and was rewarded with a light caress from several of his fingers. "Gentle is good, but I'm not made of rare porcelain," she added.

Dolan swallowed and let his fingers trace the outline of her folds. He marveled as the skin grew damp and her breath quickened. Previously all his service had been done to already damp and hard users who delighted in hurting him first before humiliating and using him brutally. These thoughts still crept around the corners of his mind but the wonder of seeing her response did not allow them in further.

"Use your mouth now," Marelda ordered as she pushed his head down with one hand.

Dolan stiffened at the push but soon relaxed as his hair was merely caressed. He breathed in her scent and felt his cock stir. His tongue jutted out and flicked at the center of her folds. He continued this until his mouth was pressed against her as her hips bucked in response.

As his tongue and lips licked and sucked at her mound, Dolan found his world reduced to her, while his own physical responses seemed like distant shadows. This, however, was not the escape that his body had sought in times of abuse, but one of pleasure and relaxation. His mind focused entirely on her, his own desires unimportant as her hips thrust and her hands gripped his hair in passion, but not in sadistic control.

Marelda felt the heat focus and increase in strength as she approached an orgasm. Somewhere in her mind she managed to mutter a spell which would make whatever pleasure the slave was receiving from this act twice as desirable for him. It was a spell that would only work because she had managed the earlier ritual and would only work now if she could scream the final word when she came.

Dolan felt his body tingle as her thighs clamped around his face. For a second he couldn't breathe, and his vision blurred while his mind recalled earlier indignities at the hands of others. Then a strange rush of pleasure hit him. His body shook with hers as she screamed in a strange voice, some odd sound that seemed vaguely like a word.

Marelda came in a shudder and with a smile as she croaked out the final word of the spell. She rested a moment, breathing deeply as his breath lingered on her thighs and his fingers danced gently at her sides, then with a sigh she pushed his head back and rolled onto her side.

Dolan wiped his face on his hand, which he then wiped on the grass before crawling in next to his owner. "Did I do it right, Mistress?" he asked. His answer was her hands grasping him and pulling him down to lie closer to her. That night she rested one arm on top of his sleeping body.

Marelda traced the outline of her slave's rugged jaw and tickled his tiny bit of beard as she sat awake in the early dawn. She smiled as her attentions stirred him and his eyelids fluttered, then opened. "Good morning, Dolan," the princess whispered as she brushed his ear with her lips.

The thief half-closed his eyes against the sunlight but grinned back as he let one of his hands wander to her knee. He returned her whisper. "I didn't know it could be like that," he said as his hand journeyed up her bare thigh. He turned his own mouth toward hers and parted his lips with a moan as she kissed him.

Marelda sighed as she licked his lips, then pressed hers to them so that her tongue could plunge inside him more deeply. As she ventured into his eager mouth, her tongue dipping just slightly down his throat then teasing the roof, his hand moved to rest on her hip. The princess's eyes opened for a moment and blinked.

Marelda pushed herself up so that she was sitting, the blanket clenched over her breasts with one hand. The slave lifted his head up with a groan. "Mistress, please," Dolan whispered.

"It seems the spells are working." Another woman's voice caused him to jerk back from his owner and sit up. The older, plump blonde he had spied the other day in the water with the princess was standing over the dead campfire, her hands on her hips. "Ah, I see now that you are indeed fairly pleasing to the eyes."

"Dolan, this is Sigrid, my tutor," Marelda said with a wave toward the other woman. "Sigrid, this is Dolan, my slave and thief," she continued, reversing the gesture.

"He's seen me," Sigrid replied as she snapped her fingers. A little chair, simple yet elegantly covered with padding on the back and seat, appeared. The mage took her seat and continued smiling. "He didn't tell you he was spying on us the other day?"

Marelda glanced toward the slave, who was now looking at his hands, which were clasped in his lap. "When was this, boy?" she asked; her voice sounded slightly angry.

Dolan whistled one long concerned note then glanced at his owner. "I was searching for you and you were in the pond taking a bath, Mistress," He added the word with a pleading tone.

Marelda frowned but turned back toward her tutor. "So why didn't you tell me then, Sigrid?"

The mage shrugged. "I frightened him away simply by catching his eye with mine. I assumed you felt his presence, but since you didn't say anything to him, I know now that I was incorrect."

Marelda grabbed her breast wrap and shirt and pulled them on silently. She stood up and slipped her underpants and pants over her legs, fastening a thin belt over her shirt. She added her dagger and sword in their sheaths so that she was armed.

The tutor, clearly a powerful sorcerer herself, moved to the slave and crouched down next to him. Without a word she grabbed the bedding and tossed it back. "He isn't bad at all," Sigrid said as she stood up again, a leer on her lips.

Dolan let his hands fall to his sides, not blocking the display of his naked body. He felt his owner's eyes on him and his shame returned as she simply tossed him his clothing. *I'm just a slave after all; of course she doesn't care what happens to me*, he corrected himself silently.

"I'll tend to breakfast," Sigrid announced. She raised her hands and muttered a few words, and soon a haze appeared covering the area immediately to the slave's right. As this magical mist parted, a table richly laid with golden plates and bowls appeared, and beside it were two elegant chairs, like those the jeweler had dreamed of out loud over his own meal on all occasions when Dolan had been forced to serve his former master. Sigrid grinned and took one of the chairs. "Come, Your Majesty," she said, motioning to the other chair. "Come and eat a hearty meal. Tonight you go to your destiny."

Marelda scratched her chin then went to take the other seat. Both women now looked at the slave, who stood up quickly when their wishes became apparent.

Dolan pulled on his pants and boots, keeping his eyes lowered at all times. He didn't bother to pull on his shirt or jacket but went to the table and took one of the towels lying there by the plates. He swallowed once then laid it across one arm, which he raised and bent before him at chest height. "How may I serve you?" he asked simply of the women together. His skin burned in old anger as the tutor spoke and the princess remained silent.

"He has had some training, it seems," Sigrid stated. "I shall take a bit of fruit first, boy." She turned to her pupil, who sat looking over her hands, now pressed palm-to-palm before her lips. "What do you want, my dear?"

"Would I sense him now?" Marelda replied, drawing startled looks from both tutor and slave. She turned her eyes to them with a serious crease in her brow. "Why didn't I know he was there?"

"You hadn't performed all of the rituals yet," Sigrid stated softly, noting that the slave stiffened when she spoke. "You'd know now that you've done them all."

"I haven't," Marelda said.

"What?" The tutor's face turned as pale as the snow that was keeping the melon cold in the bowl, which the slave now offered her. "What has she done to you, slave?" she demanded, grabbing his arm roughly.

Dolan stood still and silent, his mouth clenched shut but his chest heaving with dread as the sorcerer raised her other hand.

"I've done them all but the third," Marelda quickly added.

"That may be the most important one," Sigrid replied as she stood, her hand still holding the boy captive. Dolan set the bowl down on the table with his free hand as he glared at both women.

Marelda shook her head. "Did you stop to think that might have been what I was doing this morning when you interrupted us?" she said slowly.

The older woman nodded, released the slave, and stood up. "Ah, I understand. I'll leave you to it then," she said.

"Ouch," Marelda responded tiredly to the disappearance of the chair and her landing on the ground.

Dolan looked around him with a gasp as the table and everything upon it disappeared. At his feet rested two large leather bags that had not been in their camp before.

"Why didn't you tell me that you were spying on me?" Marelda asked as she stood up, brushing the grass and dirt from her rear.

"It wouldn't be spying if I told you, now would it?" Dolan replied quickly. He found his chin lifted by the sharp tip of her dagger. "I was afraid you would be angry, Mistress." He stepped back as she snorted and returned the dagger to her belt. "Plus I didn't do it on purpose; I just saw you and watched for only a minute," he added defensively.

"What's in the bags?" Marelda changed the subject.

Dolan knelt on one knee and opened both bags. "Food, like was here before on the table."

The princess chuckled. "Then I guess we can eat now, and eat well, it seems."

"Isn't there something you wanted to do?" Dolan asked carefully as he stood up, both bags in his hands.

Marelda glanced back at him and sighed. "Not now, boy."

Dolan swallowed then ventured another question. "So why don't you make us food and stuff too?"

"You mean like Sigrid?" Dolan nodded. "I could but that isn't my specialization and it would take more energy than just catching whatever we can out here."

"But it's magic," the slave replied with a shrug.

"Not all magic is the same. Remember what I told you about these three we're going after? How they each use a different type of magic?" Marelda asked and he nodded again. "Sigrid's specialty is conjuration; mine isn't. Theoretically we could do the same things just some of them are more difficult than others and they derive from different energies."

"Energies?" Dolan pushed again though he could see she was getting a bit flustered by his questions.

"Stop with the questions," Marelda finally said with a tired and stressed sigh. He wasn't going to understand the technicalities of magic so why was he wasting their time; he least he just held up his hands and was silent now. "Let's just eat. I have a lot to read to you before tonight."

"The gate will appear?" the thief guessed as he joined her by the dead campfire and took his place opposite her on their bedding.

"Yes. It begins tonight. If we are lucky, it won't end tonight," Marelda simply stated as she took one of the bags and started dividing the food between them.

"So he has the ring," Dolan repeated as he looked at the images and letters in the old book he'd stolen, which the princess held open on her lap. "He looks like this?" he asked, placing a finger over the black ink image of a young man with long hair and an equally long mustache. "Whose slave is he?" he mused with a grin.

Marelda shrugged seriously. "Once he was apprenticed to the other two, but now I suspect Mir would claim him as his property. If we're lucky we'll get to send him to his master before the night is over."

Dolan rubbed one hand over his eyes, then rested on one cheek. "Like the priest, I assume."

Marelda nodded. "This is the best map available for his castle. Study it well. We may get separated, and your job is to get that ring. I'll find you, but you get that ring, boy." She turned the page to one with nothing but letters on it. Dolan looked up at the sky as she read.

A knot of apprehension was forming in his stomach, but he focused on her words.

"His specialty is illusion, so be careful and check things out before rushing into anything," Marelda added. "If I succeed in killing him, we'll have only ten minutes to get out. His power isn't strong enough to last long after his death, and his realm is held together by it."

"You said there was only one way in or out," Dolan reminded her as he looked at her. In the hours since her tutor had vanished his unease with her had decreased again to almost the same level the first few evenings had created. "I guess I better find that ring damn fast and get back to you then."

"It would be advisable," Marelda agreed. "However, and this is important, so listen: if you can't find me and the place is crumbling, just get back through the gate. Sigrid will take the ring and make sure it gets home." She set the book aside and took one of the leftover cherries in the bag in front of her. They sat silently for a few minutes.

"Mistress," the thief spoke suddenly. "May I ask about the third ritual you mentioned this morning?"

"Do you have a particular question about it?" Marelda replied as she turned back a few pages to the map of the gate.

"Were you going to do it this morning, as you said?" Dolan asked, the knot in his stomach dulling into the more familiar kind of fear he had felt for years.

"No, I wasn't. I thought I might this evening before the gate appeared," Marelda admitted, her voice a bit tight. She let her eyes drift over to his leg, stretched out next to her knee. The fabric of his pants was tight across the muscles, revealing all of his form.

Dolan looked back up at the sky, not glancing at the princess as he inquired further. "May I ask what it entails? Just so I can be less, ah, tight," he offered finally.

"It will be a cutting," Marelda stated as she tore her eyes from his leg and back to the book.

Dolan's head dropped down at the news. He pulled his legs up to his chest, then spoke. "Cutting? I'm not sure I understand, Mistress. What's going to be cut?"

"There is a special pattern that needs to be traced into your skin, specifically on your ass or a thigh," Marelda replied. She turned toward him as she felt the air between them cool. "The cuts aren't that deep; there's very little blood, and there's an ointment to go over it to heal them quickly."

The thief sat for a few seconds hugging his knees, his eyes wide and looking far away. Suddenly he was on his feet and striding away from the camp.

"Are you running?" Marelda demanded as she hurried in front of him so she could walk facing him.

"I'm tempted," Dolan admitted as he stopped and glared at her. He spread his hands and frowned. "But then you'd just find me, burn me," and at this he shook his hands to indicate the cursed cuffs, "beat me again, tie me up and do it anyway. Right?"

"Yes."

The slave's mouth fell open in shock at her blunt answer. He placed one hand over his chest and gasped. "You would do that to me even now?"

"Why shouldn't I?" Marelda replied. She hurried as he returned to the center of the camp. Her hand was resting on her dagger when he stopped and faced her again.

Dolan's black eyes lost a bit of their anger as he noted her defensive stance. Then he looked into the princess's eyes and set his lips in determination. "Why shouldn't you?" he repeated then shook his head for a second. "Just a foolish slave's thoughts about his relationship with his owner, Mistress," he replied with a deep and exaggerated bow.

Marelda cursed under her breath and threw her dagger so it landed sticking straight up from the ground between his feet. "Why must you take something that could be enjoyable and make it horrible?"

Dolan stood up straight and placed his hands behind his back, grasping one wrist in the other hand as he snorted in despair. "Having my flesh cut up seems to be a horrible experience, My Lady. But then, I'm only a slave; what could I possibly know?"

"You know very little when it comes to sexual pleasure and magic," she replied flatly. "These rituals are for your benefit as well as mine," she added when he cocked one eye at her.

"Really?" Dolan stepped back and knelt on the ground behind her dagger. "Then enlighten me, oh, my most gracious owner. I will listen with full eagerness to your sacred words," he added with a growl.

"This isn't good," Marelda muttered to herself as she picked up the dagger and turned away from him. She listened to his breath as he just knelt there waiting, his anger and fear radiating from him, sapping her emotional energy, not feeding it as it had in the marketplace. "Let me explain the rituals to you, Dolan," she began as she faced him.

"My ears are yours, Mistress," the thief replied as she sat across from him. His face twitched as she used her dagger to tap on her boot heel as she spoke. He released his wrists and let his hands drop to his sides as he waited impatiently for her begin.

"The first ritual was to place my ownership claim inside you," the princess said softly.

"Clearly I am yours," Dolan muttered as he pulled up a blade of grass and twirled it between his fingers, his eyes never leaving her dagger.

"It does more than create an emotional tie," Marelda continued. "By using my magic I have assured that you will not be penetrated by anyone without my explicit consent. Anyone wishing such contact with you will have to seek my permission first, because a short-term spell will be required to breach the barrier I have placed in you. It is for all penetration, that which you receive or give," she added, looking up at him and meeting his eyes briefly before he lowered them to her dagger again.

"So, that means that only your friends can rape me," Dolan stated with a wary grin. "What a great gift you honor me with, Mistress." His voice displayed the strong feelings of humiliation this news caused him.

"You may wish to sincerely thank me for it later," Marelda countered, shaking the dagger at him briefly before using it to flick another bit of dirt from her boot.

"And the second ritual," the slave prompted after a few tense silent moments. "That was when I pleasured you last night?"

"Yes, I used my skills to make it so that part of my pleasure gets transferred to you, so that you will feel a greater tie to me and desire sexual contact with me more than you might normally," Marelda stated. "Basically, you'll get more from any sexual act with me than you would with anyone else."

"Which is why I," Dolan paused and looked away before continuing, "why this morning happened?"

"Partly," Marelda admitted, her own feelings now bruised by his thoughts. "The cutting would protect you from another's magic, to a great extent at least. I'm not the world's strongest mage, but you would always have a bit of free will if someone else tried to enchant you."

"But not with you," Dolan quickly added. He smiled tightly as he sighed. "But then, you own me, right?" His eyes rolled up as he clenched the fabric of his pants in his fists, his mind working through every method he could imagine to change his fate. "Couldn't it be an amulet or something like that?" he asked, holding his hands out, pleading in his eyes.

"Amulets can be removed or lost," Marelda explained. "Someone would have to overpower you and restrain you to physically remove a cutting. I suspect you'd fight pretty damn hard to save your leg or your ass."

Looking around, he nodded for a few minutes. *I can't argue with that, what good would it do me?* Suddenly Dolan sat back on his butt, sticking his legs out so that they rested on either side of the princess. "How do you want me, Mistress?"

"I think we should rest and get ready for tonight," Marelda replied as she stood up and tucked the dagger back in its sheath. "The cutting can wait."

"Are you sure?" Dolan asked, then held his breath until she responded.

"It can wait. How strong can this first evil sorcerer be? He's only an illusionist," she added with a forced short chuckle. The princess went to their bed rolls and lay down. Neither of them spoke as the slave joined her to sleep. Neither slept well as they each worried about the choice that had just been made.

Dolan woke up to find the princess standing and looking at a bright hole in the sky about two feet from the ground. He grabbed his vest and jacket and hastened to join her. "Is that the gate?" the thief asked as he slipped on his clothing.

"Yes, it opened a few moments ago," Marelda replied. She lifted up her hands, palms toward the hole and chanted a few words. After a few minutes she lowered her hands. "It will remain open for twenty-four hours unless something happens to the sorcerer. Then we'll have very little time."

"Ten minutes. That's what you said," Dolan reminded her. He checked his dagger and boots, then motioned to the hole. "After you, Mistress?"

Marelda tilted her head, then jerked it back toward the hole. "You first, slave," she insisted. They stepped up into the hole and were momentarily blinded by the light. The princess pushed the thief ahead of her until they had passed through the bright part into an alien terrain. "Well, it's just like the book," Marelda exclaimed as she looked at the twisted silver trees, the golden sky and the purple castle just ahead of them.

"I really wasn't expecting it to be like that book said," Dolan admitted as he bent and pulled a blade of pink grass into his hand. He held it out and shook his head at it. "Unnatural," was his only further comment.

"It's going to take us a good ten minutes to get there," Marelda announced, pointing to the castle. "There's not supposed to be anything dangerous out here, but I'd rather be prepared," she added, unsheathing her sword. "Lead the way, my thief," she ordered, using the blade to reiterate their destination.

Dolan likewise unsheathed his dagger and held it tightly in his hand as he moved up the trail toward the castle. Every now and then he glanced back to find the princess grim-faced and determined. He decided against any of the snappy comments that were running through his mind in favor of silence.

"We don't go in the front door," Marelda stated as she pulled the slave off the main trail and steered him through the brush and grass.

"I thought there was only one way in or out?" Dolan countered as his mind retraced the information she'd shared with him earlier.

"No, there should be a secret door. I can feel it." She moved very slowly, her eyes scanning the magenta outer walls. "It should be here," she said as they stopped. After a few minutes of pressing her hands against it one of the bricks gave way and the hidden door opened up.

Dolan looked back toward the circle of light that marked the gate and sighed. "Could I look at the map again?" he asked.

Marelda dug into her jacket and pulled out a piece of paper. "I made you a copy. I thought you might ask." She unfolded it and pointed the features out. "This is where we are now. The ring is here, and I hope the wizard isn't. We'll go together, but if we get separated, you head for the ring. Don't put it on; just put it in your pocket and get yourself back to the gate."

"I understand," Dolan replied. He took the map but looked at the princess. "What if something happens to you?" he asked one of his previous questions again.

Marelda grinned. "I didn't know you cared so much," she teased. "Like I said, if the castle starts to crumble around you, you go through the gate. If something happens to me, Sigrid will come and fetch you so at least the jewels get back home. They are more important than I am."

"And what would happen to me, Mistress?" the thief ventured quickly.

"Yes, I thought that was your real concern," the princess commented. "That would be for Sigrid to decide."

"Great," Dolan said, softly recalling how cold and superior the senior mage had behaved toward him.

Marelda just frowned and waved toward the door. "Now let's go!"

They walked through the dungeons the door led to, surprisingly empty of prisoners, and to a stairway leading only upwards. "Be careful of illusions," Marelda cautioned as she pushed her slave up the stairs before her. They surfaced in a corridor with four hallways branching off. She looked at her bracelet for a few minutes, turning in a full circle then stopping again when it glowed. "That way," she pointed toward the east.

Dolan shook his head as the gaudiness of the outside world was surpassed by the colorful banners hanging from the ceilings and multi-colored bricks which made the walls. His boots made no sound on the odd, soft, light blue floor underneath him. "Did he do his own decorating?" he mused quietly.

"I'm surprised he hasn't proposed to my sister; they'd probably get along real well," Marelda replied with a smile as she looked around with every step, her sword held defensively.

The slave was about to speak when a sound made them stop. He moved back to stand next to the princess as two large creatures, bipedal like a human but clearly not of their own race, advanced with large maces in their hands.

"Go!" Marelda ordered as she used her hip to shove him in the direction they had been going. "Go!" she repeated when he looked at her.

One growl from the creatures was all that was needed to start the thief's feet running down the hall. He paused at the turn to glance back, allowing himself a slight grin as he saw his owner cut one of the creatures in half before attacking the other.

Dolan looked at the map checking his direction as he ran. After several moments he paused to catch his breath and glance behind him. "Where is she?" he wondered out loud.

"I'm right here."

Dolan turned around to find the princess standing before him, her sword cradled in the crook of her arm.

"You're heading the wrong way," she said.

Dolan began to nod, then stopped when he noted her blade looked perfectly clean. Though no expert, he assumed that, having seen her kill at least one of the creatures, there would be blood or some such liquid on the blade or on her clothing.

"Come on," the princess urged. "You want that ring, don't you?"

"We're going fifty-fifty, right?" Dolan asked. He frowned as the woman nodded; something wasn't right, and anyone should have seen from the beard on his face that this kind of arrangement wasn't likely.

"That was our agreement, wasn't it?" the princess replied.

"Oh, yeah," Dolan replied as he approached closer. The creature screamed as he buried his dagger in its chest. The slave pushed it from him shuddering as it turned into a slimy green mass before sinking to the floor and dissolving into a stinking green puddle at his feet.

"Shit!" he muttered as he double-checked the map again and inched his way around the puddle. "At least he can't read my mind," he whispered as he continued down the hall at a jog.

Marelda walked quickly in the same direction as her slave, her blade dripping the green slime that the creatures seemed to be made of. Her bracelet glowed, confirming that she was headed after him and that they were both headed toward the ring. She jumped when she heard his voice off to the side of her.

"Thank goodness you're all right," he said as he stepped forward from the shadows and took her into his arms. "Ah," he gasped as he stepped back and off of the sword she had shoved into his gut.

"Very weak," Marelda commented as the creature crumbled into a green puddle. She hurried toward the chamber where the ring was. As she passed another green puddle she nodded her approval at her slave's work.

Dolan pressed his back against the wall as he edged closer

to the pedestal where the ring was elegantly displayed. He moved whenever the guard looked a different direction but froze when the ice cold eyes swept over the area where he was hiding. *Why am I even thinking about doing this? Because she told me to*, he reminded himself. He flipped the dagger into what he hoped was a good attack grip. Then, praying that the guard was just another creature of illusion, he ran the short distance to the platform from the wall.

Once on the floor, his back pressed tightly against the steps that led up to the pedestal, he took several silent deep breaths, thanking every deity he could remember that the guard hadn't seen him. He froze when he heard what sounded like the princess's voice call out to the guard.

"Yeah, you ugly bastard!" Marelda rested her sword on her shoulder as she walked slowly toward the guard. "You know, you should really talk to your boss about the security around here. It's pathetic. And his magic, oh! A child, a half-witted child, could do better."

Dolan bit his lip and waited until the guard had moved a few feet from the pedestal. As he jumped up and grabbed the ring he caught sight of the princess once more cutting her foe in half. The thief froze as ice seemed to cover his hand.

"So, you're a slave," the wizard chuckled as he held tightly onto the hand which grasped the ring. "Oh, I know how nasty that can be, my friend. Let's see how well you handle your worst memories."

Dolan swallowed as he found himself staring into the violet eyes of the sorcerer. He blinked and tried to clear his mind as the room seemed to spin and change into a familiar nightmare. Dolan found himself back in the slave quarters, crowded with teens and children crying and yelling around him as the adult overseers herded them toward the workshop. He looked down and saw his body, bruised and naked except for a torn and dirty loincloth; on his ankles were the chains he would have received if he hadn't run away when he did. "No," he whispered as he looked up to find the jeweler and his friend advancing toward him with hungry, horrible grins on their faces.

The wizard turned his violet eyes to the princess. "Stay where you are, bitch, or he dies. You wouldn't want to throw all that gold away, would you?"

Marelda narrowed her eyes. "I see now why you have the ring. Without it, you're no better than a second-rate magician. Hardly fit to wash the feet of your teachers," she spat out. She took the opportunity to jump forward onto the platform so the point of her sword was pointed at his neck. "How did you ever end up with the other two? Let me guess, you were their slave or their servant?"

The wizard snarled and released the thief's hand. He screamed as the princess sliced his own hand from his arm before he could touch her. "No! I was promised power!" were his last words as his head followed suit and landed on the floor.

Marelda grabbed her slave's hand and forced the ring from his grasp. Overhead the first shudders of the building could be heard as the magic which had created this world died with the sorcerer. "Come on, Dolan!" she ordered as she jumped off the platform. She turned and looked at him as he stood frozen, his body shaking.

His legs dragged as he tried to back away from the jeweler. "Now boy, you just open up and be nice to my friend and me here, and you'll get a bit of sleep before you start on that necklace tomorrow," the jeweler cackled. The pudgy oily hands reached out to him, pulling him forward.

"No!" Dolan screamed out loud. "Sir, please. I beg you, please," he cried as he shook his hands wildly as though fending off an attack.

"Fuck!" Marelda exclaimed. She stuffed the ring into an inner pocket of her vest and sheathed her sword. "Come on, boy! Come along now!" she ordered as she grabbed his hands and dragged him off the platform. "Faster!" she screamed as she pulled him by his wrist after her.

Dolan looked around at the slaves around him. He tried to reach out with his free hand but all turned from him. The jeweler and his friend laughed as they hurried him through the dank narrow hallways that separated the slave quarters from the work rooms. They didn't stop there, and Dolan saw the pair whom he'd been told were his parents watching helplessly as he was rushed past them and upstairs to the main house.

Marelda dodged the falling walls as best she could with the dazed slave in tow. "Damn!" she cursed. "I thought it would wear off once I killed that bastard," she muttered. Once outside she paused just long enough to pull her silver whistle from under her shirt and blow it three times.

Dolan screamed at the song of the party whistles as he was led through two large double doors. There, waiting for him, were all of the jeweler's friends, his wife and her friends. As he was led into the enormous room they all reached out and grabbed his body, ripping the loincloth from him so their nails could scratch him everywhere. "Open up!" they began to chant. The slave screamed as he saw a table frame just ahead of him. He had spent hours strapped to this frame, his legs parted and his arms tied down so that his ass and throat could be used at their whim, each guest competing it seemed in a contest of sadism and perversion. He whimpered as he felt himself being lifted up.

Marelda grunted as she tossed him stomach-down over Sugar's saddle. She grabbed the leather thongs from her jacket pocket and quickly tied his wrists to his ankles. "Let's go!" she ordered, grabbing the reins and mounting Magefinder. She spurred her steed once, and they took off toward the gate as the sky began swirling and flickering. She ducked as she jumped the mares through the gate.

Quickly dismounting, Marelda stood facing the gate. She took out the ring and held it out toward the pulsing circle of darkening light. After several minutes of chanting the gate shuddered and folded in on itself, sending out a shock wave which knocked both her and the horses back a few feet.

Now that the portal was closed and she felt they were relatively safe the princess turned her attention to her slave. She cut the leather straps and eased him off the horse so she could lay him on his back on the ground. Next she spread his shirt and vest back so his chest was bare. Marelda sighed as she laid his nipple rings down flat against his chest, noting that his nipples were erect even though he was obviously suffering from the illusion.

Marelda removed her own jacket and vest, folding it up to protect the ring, as she stood up. "I'm going to have to do some combative spell rituals," she announced to the mares as they watched her. Slowly with measured steps she began circling his body, chanting and gesturing with her arms and hands.

Dolan moaned as he was lifted from the table frame and flipped onto his back. He closed his eyes but was rewarded with a slap from his owner's wife as she crouched next to him. "Now you gonna service my friends," she ordered. The slave groaned and tried to turn his head from her as she touched his lips. He screamed as his nipples were twisted brutally. "You do as you're told, slave!" she commanded, forcing his head straight. Dolan shuddered as a dark, moist mound descended over his face.

"You have to take this," Marelda whispered as she tilted the vial of amber liquid to his lips. When he attempted to turn his head she braced it between her thighs and pinched his nose shut. As his mouth popped open, she poured the contents into his mouth and watched him swallow it with a cough. "Come on, you have to fight it," she said as she laid his head back down. He didn't stir, so she resumed her chanting and circling.

Dolan sputtered and coughed as the cock spurted into his throat. He was dizzy with all the cocks and fingers entering him, all the liquids covering him, all the bodies demanding his attention. There were no more faces, just smells and an ache in his body that reached into each part of him. "Come on, fight it!" another voice said. The slave opened his eyes a bit and looked through his owner's pudgy legs to a beam of green light forming. The light moved and grew into a familiar form of a woman with long red hair billowing out behind her. "You have to fight it," she repeated. The slave struggled and pulled one of his hands free so he could reach toward her. "It is an illusion, only an illusion," the green mist woman told him softly.

"An illusion?" the slave repeated as he pushed the bodies off him and began to sit up. He blinked several times; each time the room spun and grew fuzzy until it was replaced with the night sky above him. Dolan pulled his hands close to his body as he glanced around cautiously.

"Thank the Lady and Lord," the princess sighed as she knelt on the ground in front of him. She wiped her brow of the sheen of sweat her labor had produced. "Dolan? It's me, Marelda. Are you with me now?"

The thief swallowed, and his hands went to his throat as though to ease the pain there. "How did you get me back?" he whispered hoarsely.

"I just had to break the spell," the princess said. "He was stronger than I'd predicted, unfortunately, but that was probably because you had the ring in your hand. He was channeling most of his powers through it, I'd guess."

Dolan looked now at his clothing and pulled his shirt tighter about him. "You got my clothes on me too?"

Marelda tilted her head and frowned for a moment before smiling and shaking her head. "You weren't really, wherever."

"The jeweler's," Dolan interrupted. "It was another of his parties, but worse than any before."

"It was just an illusion," Marelda tried to explain. "You weren't back there, you were here, just trapped inside bad memories."

"No," Dolan insisted as he staggered to his feet. "I was as old as I am now, he sent me back there. I could smell everything, feel everything. It was very, very real."

Marelda let him rant for a few moments as he wandered around their camp. Finally he stopped and looked carefully about him. "Yes, it was just an illusion," she repeated when he asked for clarification. "All of your worst fears made real in your mind. It's a very easy thing to do, but usually it dies with the source. I'm afraid this is going to be a bit more difficult than I thought," she added with a sigh.

Dolan returned to sit on the ground next to his owner. "More difficult? I don't think —" Suddenly he stopped speaking and checked his pockets quickly. "The ring? I had it, I swear I did, Mistress. That's when he grabbed me," the slave offered.

Marelda placed her hands over his and held them still. "I have it. It's safe." She pulled him closer to her so that his head rested on her chest as she rocked and held him. At first he was stiff in her embrace, then he relaxed and put his arms around her waist. They sat for several minutes until she yawned, gave him a slight push away, then stood up. "We should get some sleep. There are a few hours before sunrise. Sigrid will be here in the morning."

Dolan rolled his eyes at the tutor's name.

"Are you angry because she told on you?" Marelda asked with a smile as she tossed him his bedroll.

"I should have told you, and I shouldn't have spied," Dolan admitted as he caught the bedroll and stood up. "I don't know what it is. I just feel very," he paused and chuckled, "well, that's what I am."

"You left some words out," Marelda stated, cocking one eye at him as she finished laying her bed out next to the embers of the fire.

"I felt more like a slave when she was here," he finally said. "I mean, I know I am, but I feel like I'm of value to you, real value," he tried to explain. When the princess simply looked at him, he set his bedroll down. "One who is talking way too much, obviously. I'll go get some wood for the fire," he said before jogging off to the nearby pile he had gathered earlier.

It's just her magic, he told himself as he gathered up a few logs. Glancing over his shoulder toward the princess, he tilted his head at the sight of her laying his bedroll next to hers. He stood up, looked around him, then returned to camp with the wood.

"Sigrid is very concerned with this quest," Marelda stated as the slave laid the logs onto the embers. "She doesn't want anything to distract me from the goal. And," she added when the thief crouched down and eyed her with suspicion, "she is also very class-conscious. You know that most people are."

"I'm not likely to forget that I'm your property, Mistress," Dolan replied as he rubbed one of the cuffs through his shirt. "You made that very clear to me at the beginning."

"Because you pushed me," Marelda insisted.

"Guilty," the thief plead as he held up his hands. He watched her eyes dance with the reflection of the flames in the stone circle. "You're gorgeous," he whispered hoarsely.

Marelda felt her face warm, so she looked away. "It's just the magic," she replied, certain that after the horrid illusion no one could recover so quickly.

"I don't care if its magic, if you don't, Mistress," Dolan replied; his voice sounded closer.

The princess turned back and found his face merely inches from hers; he'd moved to join her. "You're very forward for a slave," she stated.

"Tell me to stop," Dolan whispered as he brushed her neck with his tongue and lips. "Command me then; I will obey," he promised as he moved up to her ear and licked the lobe.

Marelda sighed as the wetness of his tongue, the silkiness of his lips and the scratch of his beard and mustache all tickled her skin. "Dolan, stop," she whispered. Immediately the slave moved back so he was about a foot from her, his black eyes large with desire. "Very good," the princess complimented as she stroked his face, fluffing his beard and caressing his skin, causing him to moan.

Dolan's eyes remained focused on the princess's own as his face tingled from her touches. He opened his mouth and eagerly accepted a finger, sucking on it and circling it with his tongue. Surprised at himself, he even leaned forward as the finger was withdrawn. Swallowing, he sat back and glanced down. "Do you want to do the cutting now?" he offered, partly out of fear the earlier illusion had created in him and partly from fear of his responses to her finger at that moment. It was wrong to want an owner so much; it could prove dangerous in more ways than one.

"Let's just get some sleep for now," Marelda replied as she wiped her finger on her bedroll. "We'll discuss it in the morning." She watched him closely as she lay down, then smiled and patted his own bedroll when he didn't move.

Dolan nodded and pulled off his boots. He set them with his jacket and vest at the foot of the bedroll. Just to be certain, he double-checked his ankles, but found only the healing marks from the shackles he'd worn before being sold. His mistress lay inches from him, her eyes already closed, her breathing slow and steady. Controlling the hand which wanted to reach out and touch her auburn hair as it laid about her head like a halo, he snuggled down so he could watch her sleep until his own exhaustion overcame him as well.

Chapter Four:
The Path Embraced

"You realize, of course," Sigrid stated as the slave blinked his eyes open to see the early morning sunlight, "that you should be up and have her breakfast ready for her."

Dolan sat up immediately and looked around him. He was about two yards away from the campfire and the princess, still asleep. He and his bedroll had been moved without waking him, until now. "How did I get out here?"

"Magic," Sigrid replied as she sat beside his bedroll in a far more elegant chair than the one she'd created the day before. "I understand that you were not trained to deal with royalty, so I'm here to help you learn," she said with a serious look on her face.

Dolan swallowed all the uppity responses that flitted across his mind and simply stood up. His boots, vest, and jacket had been moved as well, so he pulled these on. He sucked in his breath as the sorceress grabbed his chin and turned his head left and right, examining him.

"You had a bad enchantment last night," Sigrid announced as she released him. "She should have done the cutting. Now why didn't she?" the tutor asked in a deep, threatening voice as she leaned back in her chair.

Dolan brushed his hair back with both hands as he eyed the sorceress silently.

With a wave of her hand, the slave was tossed up into the air, then allowed to fall back down to the ground. "I find it hard to believe that the princess would allow you to not answer her promptly, slave. You will afford me the same basic respect," Sigrid ordered as the slave shook his head and glared at her. "I am your better, boy."

Dolan bit his lower lip as he stood up. "I'm sorry," he managed to say with only a hint of anger in his voice. When the sorceress began to raise her hand again he held up both his hands and hastened to add,

"My Lady is very kind, very caring. She didn't want to push another ritual on me." He sighed when the tutor lowered her hand and halfway nodded. "Cutting is very scary," he admitted. "My Lady says it will work better when I'm less afraid."

"More willing," Sigrid corrected. She stood up and immediately the chair disappeared. "It's true; spells done under fear or against the subject's wishes are weaker. She," and as Sigrid spoke she looked toward the princess, "should do it before the next gate."

"I want the cutting. Believe me," Dolan stated as he knelt to pack up his bedroll. "I don't want to be at the whims of others anymore."

Sigrid chuckled, both at his comment and the glance her response was earning her. "Fix your mistress breakfast, boy. Learn your place," she added firmly before disappearing in a puff of smoke.

"Fuck!" Dolan stated softly as he jumped involuntarily from the display of magic. "Damn! I am never going to get used to that," he told himself as he picked up his bedroll from where it had fallen when he'd been surprised. After a glance at the position of the sun, he walked back to the saddlebags.

Marelda lay awake for several minutes watching as the thief fried up several biscuits in a pan over the fire he had obviously built up. The light of the rising sun was behind him, the fire lighting up his face as he sat sideways to her. Together they created a halo around his black curls as they hung down. With a sigh, he pushed one lock behind his ears. "Making breakfast?" she asked finally.

Dolan looked over at the sound of her voice and smiled at the princess. "Am I making too much noise, My Lady?" he asked, tilting the pan so she could see the biscuits turning golden brown.

"No, I think it's the smell that has my stomach awake," Marelda suggested as she grabbed her boots.

The slave watched her pull them on, recalling pleasantly how the leather had felt in his own hands when he had removed them. The fat in the pan hissed, drawing his attention back. Using one of the forks, he flipped each biscuit over, nodding at the color on the bottom. "Almost ready, Mistress," he announced.

The princess stood and stretched a moment, shaking her hair about to loosen any grass which may have gotten tangled in it during the night. She hurried into her vest and jacket to protect her against the cool morning breeze. "Biscuits, huh? Anything else? I'm starved,"

Marelda declared as she sat down on one of the short logs sitting around the fire.

"I got out more of our fruit, and there was some leftover rabbit from last night, so I made a gravy," Dolan said as he divided the biscuits evenly onto their plates. He took the cloth he had been holding the frying pan with and used it on the handle of the pot he had sitting to the side of the fire. After setting the pot between them he stirred the gray gravy with the ladle a few times. "I hope it's good," he added with a slight frown as he dipped some onto her biscuits.

Marelda took her plate and held it under her nose so she could take a big whiff. "Smells like rabbit; that's usually a good thing for rabbit," she commented. She watched the thief as he lifted his own plate but didn't move to eat. "You know, where I come from we make the slaves eat a bit of everything first, to make sure it's fine. In fact, we often have one particular slave do that for each of us."

"Oh, I guess being royalty you have to worry about poison, huh?" Dolan said. He picked up his fork and scooped a large bite of biscuit and gravy into his mouth. His eyes darted around as he slowly chewed pausing when he caught the princess's gaze. Dramatically he rolled his eyes and started to faint then regained his composure and shrugged. "It's okay. I'm not a chef, though," he cautioned with a grin.

The princess laughed and had to grab her plate tightly to keep from spilling her own food. "Just don't do that when we get home. You could get into a lot of trouble."

"He should be beaten," Sigrid dictated as she appeared, sitting in the same elegant chair she'd used earlier that morning, off to the side nearest the princess.

Marelda rolled her own eyes as she took a bite. "We aren't home now, so just relax a bit," she said. The tutor didn't comment further but simply sighed and waved her hand so a piece of fruit drifted up to her. "So, did you get him up this morning, Sigrid?"

"Yes," the senior mage replied. "He is supposed to be serving you on this quest, you know."

"He is. Just in the ways I want him to," Marelda added with a wink toward the slave. The emotions feeding the blush on his cheeks made her eyes twinkle. She glanced up at her tutor. "Did you ever think I might have needed him this morning?"

The senior mage shook her head and waved her free hand. A small, iron trunk with jewels on it appeared on her lap. "You got the ring?"

The princess handed her plate to her slave and dug into her vest pockets until she found it. "Here," she indicated as she placed it into the now-open trunk, "it's wrapped in the cloth like you instructed."

"Wonderful. One third done, then," Sigrid replied as she closed the trunk before sending it on its way.

Dolan opened his mouth to comment, but refrained as he returned the princess's plate to her.

"What were you going to say?" Marelda asked, noting his gesture.

"I was just wondering where it was going and if it will be safe, Mistress?"

"Are you implying that my own student shouldn't trust me?" Sigrid demanded angrily before the princess could respond.

"Of course not," Marelda interrupted immediately.

"Then why is he just glaring at me?" Sigrid pointed out. "You need to learn some manners, slave," she threatened as she stood up, a nasty-looking whip appearing in her hand.

"No one touches him without my permission," Marelda stated. She looked angrily from the thief to the tutor and back until Sigrid sat back in her chair. "You weren't implying that Sigrid can't be trusted, were you, Dolan?" she demanded first.

Dolan looked down at his plate as he softly agreed, "No, Mistress. I wasn't. I was just concerned after all the trouble to get it."

"So, I think he deserves an answer," Marelda now said, more to the tutor, as she looked directly at her. After the senior mage simply nodded and sent the whip back to where it had come from, the princess continued. "The trunk is what the crown jewels were kept in originally. I've placed a spell on it, tied it to me so anything that goes into it can only be removed by me or my sister in case I should die. I believe Sigrid sent it back home where it will be safe."

"The most dangerous thing for this quest would be to let these fall into one of those wizards' hands," Sigrid announced.

"Why didn't one just take them all?" Dolan asked, receiving another glare from the tutor but a nod from his owner.

"The magic protecting them was still strong when they were stolen," Sigrid replied. "It took three very powerful wizards wielding the powers of the old religions to take them. It cost them their souls, so each demanded a treasure in payment."

"Actually, I'm surprised they haven't fought over them in these centuries," Marelda commented. "I would have thought the third one would have had the strength to take them for himself."

"That was not the deal they made with their masters," Sigrid explained. "One never goes back on a deal with the old gods." The tutor nodded to the princess and waved both arms.

Dolan shook his head as the tutor disappeared again. "I'm not going to get used to that," he repeated as he poked at his last bite of biscuit.

"Sure you will," Marelda said. "Toss me an apple. We need to do the cutting this morning. I don't want Sigrid whisking you off so easily, even if it was under good intentions."

"Sounds good, Mistress," Dolan replied slowly as he handed her the best of the remaining apples and took one for himself, his hands shaking.

Dolan bit his lip and closed his eyes, pressing his body into the tree stump. His fingernails dug into the bark as the knife made another cut. He concentrated and repeated the chant she had dictated, his voice wavering a bit.

Marelda ran a gentle hand down his outer thighs as she repeated her own chant. He didn't have to be naked for this ritual, but it didn't hurt the ritual either, so when he'd disrobed she had just smiled and told him to grab the stump. "That's good, Dolan. Just two more lines and we're finished," she whispered. She gripped the ritual knife in one hand and poured more wine over it.

The thief felt tears at the corners of his eyes as another line was added, parallel to the last. His throat felt so parched as he muttered the words, trying his best not to slur them, but he croaked out the last syllable. Her chant gave him a few moments of rest before the last promised line; this one felt like it was cutting across the first two. His final chant broke at the end with a hoarse sob.

The princess repeated her cutting chant, then laid the knife aside. She ran both hands down his outer thighs, then up the insides. As he parted his legs with a groan halfway between pain and desire, she began a new chant. "Repeat the next three words," she ordered.

As Dolan repeated the words multicolored lights seem to dance in the darkness of his closed lids. His ass tingled and seemed to burn as his owner said more magical phrases. "Ah!" he cried and jumped further up on the tree stump as something cold and wet was poured over his ass.

"Just to prevent infections and help it heal faster," Marelda assured him. She sat back a bit, stroking his thighs lightly as she surveyed her handiwork. The cutting was a larger version of the brand on his ass. A large stylized M had been placed first, then inside, under the peaks, were a stylized V and H. The blood was clotting now, so she added another wash of the cool water she'd had him collect from the well earlier that morning. She handed him a small cup of the water to drink as well.

Dolan relaxed as the heat started to dissipate, and his muscles loosened under her hands; the water felt wonderful as it slid down his throat. He looked back as he felt something cold but semi-solid on him. The princess smiled and applied a bandage to the cutting; her naked breasts jiggled a bit as she moved. "Mistress?" he asked softly, setting the cup in the grass.

Marelda glanced up at him and allowed one finger, still covered in the ointment, to slide along the crack of his ass. A new heat, one she'd never felt from him, hit her senses, but she only grinned and teased him. "What, slave?"

"Please," he asked, his eyes fixed on her hand as it traced its way back up his crack. As one finger dipped in quickly to tickle him, he hit his head on the stump in response to the desire sweeping over him.

Marelda removed her hands and wiped them on the cloth at her side. She smiled as his ass thrust back slightly and a moan passed his lips. "What do you want, slave?" she repeated softly.

Dolan rubbed his head on his shoulder and sighed before glancing back. "Please, don't make me beg," he said.

"Just tell me what you want," Marelda insisted. When he didn't reply she gathered up the ritual knife and ointment vials and stood up.

Dolan's lips trembled as his desires fought with the bits of pride he still held. Finally, when he saw the princess was putting the ritual items away, he lifted himself off the ground and pulled his pants slowly up. His ass protested slightly at the fit of the underwear, then shot pain through him as the pants covered it. Sucking in his breath, the thief pushed himself to his feet. He jumped a bit as the princess appeared in his immediate view as he turned around. She was still bare-chested, and she had been perspiring again from the ritual.

"Here, drink this and eat this," Marelda ordered with a grin as she handed him a mug of wine and an orange she'd been hiding for this moment. "You can relax the rest of the day, boy. But we move out tomorrow, so try to take it easy on the physical activity," she suggested as she finished lacing up her shirt.

Dolan nodded and mumbled a "thank you." After a few moments he went to his backpack and took out his dagger. "May I go for a walk, Mistress?" he asked.

"Just go slow and be careful." Marelda tilted her head back and examined the sun. "Here," she said, tossing him a chunk of bread, "take some other food with you, but be back by sunset," she added. The princess felt his eyes on her for a moment before he turned and went walking toward the woods. When he was out of sight she looked at her bracelet so she could follow him just in case he fell back into old habits.

Dolan walked slowly in a straight line, eating orange slices and discarding the peel, until the pain on his ass made him stop. He eyed a relatively low tree branch then decided to simply lean his shoulders against it instead of climbing up and laying along a big branch. These woods were thin, so the sunlight billowed in, lighting up all the brush and dirt below his feet.

He took the chunk of bread he had grabbed from his jacket pocket and bit into it as his eyes focused on a line of ants marching in the dirt. A farmer he'd bunked with for a few days once had told him that ants were slaves. They had one leader, a queen, who gave them the orders which they followed blindly. But, this farmer had said, because the ants obeyed so readily it showed that they were happy with their lot in life. Everyone, the oddly philosophical man had added as though he knew who Dolan was, should just be happy with their lot.

Dolan chuckled a bit as he recalled how poor that farmer and his family had been. They worked a small piece of land they didn't own and were practically slaves themselves. Yet every night, as they shared their meager meal with him, they had joked, laughed and even sung. The slave crumbled his last bit of bread onto the ground and watched as the ants attacked and gathered it up. He watched as they returned to their line and marched back to their queen. Back to the only life available to them. *Just like me*, he added as one of his cuffs reflected the sunlight back into his eyes. After one long drink of water from his flask, Dolan headed back toward the camp.

Marelda frowned and blinked at her bracelet, then quickly lowered her hand as her slave broke from the woods at a rather quick pace, not a run but a good determined march. She pulled out the book of maps and set it in her lap as he walked toward her.

Dolan dropped his water flask and dagger on top of his backpack, then paused. He ran his hands through his black curls before approaching the princess. He waited a few seconds, but she didn't acknowledge him. Finally, gritting his teeth both from the pain in his ass and the bruise to his pride, he knelt down and pressed his face and hands to the ground at her feet.

Marelda now looked up from the book, her mouth slightly opened in surprise. His desire was still there, still edged with anger, but with fear of rejection as well; the bond between them was letting her feel him strongly. A magical green light escaped her hands as she tapped her fingers on the book.

"Mistress," Dolan whispered, barely loud enough for her to hear, "please fuck me."

"What?" Marelda asked, a smile starting at the corners of her mouth.

The slave groaned and clenched his hands around the grass, his nails digging into the soil beneath. "Please fuck me," he repeated a bit more loudly.

The princess tilted her head and looked at the thief carefully. In this short amount of time the slave seemed radically changed, but was it from her magic or from her treatment? Marelda set the book next to her and set her face into an unreadable expression. "What did you say?"

Dolan sighed and lifted his head just slightly so his voice would carry better. "Please fuck me, Mistress," he restated slowly and clearly.

"Hhmmm. No," Marelda said.

The slave sat up suddenly, his mouth hanging open for several silent moments as the princess simply stared back, her arms crossed over her chest. Dolan swallowed then offered his hands, wrists together and palms up. "Please, Mistress," he begged, his eyes unable to look directly into hers as he spoke, "fuck me. Please," he paused and swallowed, then added an extra "please" with a quiver in his voice.

Marelda tilted his head up by his chin and looked into his red eyes. "Are you sure that's what you want, boy?"

"No, Mistress," Dolan replied, then added softly, "it's what I need."

Marelda gripped his chin tighter to keep him from lowering his head again. "You must give me an honest answer to this question. Do you need it because you feel this urge in your body?"

Dolan blinked. "Yes, but it's more than just that, Mistress. I just can't keep fighting what I am anymore," he whispered, and tears fell down his cheeks. "I can't run from you; I can't be what I'm not. I'm so tired of being angry and unhappy. Please, just use me now, let me know that I can matter to you."

Marelda brushed the tears away with her hand and pulled him into her arms with the other. "That's wonderful," she whispered back, her mind thinking over the prophecy about the thief who steals that which cannot be stolen and learns that he is what he cannot be with anyone else. It made sense. There were two types of slavery. That which dictates our actions because of who we are and that which is forced upon us. To be both at the same time was rare, just as the leader who is a natural and recognized leader was rare. After his tears had stopped and he rested motionlessly in her arms she gently pushed him back. "Take your clothes off, all of them," she ordered as she stood up.

The thief's hands shook as he slipped his jacket and vest off. Next he pulled off his boots and socks. Standing on slightly wobbly legs, he unbuttoned his pants and slid them and the underwear to his feet, where he kicked them off. He blushed as he shed the shirt so that nothing was left to hide the erection he now had. A moan broke from him as the princess's hands took hold of his shaft and stroked it to its full length.

"Since you asked so nicely," Marelda whispered, "you'll get some pleasure from this, slave." She caressed his balls and inner thighs briefly, then withdrew from him. It had been several days since she'd been home to use one of the skilled sluts on staff, and her own desires pulsed in her guts. "On your hands and knees," she directed softly, curbing her own desires to ease his journey.

Dolan lowered himself and felt a double wave of shame and excitement wash over him. He closed his eyes by reflex but saw images of his former life flash before him, so he opened them. His muscles tightened automatically as her hands returned to their caressing of his thighs, balls, and cock from behind.

"In my home," Marelda said softly as she worked his muscles firmly so they relaxed and heated under her palms, "we have mirrors which we sometimes place before slaves so they can watch themselves being fucked. They seem to enjoy that. Of course, we also have some trained specifically for sexual pleasures. But we don't deny ourselves the others, nor do they shirk any duty demanded of them."

Dolan looked down back between his legs so he could observe his red cock as it melted into her hands then bobbed up and down as she worked his thighs and ass cheeks. He looked up with a sharp inhalation of air as he felt a finger slide into his ass. He waited, expecting the pain and humiliation he was familiar with, but instead a full, calm feeling rose inside.

Marelda smiled and slipped her finger out, pleased when he moaned and thrust back toward her. She placed a palm over each cheek and began rotating them in opposite directions, her thumbs next to the puckered hole. As she massaged the hole was opened and closed, the skin flowing open and even seeming to struggle to stay that way as it was pushed closed.

Dolan lowered his head again and bit his lip as he felt a strange emptiness when his hole was opened and then a feeling of despair as it closed on nothing, this new longing displaced the rare pain from the cutting. The minutes seemed to drag by as she continued her tease. Every promise he had made to himself, every consolation he'd given himself when forced by the jeweler vanished when she blew her warm breath onto the opened spot. Dolan swore silently then opened his mouth in a plea. "Please fuck me, Mistress."

"Like this," Marelda asked with a grin as she pressed one finger just in to the first knuckle and wiggled it a bit.

"Oh, yes," Dolan replied softly, a slight moan indicating his feelings.

The princess pushed it in to the second knuckle and wiggled it a bit more. "Sure you don't mean like this?"

The slave moaned and thrust back a bit. "Like that. Oh, yes," he agreed eagerly.

Marelda thrust her finger in deeply, then pulled it out to the tip and thrust it back again. "Or do you want it like this, slave?" she teased as she repeated the process. "Do you want it deep and pounding? Do you like my fingers or would you prefer something larger?"

Dolan's eyes widened as he felt the sensations washing over

him and the fear of what the larger might mean. For a moment he heard the jeweler's voice in his ears. "Please, Mistress," he begged, hoping it was loud enough to drown out the past's voice. "Deep and pounding, but not larger. Please, not yet," he added with a glance over his shoulder.

Marelda noted his terrified eyes and the fear radiating from him. She simply nodded as she thrust back in. "Now I want to hear how much you enjoy this, slave," she ordered, hoping that wasn't anything he'd heard before. She closed her own eyes as he began moaning and groaning, thrusting back as she thrust in. Around her finger his heat and smoothness made her skin twitch and tingle. She had to move her own hips a bit so she could press her calves against her mound as his reactions triggered her own passions.

Dolan cried in pleasure as the princess's other hand grabbed tightly onto his cock. He tried to control himself but found it jerking and spurting cum into the grass under him. With the women he'd screwed while on the run, any desire had quickly faded after such release. This was the first with the princess that wasn't tinted with magic ritual, yet he found himself hard again almost immediately.

"Wonderful," Marelda stated as he grew solid in her hand. She felt a tiny pulse in her own groin and immediately released his cock and slid her finger from his ass. She ignored his pleas as she stood up and headed toward the well. As she washed her hands she noted that he was maintaining the position, his ass thrusting back every now and then, hoping that something would fill it again. "Wonderful," she repeated to herself. *He should have been a palace slut*, she decided as she headed back; *of course, he can be once this is all finished.*

Dolan froze as he felt cold hands touch his back. They moved down from his shoulder blades to his hips, then journeyed underneath his belly. His owner's legs settled behind his own as she lay on top of him, her braided hair falling over one of his shoulders as her forehead rested on his shoulder. He tilted his head so he could nuzzle the red braid and the top of her head.

"How do you feel?" Marelda asked softly as she stroked the muscles and ribs of his stomach with her hands, now warmer from his body heat.

"So hard, please," the thief replied as he continued nuzzling her hair.

"That's not what I meant," Marelda replied with a slap to his still-long cock. She bit his neck as he moaned from the slap. "I want to know how you feel, and I don't mean this," she added pulling once on his cock.

Dolan hung his head and sighed in frustration. Several minutes passed in silence, but the princess simply returned to caressing his stomach and chest as she waited for an answer. "I don't know," he finally said.

Marelda slid off of him and sat next to him. "Here," she said as she tossed his clothes to him. "Why don't you go wash off and get dressed? It will give you time to think," she explained.

Dolan mumbled his gratitude as he got to his feet. His legs and ass felt stiff as he walked to the well. The water was cool in his throat and on his skin, even around his asshole as he tried to calm his desires by splashing some to his needy orifice. But while his thirst was quenched, his body felt tight, poised to explode, as he watched the princess start their dinner.

Slowly, sensuously he slid each item of clothing onto his body again. *What do you want?* he asked silently as his eyes focused on his owner across the grassy space between them. There must be dozens and dozens of free wealthy men, even more poor free men, and surely those palace sluts she'd mentioned, who were better qualified for this job than him. His submission up to a few hours earlier had been questionable, and even now he didn't quite understand why he'd swallowed his pride and so shamelessly begged her.

Leaning over the stone of the well, the setting sun still shone enough light to illuminate his face as he looked into the water. His hair was damp from the water, but the curls were still there, framing his lean face. His skin was darker than it had ever been, since as a slave to the jeweler his life had been indoors at a workbench, while on the run he'd spent his time in shadows and darkness. In fact, on closer examination it appeared to be a bit red. Dolan narrowed, then widened his eyes, trying to see if there was anything interesting about them, but found nothing. The short mustache and beard circling his mouth was only an improvement on what he would have looked like with any other owner, but then free men shaved clean. For a brief moment he even wondered what an earring might add as he brushed back one lock of hair, before sighing and straightening up.

She was beautiful. Even compared to every woman who had ever entered the jeweler's store or those among the crowd at the auction, she was clearly special. As royalty, though, that was to be expected, since they could get anything they wanted at any time. Except for these three sacred ornaments. It couldn't be his looks; it couldn't be a lack of volunteers nor the lack of money, he decided as he pulled on his boots. He watched the princess carefully as he laced them up tightly. There was something she hadn't told him yet, something he wasn't sure he really wanted to know.

Marelda looked up with a smile as her slave joined her by the fire. "So do you have an answer?" she asked as she stirred the stew again.

Dolan crouched down right next to her and tilted his head to one side. "How do I feel? Was that your question, Mistress?" he queried seriously. At her nod he raised his eyebrows. "I don't really understand what you want me to say."

"How about the truth? You do know what that is, yes?" Marelda responded as she placed the lid on the pot, making sure it was tilted a bit so steam could escape. The princess sat back on her elbows and looked at him. "What happened to you out in the woods that made you so humble? Must have been something amazing. Beating you doesn't do much good."

"Isn't this the way you wanted me?" Dolan stated, then flinched and threw up his hands before she could slap him for his impertinence. "Sorry," he muttered quickly. "I was just thinking that perhaps my life might be better if I just accepted the fact that you own me, that I'm just a slave."

"Go on," Marelda encouraged gently.

Dolan sighed and ran his hands through his hair before continuing. "I wasn't born lucky. I wasn't born to rule like you, or to own my own life like a freeman. I can't change that about me. I wish I could," he admitted. He sat down, pulling his legs up in front of him so he could hug his knees as he continued. "So, while I was out there, I remembered something a very wise but poor man told me. I have the ability to make my life harder or easier by deciding to resist or to obey."

"Are you sure it's that easy?" Marelda asked suddenly. "What if I decide to beat you just for the fun of it?"

"You'd do that anyway," Dolan pointed out and earned a nod from the princess. "But at least you wouldn't do it because I refused to obey, and I know I'd feel better about myself if I couldn't blame myself for my abuse. Does that make any sense?" he asked after a moment of silence.

"Yes," Marelda agreed. "It's that way with all of life. All of us have things we have to do; the choice is how we do them and how we feel about ourselves. Some of us are what we are on several levels. Which brings us back to the original question," she said as she leaned toward him. "How did you feel when you begged, when I took you, and when I stopped?"

The thief blushed as he now understood her question. "Well, um, I felt embarrassed and afraid when I begged. I felt like I lost a part of myself."

Marelda's lips and brow frowned. "Then why do it?"

"Because it also felt more free," Dolan began to explain in a far away voice. "If you had said no, then I'd have gone about my chores and waited for the next gate and the next wizard. If you'd said yes, then I might have enjoyed it. But at least I know now that I don't have to worry about how I'll react when you tease me and force me to beg you again." He rested his chin on his knees with a look of enlightenment in his eyes. "I guess it would be pointless for me to pretend I don't want your touch."

"That is very hard for you to say, isn't it?" the princess suggested as she reached out and caressed his head. "So when I took you, did you enjoy it?"

"Yes," Dolan admitted as he moved his head a bit so she could caress him more easily. "It was strange. It was like nothing I've ever experienced before. I felt so full and alive and wanted when you were in me, then I felt so alone and empty when you left," he added as he glanced up at her, his pupils wide with desire. "If this is that magic of yours, it's pretty damn good."

"And what if I told you it wasn't just the magic?" Marelda ventured to ask as she moved closer to him.

"Then I guess I'm more of a slave than I thought," Dolan said softly as he lifted his head up. As their lips met, he parted his, and moaned as her tongue flicked the insides of his mouth lightly. His hands reached out and caressed her shoulders, slipping to her waist as she placed hers around him. After a moment he turned his face away and whispered, "I'm sorry. I feel like I should ask first, because I'm just a slave."

"I'll let you know if I want you to stop," the princess informed him as she used one hand to turn his face back to hers. "Move your legs down, though, boy."

Dolan closed his eyes as his lips met hers and his legs straightened so she could climb on top of his lap. His skin tingled wherever she touched him through his clothes, the heat flowing from him into her it seemed. At one point he opened his eyes and saw a glow of green light around the princess similar to the visions of his dreams and magic-induced nightmare, but he simply groaned and lifted his hips as she slid his pants from him.

Marelda stroked his cock several times until she was sure he was about to explode. With one final kiss on his lips she pressed his chest down with one hand as she turned to his groin. Slowly she licked the length of his shaft, tickling the underside of the reddish purple head.

"What?" Dolan whispered as he felt a warm wet pocket envelop his cock. He felt a rough, moist stroking as the unfamiliar warmth was pressed firmly around him. Part of him wanted to bolt, worried about what she was doing, but the other part couldn't help but think how many times he had done such to the jeweler and his friends, which only changed the form his worry took. Owners did not do to slaves as she was doing.

She moved quickly and firmly, her hand and now one leg on his chest, pinning him in place. He had worked grudgingly, often just offering his mouth and throat for use without movement of his own. His head spun as he felt himself spasm and orgasm. Then the world turned cold and the light from the stars just rising dimmed. The last thing he saw before closing his eyes in exhaustion was that mysterious green light around the princess growing darker.

Marelda sat up, swallowing his seed and pulling his energy into her body. She shook as the last rays of his energy streamed from him into herself. As she pulled up her own pants she smiled at her bracelet as it pulsed, confirming that he still lived but deeply slept. His body was still hot at the groin as she pulled his own clothing back into place.

The stew smelled good as she lifted the lid and stirred it. Its taste mingled with the aftermath of his liquid in her mouth, becoming bitter. After two more sips, he no longer lingered on her palate. She wondered if he'd ask about her actions when he awoke but was happy when he simply held out his bowl and grinned shyly at her. That night, he lay comfortably in her arms, his head on her breasts as they slept, while Marelda calculated how many more times she'd need to drain him before the next gate. Without a direct question, she decided that keeping her need to herself was best for both of them. The less he knew, the less anyone could pull from him by magic, torture, or bribe.

Chapter Five:
The Second Gate

Dolan shook his head several times as he tried to wake up. This was getting more difficult each morning. But then, what peaceful sleep he had had these past five nights after the princess pinned him to the ground and took his cock in her hand, then her mouth — five nights of bliss and the deepest sleep. *What kind of fool would argue with this type of use? What does she need this for?* he wondered silently as he forced his eyelids to open.

The sun hit his eyes as he opened them; his hand jumped up to half-cover them as he shifted to a sitting position. He grinned and glanced down as he stood up under the princess's gaze. "Should I get anything, Mistress?" he asked when he had joined her by the campfire, where she was baking biscuits.

"Go see if any more of those strawberries are ripe, would you?" Marelda suggested. She watched him as he went toward the bushes where he'd found the fruit the day before when they had stopped. Wiggling her fingers, she nodded when the faint light drifted up. "One day and it'll open," she whispered to the fire as she poked the rising bread lying in the frying pan.

"Does he know what you've been doing to him?" Sigrid's voice made the princess jump back in surprise.

"Why should he? You said he'd recover," the princess pointed out with a disgruntled frown at her tutor.

"He will, as long as he is given enough time. And you? Are you ready?" Marelda wiggled her fingers again, causing her tutor to grab her hands. "Don't waste it like that!" Sigrid warned.

"You said it was renewable," Marelda countered.

"Yes, given enough time. The third gate will open just a week and a half from today. You'll need to drain him ten times for that one. And then once you're home, you'll need more from him. You haven't forgotten the sacred ceremony, have you?"

"Of course not," the princess replied. "And Dolan is fine. He's happy; he thinks he's the luckiest bastard alive, and maybe he is," she added with a chuckle. Her bracelet tingled, so she glanced down at it. "And he's coming."

Sigrid stood up and faced the thief as he reentered the camp site, his jacket cradling the strawberries. The tutor simply lifted her chin, ignoring the princess's tug on her skirt, when the slave stopped a few feet from her.

Dolan bowed his head once. "Good morning, Madame Sigrid," he said cheerfully before stepping around to the other side of the princess and kneeling on the ground.

"No witty comments or nasty glares?" Sigrid asked as she watched him lay his jacket on the ground.

Dolan glanced at his owner then up at the mage with an apologetic smile. "I'm sorry about how I behaved earlier, Madame. Would you like a strawberry?" He offered her one of the largest and reddest.

"Wash them first," Marelda ordered with a pinch to his arm.

Sigrid noted with pleasure that the slave's only response was to blush and to quickly stand up, taking the bowl the princess offered him. She watched silently as he went to the nearby well, this one far older looking than the one at the previous gate site, to gather water. "Have you been performing some other spells?" she asked her student.

"No need to," the princess replied. "He just realized that his life can be a lot better if he accepts his lot and obeys me. Just as the prophecy predicted," she explained simply.

"Really?" the mage responded; her voice betrayed how little she believed that. Now Sigrid believed fully in the sacred texts; she had trained her whole life and the one prior to it for this time, but still some things were hard to grasp. *Slavery: how could anyone find comfort in that?* she mused then waved her arms and disappeared in a puff of yellow smoke and light.

Dolan paused, waiting until the magic smoke had fully dissipated before he returned with the water. He glanced up every now and then to find the princess concentrating on the bread as he soaked each berry for about one minute in hopes of ferreting out any insects. When all the berries had been cleaned he set them on a clean cotton cloth in another bowl.

"Dolan," Marelda said. As he looked up she pressed a bit of the baked bread to his lips. She sighed as he opened his mouth and took her fingers inside, sucking on them as he slipped the bread off. "It's ready," she announced as she lifted the pan from the low fire.

"Mistress?" the slave asked as he handed her most of the berries, keeping about a third for himself in the bowl that had held the water. At her nod he continued. "Do you enjoy doing that to me?" he asked, venturing the question that had bothered him every day and night since she had first taken him into her mouth.

Marelda raised one eyebrow and looked at him before answering slowly. "Why else would I do it?" she replied carefully.

"Of course," Dolan agreed quickly. "I was just wondering because I always thought it must be a way that a slave serves his master, not ever the other way around," he added quickly. He caught his breath in his throat as her hand closed over one of his wrists.

"I figure that my owning you gives me the right to do whatever I want to you," Marelda said. "Don't you agree?" she demanded, her eyes narrowing slightly.

"Yes, Mistress," Dolan replied immediately. His wrist hurt a bit, he realized after she released it. His first impulse was to rub it, but he wisely just rested it on his leg as he started to eat. *Just be happy with it, you stupid fool,* he cursed himself for treading on obviously dangerous ground.

Marelda paused in her reading to lay the second sacred book aside, then cleared her throat once, causing her slave to jump a bit and focus his attention on her. "Actually, I thought this was rather frightening, myself," she said.

"Yeah," Dolan replied with a weak nod of his head. He tapped the book a few times, glancing over the maps for the next gate and the palace of the next wizard, this one a woman whose skills were in the area of physical pains and pleasures. The thief looked up to find the princess regarding him with arms crossed over her chest. "I'm sorry; my mind was wandering a bit, my Lady. But I'm fully focused now."

"Really?" Marelda responded. She took the book back into her lap and scooted closer to him. "This isn't going to be so easy, Dolan. These books were written by prophets hundreds of years ago. They were able to figure out the first sorcerer's abode because he was weak."

"He was weak?" Dolan repeated with a frightened chuckle as he remembered how the illusionist had tortured him.

"My thoughts exactly," Marelda muttered agreement. She stood up and took her sword in hand. "Stand up; get your dagger. We're going to train a bit," she explained.

The thief raised his eyebrows but stood up and took out his blade. He offered it on his palms to the princess.

"No, I want to see how you fight with it," Marelda stated. She stuck her sword back into its scabbard and motioned with her hands. "Come at me with it."

"I don't think so," Dolan replied as he stepped back from her.

"Do it!" Marelda stared at him for several minutes before kicking him in the side and knocking him to his knees. "You better defend yourself, boy, or you're a dead man!"

Dolan stood up slowly, the dagger grasped tightly in his hand as he watched the princess circle him with catlike movements. He swore out loud when she kicked him again, this time knocking him onto his back.

Marelda looked down on her slave, one boot planted on top of one of his arms. "If I were your enemy, you'd be dead by now," she commented as she leapt from him and stepped back a few feet. "Get up! Defend yourself!"

The thief got up as quickly as he could. His arm ached where her foot had been, and his back felt shaken out of joint. This time when she struck out he was able to move aside enough that he simply stumbled but didn't fall.

"I'm disappointed," Marelda stated. "You killed one of those illusion creatures before. Must just have been luck."

Dolan narrowed his eyes for a moment as he turned with her, watching her every move closely. "I wasn't fighting a warrior and a mage, neither of which I am," he said as he attempted to attack her but was easily tossed aside by her graceful moves. "Not to mention the fact that you own me, and everything I've ever been taught says I don't harm you." He turned quickly this time and rolled away as she jumped on the ground where she had thrown him.

"That's better," the princess admitted. "I wish I had more time to train you though. You might have some talent." She sighed as he attempted to attack her again. With a smooth movement she gripped his neck and wrested the dagger from his hand. Deftly she pointed it at his throat. "If I wasn't me, what would you do right now?"

Dolan glanced down at the knife and tried to step back and throw her off, but she simply adjusted her stance to accommodate him. "I'd die," he said.

"You wouldn't beg for your life?" Marelda asked sincerely. "You wouldn't promise your captor anything and everything?"

"No," Dolan simply said. He stood still as the princess released him and tossed his dagger into the ground at his feet. As he picked up his weapon he continued. "Just because I've accepted that you own me, doesn't mean I'd accept being enslaved by anyone else. I'd rather die, in fact."

"Good," Marelda replied. As she turned away from him, she allowed herself one wide, pleased grin. "As it should be."

Dolan looked back to the gate opening as it stood out as a bright beam of sunlight. He placed his hand cautiously on his dagger as he hurried after the princess. These woods looked normal — almost too normal, he decided, then a strange flower caught his eye. "Did you see that plant?" he asked softly.

Marelda chuckled as they passed more of the phallic-shaped pink blossoms. "Pleasure and pain," she reminded him.

"So this is all an illusion?" the thief stated hopefully.

"No, these are real. She's just twisted them with her magic. I'm sure she finds it very amusing," Marelda replied.

The walk seemed longer than the previous journey, and it wasn't until they had cleared the woods by a good quarter of a mile that the castle appeared on a hill. The walls were a ghostly white, pulsing with a gray fog unnaturally located only around its foundations.

"How long do we have?" Dolan asked with a worried glance back into the woods.

"It won't close until she's been dead a while or I close it," the princess stated. She took out her book and glanced over a few pages. "Her power is strong, so it should last several hours."

"Maybe we won't have to kill her," the thief mumbled as he paused next to the princess and glanced over her shoulder.

Marelda just looked at her slave, snorted and replaced the book in her pack. "You go in the front door, and I'll take that lower entrance over there," she said as she pointed with her finger to a tiny black spot on the white walls.

"The front door?" Dolan repeated as he stepped back. "What am I supposed to say? 'Excuse me, Madame wizard, I've come to steal your necklace?'"

"I doubt that will work," Marelda replied. "She uses sex to get what she wants; perhaps you should as well; you are capable of it," she further suggested. The thief stood silently for a moment before shaking his head and following the princess up the hill.

Dolan was still shaking his head as he knocked on the door with the elegant and heavy gold knocker. "What if there's no one home?" he whispered to himself. He jumped as the double doors swung inward and a man's voice ordered him inside. Glancing left and right in the darkness did no good until the doors were bolted behind him and a man, humped over on one side, emerged with a torch.

"What do you want here?" the hunchback demanded, his voice scratchy but deep.

Dolan blinked and rubbed his hands on his pants. "Sir," he began as the hunchback stepped closer with a scowl, "I'm lost."

"Lost?" the hunchback sneered. "Quite difficult to end up lost in here."

Dolan nodded a bit then motioned to the door. "You're right, Sir. I followed this woman into a strange portal. I'd been following her, hoping to steal something from her, you see, and when she did the strangest things and this circle of swirling lights opened, my curiosity got the best of my common sense and I followed her."

"So where is this supposed woman?" the hunchback demanded, fingering the heavy sword that hung at his belt and thrusting the torch closer to the intruder.

"I don't know. I lost her in here. It's very odd here, you must admit," Dolan added with a chuckle.

"I don't have to admit anything to the likes of you!" the hunchback retorted, waving the torch a bit.

"Quite correct, Sir," Dolan said quickly as he stepped back and away from the flame. "But for me, a lowly thief, a new thief, well, I started looking around myself and lost the woman I was trailing." The hunchback tilted his head further and just glared. "Of course, I saw this magnificent castle and headed here in hopes of getting some help. Is there any help you can give me?" the slave added with a bow of his head that he hoped showed how sad and desperate he was.

The hunchback snorted, then grabbed the trespasser by one

arm. "I'll take you to my mistress. Perhaps she can help you, perhaps not."

"That's most kind of you, Sir," Dolan replied as he was steered deeper into the castle. He looked around himself, hoping he could memorize the way.

Marelda paused in the dank corridor as she heard approaching footsteps. She pressed herself against the cold wet wall and watched three guards pass within a few feet of her. The sounds of their feet and the angle she saw them at indicated they were coming down a stairway.

These guards were human, or at least as close to human as anyone could be inside a magically-maintained world. The magic had left them all very hairy; the fact that they were bare-chested left little doubt of that. Their bodies were huge, as was the obscene pouch covering their groins. Each pouch had the image of a vicious snake on it, clearly a warning and a pun at the same time. Other than the genital pouch they wore only belts with two-handed swords and hard boots.

The princess counted to ten very slowly, then inched her way along the wall in the direction they had come. The maps of this place were vague; in the palace beyond the previous gate, the secret door in the illusionist's world had been several feet beyond the place the drawing had indicated, and these were worse. There was little hope that the rest was more accurate, so Marelda decided to follow the logical thought that the guards must have come out of the castle proper.

When she reached the top of the stairs the guards had descended, another sound of footsteps made Marelda freeze. She listened closely then cursed silently as she realized there were two sets approaching her, one from behind and one to the left just out of sight. With a prayer that they could see no better than she, the princess bolted to the right. There was a door several feet away, so she pressed herself as flat as she could against the wood and behind the stone frame of the building.

The set of guards she had seen met another set at the top of the stairs. The two groups exchanged words, but unfortunately in a language the princess could not understand. The guards looked down the hallway they'd just come from, then to the right toward Marelda. The three who'd come from down below pointed toward her hiding place. Soon both sets of guards split up again, the second three returning in the direction they'd come while the other group approached her.

Marelda whispered a spell under her breath and tried to fade into the wood. Around her the air grew heavier and darker. The three guards walked by her, one looking directly at her, but they did not stop. A further second of chanting and she could see the hallway no longer, only the wooden door in front of her. Looking around, she found herself in a storage room, bags and kegs on the shelves around her. The door was locked, she discovered when she twisted the knob. "Great," she muttered. "This is going to take a little longer than I thought."

The sorceress held up one hand, stopping the intruding slave in mid-sentence. She stood up, her large half-exposed breasts swinging slightly as she stepped down from the pedestal her throne was on to stand directly in front of him. "You're lying to me," she stated with a tight frown.

Dolan swallowed and looked at his feet. "Ma'am? I have told you all that I can." He glanced up at the raven-haired woman, who now seemed more beautiful than she had when he had first been introduced to her half an hour earlier. Before, she had appeared to be in her late forties, but now she hardly looked thirty.

"She's here, your mistress," the sorceress stated as she glanced around the reception hall. The candles dripping their red wax on the walls were the only sounds as both thief and hunchback stood silently. "And she's trapped herself," the sorceress said suddenly with a wide grin.

Dolan stood perfectly still as the sorceress circled him. "So tell me, little slave," the sorceress addressed him, making him jump and glance back at her as she came up behind him on his left side. "Yes, I know that you are. Not only are the cuffs not easy to hide, but your beard is a dead giveaway unless the culture has changed considerably," she added, grasping his arm and shoving his jacket and sleeve up.

"So, what does the foolish little mage want?" the sorceress demanded. She stopped directly in front of the slave and touched his hand to the pearl hanging around her neck. "Come on, tell me, my pretty one," she purred as she rubbed his fingers on the pearl. "Tell me, and you can have your freedom."

Dolan blinked and glanced up at her. "What?" he heard himself ask; his voice sounded far away. He vaguely felt her hand release him, but he continued caressing the pearl. It was beautiful, clearly far better than any he'd seen before, let alone touched, and yet it seemed familiar.

"I'll give you your freedom," the sorceress continued. She took his head in her hands and pulled his mouth toward her own. "And I can offer you more as well," she whispered, right before opening her mouth and catching him full on the lips.

Dolan let his hands fall from the pearl to her ample breasts, then one hand wrapped around her, pulling her tightly to him as they kissed. In his mind he saw a distant image of a woman clad in a voluminous green gown. Soon, however, the image faded as multicolored sparks surrounding a dark-haired beauty took over his consciousness.

The sorceress motioned with her hand to the hunchback. The deformed man cackled and hurried off. Behind him he heard the sorceress moan and the intruder return the sound.

Marelda wiped the sweat from her face as she held a tiny version of her sword. It was very easy to change the nature of inanimate things, but having to shrink her backpack, her dagger, the book, and finally her sword had taken quite a bit from her. The light from her fingers as she ended the chant was paler than it had been that morning.

The princess just stood there, her arms crossed over her stomach, when the original set of guards she'd seen returned and opened the storage room door. "I was wondering when you'd get here," Marelda said casually. "I'm lost and I could use some help." She stepped back into the shelves as one advanced with raised sword. "You don't need to do that," she stated.

The guards laughed as the princess fell at their feet, a trickle of blood at her temple when the sword had smashed down onto her skull. The one who'd hit her checked her breath and heart by bending close and placing one hand on her chest. With a nod to reassure his comrades that he had not killed her, he lifted her up into his arms.

"Well, now you have nothing to fear from her anymore," the sorceress cooed to the slave as he looked away from the hunchback, who had just interrupted their conversation to whisper into her ear. "Your owner is quite out of the way. You need not concern yourself with her any more."

"Is she dead?" Dolan asked, half expecting the cuffs to kill him with bolts of lightning. When nothing happened he half laughed in relief.

For twenty minutes he'd been telling the sorceress why he was there and what the princess was looking for. If asked he could not have said why he was betraying his owner, but the sorceress, it turned out, was a caring, loving woman. Not to mention the fact that the sight of her young curvaceous body had him harder than he thought was possible.

His suspicions, though, were not yet evaporated. "So will you enslave me now or simply kill me?" he asked as he stood up, the hunchback moving toward him.

"Oh, Dolan, you wound me," the sorceress pouted. "Truly you do. I don't want you to stay with me against your will, and I certainly don't want to kill such a lovely boy as yourself."

The sorceress stood up and slowly undid the lacings of her bodice. Once freed, her breasts proved to be larger than any the thief had ever seen before. She caressed each one with her hands, pressed them against the pearl that hung between them on a silver chain. "Let me prove it to you," she suggested as she moved closer.

Dolan focused on the brown nipples, which swung back and forth as the sorceress moved closer. They felt solid and warm to his hands as he took them from her and began kneading them. The pearl danced before his eyes as he leaned down and placed one nub into his mouth. Sucking, biting, twisting, things he could have never done with anyone else for fear of punishment, seemed to happen naturally as he surrounded himself with her breasts.

The sorceress chuckled as she pushed the slave down on the floor so she could straddle him. Her mouth twisted a bit at the jolts of pain and pleasure his attentions were causing. Soon she pulled away and sat back to unlace his pants.

Dolan lifted his hips so his pants could be removed easily. Instead of taking them off, though, they were simply pushed down to his ankles, as were his undergarments. He watched as the beautiful witch teased his thighs with her long red fingernails. He arched his groin up as her hands approached his cock. The grasp was firm and slick. When he looked he saw that the sorceress was taking the wetness from underneath her skirt and using it to grease him well.

He nodded when she asked if he wanted to join with her, be her consort, her partner, promising him wealth and power. He lay back as she moved her body forward. When she was straddling his hips, she raised her skirt and spread her legs wide, showing him the place he knew was there but had never really seen before his time with the princess. Colored lights seemed to be whirling around her thighs and swirling into her. "Oh, yeah, let's do it," he purred. He moaned as he felt the moist area touch his eager cock.

A scream from both their throats snapped him back a few feet and sent the sorceress bolting to her feet. Dolan's body felt like he was both on fire and being stuck by several hundred needles. He rubbed his eyes and looked at his would-be partner. The woman seemed different, older, wrinkled, ugly, for a moment then wavered and became the same beauty he'd been touching, though with a deep frown.

"Damn!" the sorceress yelled as she pulled her shirt from the floor.

"I'm sorry; is it something I did?" the thief asked as he stood up slowly, pulling up his pants awkwardly.

The sorceress rubbed the pearl between her fingers and counted slowly and softly before turning toward him with a smile, her shirt held weakly to her body. "No, you haven't done anything, my lovely lad," she spoke sweetly. "It seems your former owner has placed a spell on you to prevent our wonderful partnership. I should have realized she would," the sorceress conceded with a tightening of her smile.

Dolan shook his head. "I'm sorry, I should have told you, I didn't realize it would last so long."

"Unfortunately it appears to be a very strong spell," the sorceress decided. "But it can be cured." The sorceress smiled, then held out her hand, the one that had been holding the pearl out toward his face. The slave came to her and sighed as she caressed his face. "You'll have to do it, of course. It will be quite simple; my guards will help," she suggested.

"Do what?" the thief asked as he turned his head and kissed her hand.

"You'll have to kill her. It will be so easy, and it is the only way for us to be together and for you to be free," the sorceress coaxed with a soft voice and caresses of his body with her hands.

"I thought she was dead, I don't know if I can kill her," Dolan said softly with a slight frown.

The sorceress tilted his head up and fluttered her eyelashes at him with a pout. "Don't you want me? Don't you want your freedom?" She patted his head as he nodded. "I knew you felt the same way about me," she cried, false tears just forming in the corners of her eyes. "It will be so simple," she whispered as she kissed his mouth.

The third guard rubbed his arm and glared at his buddies as they stood at the end of the cell furthest from the woman they'd captured. Every attempt to enjoy the beautiful body they'd discovered under the rough clothes had been met with shots of pain as though they'd been struck by lightning. "You said we could have at her before killing her," the third guard growled to the first.

"Aye, so I was told," the first insisted. He shook his head, then offered a strategy. "If we all go for her at once then it will work."

"No, it won't," Marelda said as she sat up. Truth was that she'd been awake for the last two attempts but was enjoying the effect her protective spells were creating; she also knew they wouldn't last. She stood up now, her jacket and shirt parted, her breast wrap askew, her pants around her ankles. As the guards watched she unfastened the wrap and slipped her jacket and shirt to the floor so the undergarment could follow. "Don't you think it might be better to have a willing partner? And if your pouches are any indication," she added with a nod toward the obscenely decorated coverings, "I'd like a good bite from your serpents."

The leader of the guards sneered and elbowed his nearest friend. "We don't need your permission, girl, and we don't give a damn whether you want it or not," he announced as they advanced.

Marelda just held out her arms as they each grabbed one. "I wouldn't do this if I were you," she warned them again. She frowned as one shoved his hand into her mound. The frown became a smile as both guards screamed, their bodies jerking violently before collapsing onto the ground.

The princess shook her hair back and smiled at the third guard. "Now, surely you're a wiser man than your friends?" she teased. As he nodded and stepped forward, Marelda took her hands and ran them down the sides of her body. Her hands parted her thighs, and she sighed as they traveled back up via her center, trailing moisture up her stomach.

The guard smiled. "You want this?" he said as he loosened his pouch and brought out his organ, red and hard. He stroked it twice as he moved forward. His eyes widened as the prisoner knelt before him.

Marelda looked up, her eyes wide and her smile genuine. "Oh, I need this," she declared. She took his hand from his cock and touched it with her own. With just her lips she kissed the crown and the shaft, giggling as the big burly guard began to moan. His moan turned loud and animalistic as she took him into her mouth.

He was large, but the princess only needed to get him past her lips to get what was required. Her hands slipped behind him, and with little difficulty she was able to slip several fingers into his ass. Stroking the head with her tongue and pressing with her mouth she used her fingers to massage his insides until he was bucking into her.

The guard screamed when she used her teeth to hold him into place but the sudden spurting of his orgasm made the pain and worry secondary to the pleasure he felt. He fell to his knees as he felt a rush from his groin. He looked down and saw blood flowing from his cock then in horror at the floor when he saw that the tip lay there in a pool of blood. He glanced up to find the prisoner grinning grimly, her mouth ringed with blood, as a knife descended.

Marelda chanted as she quickly slit the guard's throat. She spat out more of the blood and cum, then pulled her pants up. Bare-chested, she turned to the other guards and killed them as well as they stared at her, unable to move yet because of the shock over their comrades sudden, violent death. Quickly picking her shirt and jacket up from the floor before they were soaked in blood, the princess hopped over the bodies to the bars of the cell.

She managed to keep her stomach in check as she returned the dagger to her boot and put her clothes back on. Then, her guts wrenching, she turned to the corner nearest her and vomited several times. "Damn, it's going to take hours to get cleaned up," she swore, spitting a few extra times.

"What happened here?" The voice of her slave made the princess turn toward the bars. He was standing, his dagger in his hand, frowning at the bars, the bodies, and then her. His face was pinched up and he rubbed his eyes with the back of his free hand.

"Dolan?" Marelda began cautiously and gently as she stepped toward him. "I'm Marelda, your owner. Remember?"

The slave nodded then turned his dagger toward her. "I'm supposed to kill you," he muttered with a shake of his head.

"Really? She is very strong, then," Marelda replied softly. She moved closer and placed one hand outside through the bars. "Give me the knife, Dolan."

Dolan looked at the knife, then at the princess. Something in the back of his mind was screaming at him to kill her, but it battled with the memories of serving her and her using him in very pleasing ways as well as her vicious and immediate punishments.

"You can't kill me with that dagger, Dolan. It's magically charged to prevent that," she reminded him. "See these boys?" she added, motioning at the bodies behind her. "They thought they could hurt me, and they're much bigger, much better trained than you."

Dolan looked, then gasped as the dagger was taken from his hands. "But she told me I'd be free!" he exclaimed as he put his hand through the bars to try and grab it back.

"I seriously doubt that," Marelda answered as she added the dagger to her own belt. She took her sword and muttered a few words as she watched her slave stand there and hit his head on the bars a few times. "You better not do that. You'll hurt yourself, and I'm the only one who's truly allowed to do that now," she informed him as she strapped the now full-sized sword to her side.

"What does it matter?" Dolan retorted as he stepped back from the bars, marveling that he was still obeying, though he felt so confused.

Marelda didn't reply but ordered, "Pick the lock. This place is getting sticky and its starting to smell horrid."

Dolan crouched down and took the thief's kit from his jacket pocket. As he worked at the lock he watched the princess restore the rest of her property to full size and put the backpack on. He moved back on his knees as the door swung up and she exited. His bowed head jerked up when the dagger was held under his nose.

"Better take it back; you may need it," Marelda hinted with a flat tone. She waved the dagger until his hand closed around it.

The thief frowned, then tucked the dagger into his belt. "You're giving this back to me?"

"I gave it to you," Marelda said.

"But I tried to kill you," Dolan stated.

Marelda gave him a tired and amused look. "No, you were told to, but you hadn't really decided to, and you were obedient after just a few moments. So it doesn't really count," she assured him with a pat to his blushed cheek. "Besides, you were under her spell."

Dolan followed his owner to the door, where she checked the hallway outside. "Wait a minute! I thought that cutting was supposed to protect me from that!" he challenged.

"Tell me," Marelda countered, "is she wearing the necklace? The one that looks like a huge perfect pearl?"

The thief frowned, then focused his mind. His time with the sorceress seemed so fuzzy now, but he clearly saw the same pearl the princess had shown him in her books around the witch's neck. "Yes, it's around her neck," he said with a confused shake of his head.

"Then that's how she got through my spell," Marelda theorized out loud. "Though I bet she didn't get to have sex with you, did she? That's good; it means that I'm stronger and we have a good chance at this," she replied to his nod. The princess clapped one hand on her slave's back. "Now we need to go get that necklace from her."

"That's not going to be easy," Dolan stated. "There are six guards up there, and her number one servant is waiting for me at the top of the stairs to make sure I did this," he admitted with a sigh as he hit his head on the door.

"Well, then, this will require a bit of trickery," Marelda stated. She thought for a few moments, then took his dagger from his belt.

"No, don't," Dolan pleaded as he tried to stop the princess from cutting her own arm. He watched as she traced the blood around her neck. He took the soiled blade and began to wipe it on his sleeve when she placed her hand over his.

"Just put it in your belt. Now, I hope you can lift me and carry me up there," Marelda whispered as she tore at her shirt and added more blood there.

"Why?" Dolan asked as he swallowed and watched her ready herself.

"You're taking my dead body up to show your dear sorceress." Marelda then took a deep breath and let out a wail of anguish as she fell into his arms. She winked as he lifted her up, then she let her body go limp so that her arms and head trailed back. Her years of meditative training allowed her to slip into a deathlike state while remaining fully aware of the world around her.

The sorceress stood up as her hunchback led the slave forward, flanked by six guards. The hunchback bowed, then approached to whisper into her ear. A smile crept onto her face as she listened to her hunchback's raspy voice and watched the slave's eyes glaze a bit as he set the limp body on the floor before him.

The sorceress pushed the hunchback aside and descended the

steps to look more closely at the body. The princess had blood around her neck, which was twisted at an odd angle, as well as a torn blouse spotted with more blood. The sorceress looked up and frowned as she counted only six guards. "Where are the ones who were guarding her?" she demanded.

Dolan blinked as his mind tried to fight the spell, which hung in the air like a heavy blanket. He hadn't noticed it before, but when he'd entered the room a second time it had hit him like a wall. Looking down at the body at his feet, he bit his lip to keep from replying.

"My Queen," the hunchback croaked as he scurried down to her, "the boy says that the woman killed them herself."

"Is that true?" the sorceress asked with a tight smile as her hand caressed the pearl again.

Dolan looked up and noted that the witch was indeed using the pearl. He buried himself as much as he could deep inside himself but had to reply as she repeated her question. "All three were dead when I arrived in the dungeon. She said she killed them."

The sorceress raised her eyebrows, then shrugged. "Oh, well, I can always make more guards." Her statement caused the six there to fidget uneasily. After her glare made them quiet, the sorceress turned to the slave with a warm smile. "Did you use your dagger on her?"

"I ... did as you asked as ... best I could," Dolan haltingly replied. He looked down at the body and shuddered at the thought of what he had been so willing to do.

"Ah, you feel sad about it," the sorceress mocked with over-pouting lips. "I'm insulted," she stated angrily.

Dolan looked up and swallowed. "It's just that I've never killed another person," he reminded the sorceress.

"Such a lovely, delicate boy," the sorceress announced as she looked at her guards. She turned her face to the body and considered it for a moment. "Yes, I think the head will look lovely up on the wall," she decided with a wave of her hand that lit up the wall behind her throne.

Dolan's eyes widened at the sight of several dozen human heads on the wall. Out of the corner of his eye he saw one of the guards approach with drawn sword. "But what about your promise?" he blurted out as he stepped between the guard and the body.

"My promise?" the sorceress repeated.

"Yes, my freedom, our love. Surely, my most beautiful lady, you have not forgotten," Dolan prayed with tears forming in the corners of his eyes. It was odd, but even though he was trying to distract them he felt that he would die if the sorceress turned her favor from him. "Please, she can wait, I cannot. My body aches for you," he whispered as he grabbed the sorceress' hands in his own.

"Release her!" the hunchback ordered as he raised his hand to strike the slave.

"No," the sorceress said as she nodded to the head of her perverted staff. "The boy is right, I did promise, and he has earned it," she chuckled as she ran her hands up the slave's arms to his shoulders. "I too deserve a bit of relaxation before finishing this thing."

Dolan made sure the witch was close to the princess as he stepped back to the other side of her body. He opened his mouth and accepted the sorceress' probing tongue. As she moaned into his mouth she allowed his hands to caress her hips, then slid up to her waist to cup her breasts. His hand brushed the pearl as he turned from her mouth to nuzzle her neck.

"Do you feel the pleasure, boy?" the sorceress asked as she opened her eyes and winked at her hunchback. "Just think of how much more wonderful freedom would be if you were granted it."

Dolan opened his own eyes and looked at the guards approaching him. He felt the remnants of the magic ebbing away as the truth of the matter over-rode it in his mind. "You mean that you don't intend to free me?" he asked. He edged the hand not touching the pearl to his belt.

The sorceress roared with laughter as she pulled back just enough to see the slave's face. "Of course not. But don't worry, I intend to enjoy you thoroughly before adding you to my collection up there."

"That's too bad," Dolan replied with a sigh. He pushed the sorceress back with the dagger, drawing a bit of blood as he yanked the necklace from her. The force of the witch's return kick sent him to the floor.

The princess jumped to her feet directly in front of the sorceress. As the surprised woman stepped back, Marelda grinned. She held out her hand and grasped the pearl as Dolan placed it in her palm. "Is this the beauty you were addressing?" she smirked as the thief stood up next to her.

Dolan made a sound like a choking man as the spell dissolved. Instead of the young lovely he'd seen before, there now stood an old, old woman, shriveled with more wrinkles than he'd ever seen, thin white knotty hair falling around her head. "By the Lady and Lord," he cursed as he brought the dagger up in front of him.

Marelda quickly deposited the pearl into the cleft between her breasts so it was out of easy reach. She brought her sword up, pointed the tip at the sorceress' throat and stepped forward as the frightened crone hobbled backward.

"Don't! I can give you riches and power beyond your imagination," the sorceress promised. When the princess just continued to advance the sorceress shrieked, "Kill them, you fools!"

Dolan turned and bolted to his owner, his back to hers, his dagger shaking in his grip as the guards and the hunchback surrounded them.

"You kill me and they'll kill you!" the sorceress declared. "I'm the only way you'll get out of here alive!"

Marelda lowered her blade just a bit and rolled her eyes to one side as though thinking about the words. "What do you think, Dolan?" she asked, lifting the sword back up to the witch's throat.

"They'll kill us anyway," the slave said.

Marelda shrugged. "I think I believe him over you," she told the sorceress, then plunged the sword through her throat. The blood spurted as a dying curse accompanied the dying spasms from the sorceress. The princess turned the sword, sliding it clear though one side, then slashing back to decapitate her would-be murderer. She stood still, watching the body turn to dust in a haze of reddish black light.

"Mistress?" the slave asked as he poked the princess in the ribs with one elbow. "We still have problems," Dolan pointed out as his owner turned around.

"I don't think these boys are going to be a problem for much longer," Marelda speculated, leaning on the hilt of her sword as it stood point downward.

"Kill them!" the hunchback stormed as he hopped from one foot to another. The guards looked at him with open mouths, and the hunched-over man faded and changed before their eyes into a much smaller boy, his face wrinkled up with crying and screaming as his high voiced demanded revenge.

Dolan lowered his dagger as he saw the guards change as well. Now instead of six huge monsters of men there were six fat little boys who still filled their pouches but only because they were now taut around bulging stomachs. The six dropped their heavy swords and looked around in confusion. "What is this?" Dolan asked with a glance at the princess.

Marelda's lips curled up in disgust as she took her slave by his arm and led him toward the double doors and out of the throne room. She didn't reply as she hurried him down the corridors and out of the castle.

It was several yards before the thief pulled free and stepped in front of her. "What was that back there? You never mentioned her turning children into men!"

"It's just perverted, unnatural magic," Marelda retorted as she pushed past him and went at a fast pace toward the gate.

Dolan looked back at the castle and saw the towers starting to shake. The seven boys were wandering around outside now, but the thought of what they might become if he stuck around made the thief hurry after his owner. The plants he briefly noticed as he trotted were no longer replicas of penises; their colors were fading into dull green and brown as they literally decayed before his eyes. The princess jumped through the swirling gate then called after him.

Marelda was taking off her clothes when Dolan jumped through the gate. He stood up and watched as the hole in the sky started to shrink and close. When he turned again he saw the princess stomping off toward the well with her saddle bags.

Setting her bags on the side of the well she began drawing up buckets of water. She drew up three and dumped each over her naked body. The fourth bucket she set next to her bags and dumped the contents of a flask into it. Taking her scrub brush she dipped it into the solution and then began rubbing her body harshly.

"Mistress, may I help?" Dolan asked as he stood a few feet from her.

Marelda looked at the suds on her body then at just how much she was shaking. She glanced back at her slave and was relieved to see his face held only confusion and perhaps concern and not lust. "Yes, would you take those dirty clothes and wash them for me?"

"Of course," Dolan agreed. He picked up the clothing and immediately his nostrils were assailed by odors he hadn't smelled since the slave pens. There was of course the blood on her boots and the clothing, both her own and the guards'. As he washed, he glanced back at her, frowning as she started sniffing at her own arms and hands then took another flask from her bag. She seemed determined to get herself clean.

He returned his attention to her clothes and recognized the further smell of urine and vomit; vaguely he recalled that she'd been doing when he'd seen her in the dungeon. There was also a smell that made him sick to his own stomach, the musky scent of ejaculate, which he'd himself been forced to accept in the jeweler's shop. No accompanying scent of the princess herself was on the clothing, and that knowledge made him growl in anger as he watched her scrubbing herself again. As a slave it was easy to be raped, even if it wasn't called that, but at least you knew the risk was high and so would be somewhat emotionally broken before the violation occurred. A princess, though, a powerful warrior and mage, wouldn't be prepared. It must be a hundredfold worse for someone so powerful to be forced so low.

Marelda had just finished the second rinse when her slave came up to stand on the opposite side of the well. The look in his eyes was miserable, and she jerked back as he spoke.

"I could just burn them, my Lady, if that would help."

The princess's lips trembled for a moment, then she slammed her fist down on the stones of the well. "Just clean them and don't give me your stupid advice!"

"I know how hard this must be," Dolan began as he had several times with younger boys and girls who had just been up to the jeweler's private suite.

"You don't know anything!" Marelda growled. "Just get a bucket of water, boil it and clean everything! And no talking!" she commanded as she picked up her bags.

Dolan just stood perfectly still as he watched the princess stalk away to the other side of the fire. "I should have expected that," he muttered to himself as he recalled that his own reactions and all the reactions of his fellow slaves had been the same. You didn't want to remember it, and you told yourself that ignoring it would work. As Dolan lowered the bucket and brought up water he shook his head. *No, it's not the same at all. She won't ever suffer though that again,* he decided as he unhooked the bucket to carry it back to the fire.

Marelda was dressed in shirt and underpants now and sitting on her blanket combing out her hair when her slave returned with the water. She tried not to look at him as he emptied it into the large cooking pot they had and set it on the fire to heat. After watching him sort out the clothing and accepting the pearl he found in her breast wrap, she dug into her saddle bags. "Here, this will help you clean the clothes and shine the boots," she stated as she handed him two flasks and a small wooden case. "You might as well do your own while you're at it."

Dolan looked at her then bowed his head and accepted the items. He added the first flask to the water. As the bubbles started to form on the surface of the water he took her shirt and emptied some of the contents of the other flask onto a blood stain. "I'm not trained to clean clothes," he said softly.

"Just do the best you can," Marelda replied softly. She sat gazing at the pearl she held. It was beautiful, but the green light that pulsed from it as she held it was dirtied by its past abuse, it would have to be cleansed before it could be used. She sighed and stood up. When she was a yard from the fire in the opposite direction from the well, she threw back her head and screamed.

Dolan jumped to his feet at the sound. He grimaced as the princess's voice turned from rage to sorrow and she fell to her knees sobbing. Part of him wanted to run to her, to somehow make her feel better, but that part made no sense when he moved his arm and saw the glint of the fire's flame off the cuff at his wrist. She would only be insulted if he tried to comfort her again; free people hated anything that might resemble the lot of a slave, and rape was certainly a resemblance. He removed his own clothes and added them to the pot, then changed into just pants. With a determined frown he sat down and continued cleaning her boots.

A good half hour later a semi-familiar voice made the thief almost drop the boot he was just shining into the fire. "Well, slave, did you two get the necklace?"

Dolan bit his tongue as he picked up the boot. He sighed then smiled and tilted his face up toward the mage, making his voice as light as possible. "Madame Sigrid, what a surprise to see you tonight."

"Didn't mean to scare you, boy. If I had, you'd be aflame right now from falling into the fire yourself," chuckled Sigrid as she bent over and messed his hair up. "So where is your mistress?"

"Over there," Dolan indicated with a nod toward the direction he'd last seen the princess. He watched from under his curly locks of hair as he absently rubbed the boot in his hands. The mage went to the still-crouching princess, but when she touched her pupil's shoulder the response was a violent jerking away. Their voices were low, and the thief couldn't tell what they were saying as he tried to eavesdrop and finish his job at the same time. He straightened up, though, when his name came through loud and clear, along with a few words about the princess's "rights" to him.

Sigrid sighed as the princess held up her hands and refused to talk any more. She walked back to the fire, conjured a chair and sat down where she could easily go through the saddle bags. The slave watched her attempting to use his hair and the boots as barriers to hide his spying. The mage found the necklace and examined it closely. "Was hard to get, was it? Things didn't go quite as she planned?" she asked with a voice that sounded sincerely sad and concerned.

Dolan slowly looked up to find the mage looking at him. She repeated her question with a frown. "Yes, Ma'am, things didn't go as planned," the thief replied as he turned his eyes back to the boots. They were clean, smelling only of leather now and shining in the fire and moonlight. He took the stout stick they used to lift the pot from the fire and removed the pot to set it to one side.

"So, do you know what happened to her, boy?"

"She hasn't told me anything, Ma'am," Dolan simply said as he stood up. As he turned toward the well, he was stopped by the mage's harsh grasp on his arm.

"Don't you think you should do something for her?" Sigrid hinted, her words as rough as her nails digging into his arm.

"My mistress told me to wash her clothes and boots. That's what I'm doing," Dolan stated as his eyes flashed with anger. His eyes met the mage's until he felt his body start to tremble in fear that she might force him to do something. "Please let me finish my work, Ma'am," he finally whispered, bowing his head.

Dolan stumbled a bit as the mage tossed him away. Clearly her ample form was strong, not to mention her magic. The slave hurried to the well and drew up a bucket of cold water then carried it back to the campfire. Dolan didn't speak as he lifted each article of boiled clothing and dunked it into the cold well-water.

"You should hang those up to dry," Sigrid said softly. Her frown was tilted when the slave looked up at her again. "Hey, I'm not heartless," the mage retorted at his expression of surprise. She moved her hands, mumbled a few words, then motioned behind him. There were two posts with a line between them, several clothespins waiting.

"Thank you, Ma'am," Dolan said simply. Then both thief's and mage's eyes widened at a strange sound. They both looked back at the still-open, though much smaller, gate. A moment later a scrawny hand could be seen clawing at the foot-wide swirling window. The slave stepped back, swallowing in fear, as the mage stepped forward a few feet.

"Marelda! You need to deal with this!" Sigrid yelled as she watched the hand disappear and then reappear, this time with three others.

The princess turned around and assessed the situation quickly. Silently, her bare feet running across the distance in a matter of seconds, Marelda stopped in front of her tutor. "It's just some poor boys that witch perverted with her magic. They're harmless," she began after noting how small the hands were.

"You have to close the gate now so they can't get through," Sigrid ordered.

"Look at them. They can't even get more than their hands through it, and it's collapsing as we speak," Marelda droned as she turned away.

Dolan opened his mouth silently as he saw how red-rimmed her eyes were. Without a word from her he lugged the bucket of clothes and cold water to the conveniently set up line.

"You can't risk that!" Sigrid insisted as she grabbed her pupil by both arms.

The slave turned his head to watch as the princess roared out and pushed the mage away. "It's not your problem!" Marelda screamed. Her glare paused on Dolan until he turned his attention back to the bucket at his feet before she continued back to the gate. In a few minutes more the cries behind the shimmering hole increased as the rush of unnatural wind ushered in the implosion with a loud pop.

The princess turned around slowly and looked at her tutor. "I'm sorry, Sigrid," she wept as she fell to her knees.

The mage knelt as well and held the princess tightly to her chest. "It's going to be all right, my dear. Just fine. You're just tired and scared still. It will pass. It has to pass," Sigrid added as she looked over the sobbing woman into the face of the thief as he returned with the empty bucket.

Dolan tried not to listen as he carried the well bucket back, hung it back on the hook, and lowered it back down until it splashed. After a second of thought he lowered the bucket further, then brought up more water. He washed himself as well to get rid of any scent of the sorceress on his body.

In the background he could hear his name mentioned again. At almost any other time since he realized that what he'd been taught was torture could be pleasurable with the right owner, he would have been smiling at the thought of touching the princess and feeling her body in return. But now he knew she'd experienced something horrible, perhaps too horrible for a free aristocratic person to deal with. Instead, he knew, she'd take out her feelings on him in the form of pain and more pain. *Well, that's what I'm for, right?* he tried to reason with himself as he splashed his face with water again. *Not like I haven't survived it time and again.*

Sigrid was nowhere to be seen, and neither was her chair, when the slave returned to the campfire. Dolan's head was bowed just enough so his eyes didn't meet his owner's. He was bare from the waist up. Marelda just stood there looking at him as he sat down on the stump. She swallowed, then tossed her head when that brought a slight arch to his eyebrows. "You finished with my clothes, slave?"

Dolan nodded. "Madame Sigrid provided a clothesline," he added with a wave toward it.

"Hand me my boots!"

With only a mental pause, the slave dropped to one knee and picked up the boots. He gasped as she forced his head back by his hair. In her eyes he saw rage, not the same intensity as he'd seen back at the hotel nor after he'd attempted to run away, but something much stronger. The calm she had shown when she'd beaten him before was missing, he noted as she backhanded him then reversed her swing and knocked his head the other direction. The blood at the corners of his mouth tasted weaker from the water still in his beard and mustache. Dolan took a deep breath but did not otherwise move.

Marelda looked down at her kneeling slave. She twisted his hair in her hand, making him gasp again. Her free hand stung from the slaps, so she shook it a few times. Still her slave didn't move or make a sound. "How does that feel?" she hissed.

"It hurts, My Lady," Dolan said. He licked his mouth lightly, wincing at the sting this caused his swelling lips.

Marelda's eyes narrowed. "Is that all you have to say?" she scowled as she slapped him once more so his head was forced to the other shoulder.

Dolan clenched his hands into his pants and thighs, trying to just accept what couldn't be changed. He sucked in his breath when she jerked his head up again. The princess's face was pale, not red in anger, and behind the rage in her eyes tears were forming. "Yes, My Lady," he muttered, then gasped as she jerked his head up and down several times. One of his hands jumped up to his waist but stopped and grabbed the waist band of his pants instead of flying up as part of him wished to ward off the attack. "Please," he screamed.

Marelda stopped the motion of his head and released his hair only to cup his chin and force it up toward her. "Please what?"

"Please tell me what I can do to help you," Dolan offered.

The princess stepped back and with the full force of her arm knocked him backwards to the ground. She caught a sob in her throat, her hands twitching at her sides.

The slave cried out as he fell back; his head throbbed, his lips felt three times bigger, and his legs were aching. He rested one hand against his head as he twisted his legs from underneath him and leaned on his side. Dolan cursed everything he could think of as he just lay there trying to remain as calm as possible. He pulled back with a whimper when her bare feet moved in front of his face. She didn't speak, and she didn't kick him; in fact, her legs looked a bit wobbly. "Do you want me on my knees again, Mistress?" he asked suddenly.

"Why aren't you fighting back? Why aren't you pleading with me to stop?" Marelda yelled, but her voice didn't sound as angry as it had mere minutes before.

Dolan looked up just enough to wonder at the tremble that seemed about to take over the princess's body as she stood there. "It wouldn't stop you," he theorized in a flat tone. He flinched as her foot swung back, then forward to ram into his stomach. He moaned but grabbed her foot with his top hand, though not very tightly; then he let it go so she could regain her balance. "I can't stop you," he pointed out as she hopped back with a threat in her voice. "Mistress, I am but a slave, your property. I know that, and I know you will do to me what you want. I want you to do what you need, what you wish. I accept it all."

There was silence and then sniffles that made the slave look up. The princess was standing with her hands on her face, her hair fallen down to cover it, but the weeping was clear. Dolan turned on hands and knees then pushed himself back to his kneeling position. He took several shallow breaths as he watched in confusion.

"I don't know what I'm feeling," Marelda bawled.

The thief blinked and leaned back from the shocking sight. With an internal question of whether what he next did was wise or foolish, he hinted at the question that had been in his mind since seeing her in the dungeon in a pool of her victims' blood. "Did you do something you didn't want to do?"

The weeping stopped immediately. Marelda let her hands fall as she looked back at the kneeling slave. *He knows. He's making fun of me.* She used both hands to push her hair back from her face. "Take all your clothes off," she growled as she stomped past him.

Dolan froze as she bumped into him. He stood up when he heard the buckles on one of the saddle bags being unlatched. As he pulled off his boots, he glanced back to find the princess looking into her saddle bags. She seemed uncertain as she removed one thing, replaced it and then removed something else. The slave stepped out of his pants and underpants. Once he'd folded these and placed them in his own backpack, he went to the same spot and knelt again.

Marelda replaced the dildo, looked through the bag again then fingered the fake cock once more. "Damn!" she screamed as she threw the bag about two feet. She rocked back and forth from the tips of her toes to the heels of her feet, her fingers tapping her chin as she thought.

The night air was filled by the sound of insects, owls, and occasional crackles of grass and twigs under animals' tread. Dolan watched silently, moving only when a bug decided to taste him. He had been scared many, many times in his life, a common condition for slaves and runaways both. But as he heard the princess continue cursing and crying the fear changed into something else. At first he wasn't able to identify the thoughts; the feelings urged him to talk, to do something, even though his mind and body argued not to push her any further. The conflicting viewpoints fought for a few minutes until the princess fell onto her knees and doubled over with a wail.

Dolan leaned down and crawled on hands and knees until he was facing the princess. "Mistress," he whispered as he bowed his head low, his body still supported by knees and hands. "Please do whatever it takes to make you feel better. Whatever your pain, give it to me twice over if it will comfort you."

Marelda sniffed back the tears, blinking until her vision cleared. The thief's body was trembling as he offered himself to her, not as a palace slut would when summoned for the night in hopes that they would receive not only a moment's pleasure but any privileges that the royal family could grant. She herself had used several of the staff, mostly young men but occasional young women as well. Of course, they were not targets of her magic and thus were purely motivated out of their own desires. Dolan was motivated by the feelings her own sexual pleasure would create in himself. Except he was offering himself to be beaten, to be hurt, and she doubted that would give her sexual pleasure right now. No, his stance, his words, were far more open, far more vulnerable, and his motivation was far from clear.

"What if I want to hurt you really, really bad?" Marelda demanded, her voice still weak with crying. "What if I want to kill you?"

Dolan glanced up at the second sentence and licked his lips. "I hope you don't," he replied softly. It took all his willpower to stay still as her hands reached out and caressed his hair. Her petting continued as she added the other hand and smoothed back his hair, releasing it from the leather band which held it back. He sighed as she moved so she could press her body against his own and her hands could reach down to his ass. The sigh became a grasp, drawn out as her fingernails scraped up over his back.

"Dolan," Marelda said softly as she laid her head on his hunched-over shoulders, "I need to tell you something."

"Anything, Mistress," the slave pleaded back as he was pushed up to face her. He reached out but did not touch as she pulled her hands free of him and folded her arms across her chest. "Princess?"

Marelda closed her eyes as she spoke. "I've been taking life force from you when we have any type of sexual contact. I need it to help my magic. I'm," and she paused to tighten her grip on the sides of her shirt. "I'm taking your life from you." When she opened her eyes the slave's darker ones just stared at her, no real identifiable emotions there. "I did the same thing to one of the guards before killing him."

Dolan tilted his head to one side as he considered the words. Part of him was surprised, but another part of him had been suspicious for days as each morning awaking seemed to come harder and harder. The slave narrowed his eyes as his owner looked at him silently. "I'm not sure I understand what you're saying, Mistress," he replied slowly.

Marelda rubbed her forehead with one hand as she tried to find the right words. "I'm not supposed to kill the person I take life force from; it just takes what you have at that moment, you rebuild over time."

She sputtered to a stop, then sighed and set her hands back onto her thighs. "I killed him after I'd taken it, and I killed the other ones so we could get free. But, I didn't want to take the life force from him, not that way, not that way. I didn't know what he really was," she added softly.

"Did he force you, Mistress?" Dolan asked, then sat up straight as she glared at him. "I know that must be very hard for a free woman, an aristocrat, a princess, to experience," he offered weakly.

"No, he couldn't force me," Marelda replied, shaking her head. "The spell I cast on you is very similar to one on myself. It protects me from all sexual interactions I don't want ... or need," she added in a faint whisper.

"Need?" Dolan repeated. He edged closer as the princess seemed to fold in on herself.

"Yes, I cast a very powerful spell earlier," Marelda began to explain. "I didn't know when I'd be seeing you, and I needed to get out of that dungeon to get the necklace. So, I used one of them," she stated flatly.

Dolan looked down at his bare thighs as he sat now within easily reach of the princess. "May I ask how it compared to me?" he ventured with a tiny smile.

Marelda frowned, then found herself smiling as well at his light-hearted question. "You're much better. You make me stronger, and you don't make me sick to my stomach," she said, trying to make her voice and her heart a bit lighter.

"I'm glad," Dolan responded. He closed his lips together tightly, then released them with a sigh of frustration and confusion. "So, do you think beating me or using me in any way would make you feel better, Mistress?" he offered slowly.

"Would you go cut me a switch?" the princess asked softly. She sat back as he nodded and slowly moved to go. "Dolan, stay right there," she ordered quickly. She embraced him, her fingers combing through his curls as he held on to her with one arm as well. "There are lots of folks back home who I can do that with; some even enjoy it."

Dolan pulled his head back slightly to give her a cynical look. "I hope you aren't waiting for me to beg you to beat me, because I just don't see that happening anytime soon," he informed her seriously. "I mean, you can do whatever you wish to me, and I might offer if I think you'd feel better. I don't enjoy it."

Marelda tilted her head to one side as she smiled. "You're still so mouthy," she whispered, "just like the book said you'd be." When he shrugged she lifted his head up with one finger under his chin. "That's why I used the beating as a punishment. And that's why I'll do this to thank you for your offer," she added just before pressing her lips against his.

The shock of the kiss was momentary, and soon the slave opened his mouth eagerly; his own tongue caressed hers as she invaded his mouth. He eased back onto the ground as she climbed onto his lap, straddling one thigh and positioning one knee between his legs. She broke the kiss long enough to push with her other leg so that his thighs were opened wide. Her mouth then resumed her kissing and licking, but this time on his neck and shoulders.

Opening his eyes he could see the wisps of green light float up from her and then change colors, so that a white trail of light formed from where she touched him with her mouth. The slave groaned as his owner's mouth now jumped down to his nipples and twisted the rings with teeth and tongue. Each tug, each jolt of pain on his chest seemed to trigger a pleasurable ache in his groin. *Am I enjoying this just like one of her palace sluts*? he wondered silently, then just smiled and relaxed as her hands caressed his thighs.

Once his nipples were erect and red, the princess worked her way down his stomach, nipping at his flesh as she descended. She pinched his thighs and chuckled as his hands jumped up to his stomach but twitched, fighting to keep from touching her. "Put your hands above your head," Marelda commanded, breathing her hot breath onto his firm penis as it bobbed with his gasps. "Above your head, cross them at the wrists as though they were tied."

Dolan moaned as he slowly raised his hands. It was too similar to the ways he'd been abused by the jeweler, and yet the feelings caused by obeying her lessened the memories flirting at the edge of his mind. When his hands were crossed and trembling he opened his eyes at the wet warmth that surrounded his cock. He tried to hold his breath as she sucked him and licked him, sending wave after wave of pleasure through his entire body. His will broke, however, when she pulled his seed from him in a violent orgasm and his scream pierced the night.

Marelda sat back and swallowed the ejaculate; her throat tingled as his energy and the remains of the spell the sorceress had cast on him were absorbed into her. She opened her eyes and watched as a dark green light issued from her fingertips. This was a bit corrupted, so while it gave her more strength she was far from satisfied. Luckily her slave was still sitting up, his arms supporting him, his eyes twinkling toward her. The princess unlaced her shirt then leaned toward him.

"May I, Mistress?" Dolan asked as he looked at the tops of her breasts rising from the opened shirt. He smiled as she nodded, eagerly shifting position so he could kneel and reach her better. First he contented himself with what he could reach from the top part of her shirt, concentrating on her neck, shoulders, and top of her breasts. With a whispered request he earned access to the rest of her body as she quickly removed her shirt and underpants. Her nipples were now his focus as he licked and nibbled on each one until she pushed his head downward.

Her bellybutton wiggled as he licked it and drew a few chuckles from her before descending further. Dolan skipped past her thighs to her feet. He rubbed each and kissed the tops and soles before twirling his tongue around each toe. His heart pounded, and his own groin responded as he took each big toe into his mouth and treated it as he had her fingers days before.

Glancing over her beautiful body his mind briefly wondered why there was no light exchanged now as there was when they kissed or she took him into her mouth. But these thoughts faded as he licked from each ankle to each knee, then slowly, in circles, worked up to her inner thighs. From his position he could see her mound moistening and opening, the edges deepening in their red color and looking much like a happy grin.

She smelled wonderful, so comforting and natural, like the safety she offered him and the earth offered her people. Not that he'd ever paid any attention to how women smelled other than the ones who knew the jeweler and his wife, and that wasn't a pleasant memory in any way. No, her scent was intoxicating to him, urging the slave up and into her folds. He licked eagerly; any thought of teasing and prolonging the moment disappeared as he tasted her. Quickly he swallowed her juices as her hips pumped up and down in rapid succession and her thighs clasped his head.

Marelda's mind had still been flickering from the dungeon and the blood-covered guards when she'd taken her slave's cock into her mouth. The draining had replenished her, emptying the poison from the perverted guard and clearing Dolan of any traces of the sorceress, but she had felt hollow still. Now as she tossed her head from side to side and her body tightened further and further, all thoughts fled. Her blood raced from her limbs and head, making her dizzy and light, as her hips bolted up and her thighs clenched tightly.

The orgasm was the most intense the princess had ever had, far better than she'd ever imagined was possible with a mere slave. The world spun as all the pressure built up inside of her rushed forth in sharp contractions and loud cries of surprise and joy. Several minutes of repeated contractions of lessening degrees left Marelda sighing.

She finally felt her legs sliding down to the ground and her slave sitting back from her. When he moved up to lay at her sides he could smell her scent on him as their lips met. "Damn, that was good," Marelda confessed with a giggle.

"It was," he agreed then looked away and swallowed. "I mean, I'm glad, my Lady," Dolan said as he lay back onto one hand and watched what appeared to be a smile on his owner's face settle into her body as it relaxed further. "You know," the slave offered when she turned to face him, mimicking his body as a mirror image, "I think I could be a decent whore, so if you ever need extra money ..."

"Oh, no," Marelda said as she pushed him flat onto his back. She slid right up next to him and wrapped one arm and one leg around him. "You're entirely mine. My slave, my thief, my personal plaything."

"I'm glad," Dolan replied as he lifted his head and placed a kiss on her lips.

Chapter Six:
The Third Gate

The horses neighed before running off toward the nearby creek. The princess and her slave laughed as the two mares jogged into the water and splashed around. "This is the place?" Dolan asked, taking the reins, bit, and saddle from his owner's hands.

Marelda looked at her bracelet as it continued to glow. "Apparently," she said uncertainly.

The slave noticed her voice and the frown on her face as she continued to stare at her bracelet. "This isn't what you were expecting, is it, Mistress?" he guessed as he set her saddle next to his own. Dolan looked around at their new campsite. The trees were thin here, the grass dry and breaking under his boots, and the creek's banks even from this distance showed it had once been a much larger river. After five days' journey he had been hoping for something nicer, or at least more alive.

"Something's wrong," Marelda stated. She sighed and lowered her arm. Closing her eyes, she concentrated on the air around her, flinching when the unmistakable stench of magic hit her. The smell was old and suggested no immediate danger, though all her instincts kicked in. "I'll be back shortly," she announced.

Dolan just stood and watched as she drew her sword and went off into the trees. The poor coverage allowed him to see her for several minutes until she disappeared into the shadows. Next he turned his attention to the horses as they left the creek and began nibbling at the grass. "Well, best get things set up," he told himself as he stripped off his jacket.

The old riverbed provided the needed rocks to make the campfire ring. The slave pulled up the grass around the stone circle as well, recalling the fires he'd accidentally started in similarly dry grass because the embers were not completely out. Luckily he had learned quickly how to do it more safely, and at least those flames had kept his hunters back. Sitting back on his heels he searched the sky. No rain in the time he'd been with the princess; most unusual in his experience. At least finding wood to burn wouldn't be much of a problem.

When Dolan returned with his second armful of twigs and larger branches the princess was talking to her tutor. Both women ignored the slave as he knelt and added his burden to the previous pile. Neither told him to leave, so he sat down where he was and pretended not to be listening.

Marelda and Sigrid were both sitting on those chairs the senior mage conjured up whenever she visited. They were very close together, their heads bent over a couple of books, likely the ones that had led them here. Their words were far too low for the thief to hear clearly, but their body language indicated it was important. After a few moments the senior mage rose to her feet, the chair disappearing from underneath her, and lifted her arms up to the sky. Marelda likewise stood and tucked the books underneath her jacket.

Dolan looked up at the sky and watched as the clouds grew and turned gray. He jumped when a bolt of lightning leaped across the sky. He rose to his feet at the princess's command and was running with her when the rain burst forth. He paused as he saw a small shelter appear before them but found himself pulled into the tiny building.

The room he entered was much like the hut that had belonged to the farmer who had given him shelter a few years earlier. A fireplace was set in one wall, a fire blazing within already, two chairs were placed before the hearth, and a table by a basin stood off to one side near to a door. Looking left and right he saw a large bed in one corner, while the other housed shelves covered with containers. "Wow," he muttered as he shut the door behind himself.

"I'm glad you approve," Sigrid said from where she stood in the middle of room. Her hair and clothing were dripping water, but the mage simply shook herself and was soon dry. "This should take care of you," she added with a warm smile toward the princess.

"The horses," Marelda began.

"All taken care of," Sigrid replied. "Look out that window," she suggested, pointing toward the one near the kitchen area.

The princess pulled back the neat little gingham curtains and relaxed visibly. "Thanks," she said, moving aside for her slave to look out the window.

Dolan saw that the horses were secured underneath a roof; troughs of hay and water occupied their attention. *You're probably a lot more used to this than me*, he stated silently to them. He turned from the window and was about to mention their saddles and bags when he spotted these on the bed. "Did you make it rain, Ma'am?" he asked as he joined the princess and mage, who were sitting by the fire.

The buxom blonde smiled. "Yes; had to counter some bad spells," she said. "There's supplies over there, boy. Go fix us some dinner," she ordered with a motion of her head toward the shelves.

The slave looked toward his owner and received her nod of assent. On the shelves were containers which held various foods. After opening them all, the thief settled on something he knew he could deal with: potatoes, carrots, two loaves of bread, a jug of milk, and some dried meat. After pouring water from a barrel near the basin out into the kettle he diced the vegetables and the meat. The stew he set over the fire, where he could tend it and hear anything the two women were discussing.

"Your parents have returned," Sigrid informed the princess.

Marelda raised her eyebrows and leaned forward, her elbows resting on her knees, her head in her hands. "And what have they said?"

"Well, quite a few things, little of it about you, luckily." The senior mage chuckled and rocked back and forth in her chair until the princess turned her face toward her. "They reviewed the prophecy and agreed with our assessment of the situation. They ask for daily reports from me, if you give your consent."

"Of course," the princess conceded softly. "And my siblings?"

"Things are not so well on those fronts," Sigrid replied. She paused and pointed to the slave stirring their dinner while clearly listening.

"Dolan," Marelda addressed him firmly. When her slave faced her she continued, "You can listen in; there's no big secrets here you shouldn't learn about eventually."

"Thank you, Mistress," Dolan said with a bow of his head.

"My siblings?" the princess repeated her question.

The senior mage blinked a few times. Things were moving along quickly, it appeared, between the two adventurers — perhaps not as they should be. Later; she'd deal with it later. "Oh, yes. Annabel has been told to have the castle repainted everywhere but in her own quarters."

"Good. I don't think I could stand those colors for very long," Marelda admitted.

"So said your father," Sigrid reported. "Benjamin has become a monk, but he is only a few days' journey away from the castle."

"I want him there for the ceremony," Marelda directed. "I think it is best to make this transferral as family-centered as possible."

Sigrid nodded silently, then moved on to the hardest news. "Joshua has been kicked out of the castle and is living in hiding with his lover. Your mother says that you must decide his fate when you return successfully."

"Great," Marelda whispered. She rubbed her hands down her face slowly as she sat up straight. "Do I know who she is?"

"I doubt it. Just one of the upstairs maids, not specialized at all in anything, freeborn at least. It's causing quite a social problem," Sigrid added as the princess stood up. "He carries no magic in his blood; the problem is purely social and political."

"Does his promised bride know that he cannot inherit the throne?"

"Yes. I think that's why her family is demanding compensation," Sigrid confirmed.

"No," Marelda stated, "this is just a hint of things to come. You read the signs with me before I left. Blood will be shed before unity is restored. Our allies will resent their loss of liberty, or perceived loss, and fight for a while."

Dolan turned around at these words and looked at his owner. *Great! Not just fighting sorcerers, but a war too*, he thought silently.

The princess tapped her foot on the floor for several minutes, then sniffed the air suddenly. "Smells like dinner is ready," she guessed and received a nod in confirmation. "Do you want to stay with us, Sigrid?"

"I'm sure it is good," Sigrid offered with a sniff of the air as she rose to her feet. "But I need to get back, and you need to get ready. Only five more days if you're lucky," the mage said before disappearing. The chair she had been sitting on remained.

"I'll get the plates, then," Marelda stated as she went to the saddle bags. When she returned the two chairs had been moved to the small table and the pot of stew and the loaf of bread set out, while Dolan stood off to one side. "Sit down and join me," the princess encouraged as she took her seat.

"Thank you, Mistress," Dolan answered. He put the pitcher of milk he had found in the newly-refilled food sacks on the table as he sat down. Then he bowed his head and listened to the recitation of the prayer the princess said each dinner time. This was the same prayer he'd heard the jeweler say during holiday meals when he'd been forced to serve, though he doubted it was used on any other occasion. Himself, he'd only appealed to the Lady and Lord when in desperate need, figuring they wouldn't heed the words of a slave. Marelda told him that the Lady and Lord would listen to anyone with pure intentions. He didn't know anyone like that either.

Marelda smiled across the table after taking a hot bite. "You are getting better," she complimented.

Dolan nodded once. They ate in silence until the last of the stew was ladled into their bowls. "Mistress, is there a problem with this gate?" he suddenly asked.

The princess looked straight at him, then nodded slowly. "There seems to be, and I suppose it would be best if you knew a bit about the situation."

"I'd prefer to know," Dolan confessed as he crossed his arms over his chest and leaned back in his chair with a demanding look on his face.

Marelda sighed at what she would have called impudence a few weeks ago but now simply found amusing and reasonable, at least out here on her quest. "Take these bowls to the sink, then bring your chair around to this side."

Dolan rose immediately and gathered up the remains of the stew. At the window he could see the rain, now a steady light drizzle, misting up the darkened sky. The horses seemed at ease as they watched the rain and lazily munched their hay. After rinsing the bowls quickly, the slave returned to the table, where the two books were laid open. Once he'd taken his seat a few inches from her own, the princess began.

"Now you've figured out what type of magic we're dealing with here, I assume."

"I don't think so," Dolan replied with a frown.

Marelda sighed but checked her anger. "It's matter-changing magic. That means it deals with what things are and what things appear to be," she explained in simple terms. "The first could construct illusions which had only small amounts of matter and thus were easily killed. The second changed the outward appearance of living beings, an illusion of a higher degree, since they could do physical damage and not simply mislead."

"I understand," Dolan replied when she paused.

"This third, however, can completely reconstruct matter into any other form he wishes. This means he could become a horse and run away fast, or become a bear and fight with that strength, or become a unicorn and use the horn to spear an enemy. I doubt he could become that last one though, because it requires a high level of spiritual purity," Marelda added quickly when her slave frowned at the suggestion.

Dolan laughed. "But unicorns aren't real. Are they?" he asked when the princess just looked at him in full seriousness. "All right then. So what exactly can this wizard become?"

"Anything, by now, I'd imagine, as long as it need not be spiritually pure and good. Since he's near here, I doubt it is a water creature. The dryness here indicates something large, something nasty, something hot," Marelda speculated.

"Like what?" the slave asked as he looked at the book. There in the volume on the three mage-thieves was a diagram of several animals the third wizard had been known to take. These ranged from the common mouse to an odd bird with flames around it and flames issuing from its beak. "Anything?" he repeated.

"Anything," Marelda repeated. "Which is why I need lots of life force from you and you need lots of rest," she added as she closed the books and stood up.

Dolan looked at the cover of the book he'd taken from that mad priest's church his third night with the princess. The images in it had scared him then, and now at the thought of losing his life in more ways than one the figures seemed even more horrifying. He swallowed and stood up to face the princess. "Take what you will, Mistress," he whispered in a merely audible voice.

Marelda kissed him passionately, taking his ponytail into her fist and pulling him tightly to her. She nuzzled his neck but kept one hand on his face to indicate he was to just stand there as still as he could. In the last few days, draining him at least once though most often twice before the sun set, she'd taken him quickly and efficiently. The less work he actually did, the more quickly he recovered and the sooner she could drain him again.

His erect penis sprang from his pants as she slid them from

his hips. He made only gasps, his body only twitching slightly as she enveloped him with her mouth. His skin was hot and dry to her tongue, indicating her extreme use of it. Her eyes swept upward as his groans turned to a moan of pain. She placed her hands on his ass and pressed him further into her. One finger easily slid between his cheeks and tickled him from the inside.

Dolan's body arched forward as he shot into the princess's mouth. He felt her swallow and moaned with the pain it caused. As she sat back he knelt down on the floor. "Hurts," he whispered as he clenched at his groin.

"I'm sorry," Marelda replied softly. She brushed back his bangs and tried to smile at him. "Only a few more times."

"How many?"

The princess considered the condition of the land and the words of her tutor. "Only as much as I need," she promised, hoping she was correct in her estimation of this third wizard's power. "No more tonight," she added.

"Thank you, Mistress," Dolan replied as he struggled to his feet with her help. He laced up his pants as she slid them back to his waist. Her hand alit on top of his, sending shudders of desire through him. "I want to do something for you," he pleaded as he caught her hands and brought them to his lips.

Marelda only allowed herself a smile as he kissed each hand and began rubbing them with his own. "You need to rest now," she replied as he lifted one finger to his mouth.

Dolan didn't stop, but took the digit between his lips so his tongue could eagerly lick the tip, pulling a deeper smile from her. "Please, Mistress?" He tried to coax her by switching his attentions to another finger.

The princess pulled her hands free and backed up two steps. "No! Go to sleep!" she ordered, pointing to the floor by the bed. Her face felt flushed as she maintained her stance; her orgasms released too much sexual energy and would require more from him. She needed him to be able to go into the rift with her to retrieve the last item, he had to have enough strength to do that.

The thief sighed and held up his hands in defeat. He took his bedroll and laid it out by the bed, leaving enough space for her to walk between them. The princess returned to her books as he removed his clothing and sat between the layers of the sleeping bag. "Mistress? Do you wish for me to set up your bed?"

"No, I won't be sleeping tonight," Marelda replied as she turned to another section of her first book.

"But you need your sleep," Dolan countered. The princess turned toward him with a frown. "As you wish, Mistress," he said, hastening to amend his previous statement. The slave laid down and tried to watch his owner at the table. Minutes ticked by as the exhaustion her use of him had caused fought with his curiosity. The last thing he saw was the princess adding another log to the fire and taking off her jacket.

The rain had stopped the day before, but Dolan was not allowed outside, where his gaze out the window over the sink in the tiny cabin informed him the horses were running free. The princess had made it very clear that his place was inside resting while she scouted around. The slave walked slowly to the fireplace, his thighs, legs, butt, and groin still uncomfortable. Multiple orgasms in less than 36 hours would have been fine, had it been the quickie casual sex he'd enjoyed on the run. His owner's magic, though, drained him, and had left him crying that last time.

The thief sucked in his breath as he sat down on a chair. That was the last time, she promised, he reminded himself. This last time he'd been shocked at how easily he was aroused and brought to orgasm by her mouth. He rubbed one of his wrist cuffs as he thought about it. *I really have no more control. I have no control over anything. Why doesn't this knowledge make me run off from here?* His jaw still ached from the slap he'd received for requesting a few more hours of sleep that morning. He was to rest, but not sleep more; it wasn't healthy, she told him. *There's nowhere for me to go; anyone else would just be worse, so much worse.*

The sound of the horses mildly protesting outside made the slave look toward the door. In a few minutes it opened and the princess entered carrying two rabbits in one hand. "Hey, this should taste good tonight, huh?" Marelda announced as she dropped the skinned animals on the table in front of her slave. "Should add a bit of substance to that stew of yours," she added with a smile.

Dolan stood up without a word and took the rabbits by the string tying their feet together. The princess didn't stop him as he went to the sink to start cutting them into usable pieces but instead took the kettle from over the dead hearth and filled it with water when he turned to throw a few pieces into a bowl. "Thank you," Dolan simply stated without looking at her.

Marelda frowned at his pale complexion. "How are you feeling?" she asked as she set the kettle back down and crouched down to start the fire underneath.

"I'm fine," the slave replied quickly.

"I'm sorry about this morning," the princess offered as she struck her flints and started a tiny flame. There was no reply as she blew up a stronger flame and added more kindling. Marelda looked over her shoulder at her slave. He was dressed only in pants and shirt, no shoes, and his movements appeared stiff. "Are you tired? Dolan?" Standing up, she demanded, "Answer me!"

"A little, Mistress, but I'm fine," Dolan restated with a sigh. He rinsed off the good meat he had laid aside in the bowl, then covered them in water. The useless parts he gathered up into another bowl. He flinched when the princess's hand took it from him.

"I'll take it out," Marelda informed him.

"Thank you," the slave replied softly. He watched her leave the cabin again, then slammed his fist down on the narrow countertop, almost spilling the water in the bowl of good meat. He cursed the fact that the mere touch of her hands on his had made him as hard as a rock again while at the same time filling him with fear. *It used to be so easy!* He reminded himself of how any thought of the jeweler, let alone a touch of any type, had made him sick to his stomach from horror and disgust. Neither of those emotions was what he felt now.

He went to the shelves and gathered the magically ever-fresh supply of vegetables and seasonings for the stew and returned to the sink. Leaving the carrots, beans, and potatoes in the sink, he took the bowl of meat to the kettle. The water was beginning to steam as he added the meat to it. He was dicing the vegetables when the princess returned, this time with a handful of wildflowers.

"Things are growing again," Marelda announced. She took off her jacket, holding the flowers in one hand then the next. Searching the shelves, she found a taller mug. "This will do nicely, though it won't be nearly as decorative as Annabel would like," she commented as she joined him at the sink. "Beans too?" she asked with a frown as he stepped aside to let her at the water pump.

"I won't add them if you don't think it's a good idea, Mistress," Dolan whispered. His throat felt tight, his skin felt hot, and his nostrils flared at her scent; just being around her was starting to get more and more difficult.

Marelda looked back into his very wide eyes with a frown. "I promised that was the last time for quite a while, and it was," she restated.

"I didn't say anything about that," Dolan began, but found one of her fingers pressed against his lips. Instinctively he licked it and closed his eyes.

The princess pulled away and walked around him to the table carrying her mug of flowers. "I think the beans are an excellent idea. You could use the added bulk, I'm sure," she said as she frowned at the rabbit-stained table. "As soon as you're done there would you wipe off the table here?"

Dolan sighed and shook his head as the arousal he'd felt moments before disintegrated with the distance between them. "Yes, Mistress," he agreed. The last of the vegetables were rinsed and diced and placed into the bowl the meat had been in. He took the tiny packets of seasonings and went to the kettle where he added everything but the pieces of paper that had held the salt, pepper, basil, and sage. He stuffed these into his pants pocket and went back to the sink.

"This is not exactly what I was expecting to be doing," he said softly to the table as he cleaned it off.

Marelda set the mug of flowers down. "What were you expecting?" she asked.

Dolan was surprised for a slight moment as though he didn't realize that he'd been speaking out loud. Before answering he went to the sink to rinse the rag. There was nothing he had found that he could hide from her, especially if he was stupid enough to speak out loud. "Well, Mistress. If you'll recall, I thought you worked for or owned a brothel back at that hotel."

Marelda chuckled as she pulled her chair toward the fire and watched the flames. "Yes, you thought you were destined to be a whore in some ritzy establishment."

"It made sense with all the shaving and the magic that's kept every bit of hair from growing back," he defended his earlier assessment. Dolan came to his own chair and sat down with a small moan as his groin protested again. He lowered his eyes when the princess's green ones turned toward him at the sound. "I guess I was sort of right; I think I've been used as much as I might back in a brothel, but I'm much happier just with you," he added quickly. Then his mind flashed back to some other earlier events. "And those clothes I still haven't worn are very fine. What exactly are they for?" he asked immediately.

"Oh, for the castle when we get home again. I figured you'd be more comfortable if you were better dressed," Marelda replied as she turned her attention to the stew. She took the large spoon hanging from the mantle and stirred it a few times. "So what did you figure you'd be doing right now, if not this?" she urged him to continue.

Dolan sighed as he swallowed the questions he had about her home and about royalty. "Well, after you explained why you needed me, I didn't think I'd be alive this long. I mean, magic and slaves just don't mix."

Marelda glanced down at her bracelet, recalling how strongly it glowed when he was on the auction block. *You might be surprised,* she thought. "While I've faced dangers I only dreamed about in nightmares, you've protected me, my Lady, and for that I am most grateful," Dolan added with a humble bow of his head. He sniffed the scent of the stew and pointed to the kettle. "And I never imagined I'd be cooking and actually enjoying it."

The princess faced him with a wide grin. "Perhaps you'd like to work in the kitchens when we get back home? They're bigger than most houses you've seen, I assure you."

"I believe you, Mistress," Dolan said. "Is that what you'll do with me there?" he asked as he leaned forward biting his lower lip.

"Is it something else you'd like to do?" the princess countered.

"Does it really matter?" the slave replied.

Marelda swallowed then faced him as she stirred the stew again. "No."

Dolan leaned back with a nod. "Well, I was expecting that answer at least," he announced softly. "See, I have learned some things."

The princess had disappeared after supper, taking the bottle of wine from her saddle bags with her and leaving her slave to clean up as he was now used to. Dolan's body felt better thanks to a good meal and the lack of sexual demands. He cleared everything away and even pulled on socks and boots and took the remainder of the stew outside to dump in the pit she'd dug for disposal several dozen feet away from the cabin. The ground was covered with new grass, the air filled with pollen. A solid day of rain had done wonders.

A few feet from the door Dolan stopped in his tracks. The hair on the back of his neck stood up, and his breathing increased rapidly. This was a frightening sensation, almost as though several dozen pairs of eyes were watching him. Turning around slowly, he could see nothing in the setting sunlight. His skin cooled from dread as he continued turning around, certain he could sense someone watching him.

The slave yelled and jumped back in terror as Marelda appeared in his line of sight, one hand on his shoulder in a move fast as lightning. "What are you doing out here, slave?"

Dolan swallowed as he tried to calm himself down. "Just throwing out leftovers," he tried to explain. He found his arm gripped tightly as he was marched back into the cabin. "I'm sorry, Mistress," he gasped as he was shoved across the floor toward the table. The last thing his body could take in its weakened condition would be a whipping, so he fell to his knees, determined to plead for mercy.

"I would have done that," Marelda stated as she set down the bottle of wine and the bowl she'd earlier filled with the unsavory rabbit parts from the table. She ignored her slave as he merely knelt on the floor silently and fetched her own ritual mug from her saddlebags. "Sit down in your chair," she ordered as she returned to hers, setting the mug on the table.

Dolan rose and took his seat. He watched as the princess turned the mug three times clockwise then three times counterclockwise. The mug wasn't plain earthen material like those in the cabinet nor the finer wood the hotel had had. It was white and shiny, with several large stones he thought he recognized as emeralds, rubies, and diamonds laid out in three horizontal bands around the body of the mug.

Marelda took the wine and poured it until one third of the mug was full. She then added the red substance from the bowl into the mug until it was two-thirds full. The remainder of the mug she filled with more wine, then set it in the middle of the table. From one pocket of her jacket she took out a small vial and emptied it into the mug. "Give me your dagger," she instructed.

The slave rose and went to his share of the saddlebags to fetch his single weapon. "I cleaned it yesterday morning as you ordered," he said as he returned and offered it handle first.

"Good. It's important that it be free from any magic other than my own," Marelda said, repeating her earlier words. She held the dagger on her palms and began chanting a few words. Then she used the sharp tip and stirred the contents of the mug three times clockwise and three times counterclockwise. Taking a clean piece of white linen from the inner pocket where the mysterious packet had been, she wiped the blade clean.

"You need to drink this now in one attempt," the princess explained as she pushed the mug across the table. "Do not remove it from your lips until it is emptied. Drink every last drop."

Dolan looked at the mug and the blood-red wine inside, mixed with unknown matter and words of enchantment. He could refuse, but then he knew that she'd simply pin him down and force it down his throat. The slave took the mug in both hands, took a deep breath, then leaned backwards as he tilted it up to his mouth. The wine was salty, but sweet, an odd combination, but then he had little experience to be a true judge of the matter. His throat swallowed and swallowed; his lungs started to protest, but he kept his eyes focused on his owner as she watched him closely.

With a gasp for air he set the mug down. He released it as the princess took it up and examined it carefully, sniffing at it and running her fingers along the insides. "Good, you drank it all," Marelda praised him with a smile.

"What was it?" Dolan asked. His vision blurred no matter how hard he shook his head.

"Don't fight it. Just go to sleep," the princess coaxed softly. She rose and helped her slave stand, then half led and half carried him to his bedroll on the floor. She quickly removed his boots and shirt then easily she rolled him under the blanket and pushed his pillow under his head.

Marelda stood up and looked at the door. "That will help. You need to recover fast, because we've miscalculated this opening in a terrible way," she whispered.

Outside under the horses' shelter the princess found her tutor waiting for her. Sigrid folded her arms across her chest and regarded her pupil seriously. "I hope you haven't given him what I think you have? You need all your strength."

"I didn't give him anything my body wasn't already getting rid of," Marelda replied. She looked steadily at her tutor as the older woman paled a bit. "It is stronger anyway. Far more potent than the blood I'd get from opening a vein. I'll just never tell him."

"Thank the Lady and Lord for some wisdom," Sigrid muttered

softly as she crossed the distance between them. "Are you all right?" she asked, placing a loving hand on her charge's shoulder.

"Day after tomorrow it will open; that's a day earlier than we calculated," Marelda replied with a concerned frown.

The mage looked down at the younger woman's belt and the slight swelling underneath. "Will you still be bleeding?"

"No, I shouldn't be. That's why I had to give him the potion tonight," Marelda explained. "He's very tired. I just hope he's recovered enough for this."

"Did you take enough from him?"

The princess raised her hands so her tutor could see the pale green glow from them. "I'm not doing anything either."

"Well, at least not consciously," Sigrid amended. She led her pupil out from under the shelter and into the open air where they could sit in two conjured chairs. "You need to rest yourself, my dear. And you need to focus. Choose one," the mage instructed as she pointed to the stars overhead, "and concentrate on any questions you may have."

Marelda leaned back in her chair and glanced over the stars. Soon her eyes focused in on the brightest star of the flaming wheel constellation, the one that represented the eye of the Earth Mother, second of the Tripartite Lady. The light of the star grew in her sight until it blocked out all other stimuli of sight, sound, taste, touch, and smell. As the connection grew the princess could hear the flames of the star as they leapt from their fiery core. The heat touched her as the smell of burning hair and the taste of hot dry air surrounded her.

In the center of the star something black waited. Concentration did little to enhance the image, though it seemed to grow larger and darker. *What are you?* she asked the creature. The sound of thunder filled her ears as the figure appeared to move and open enormous jaws to scream a reply that she could not understand.

"What did you see?" Sigrid demanded softly as she supported the princess in her arms.

Blinking her unseeing eyes and trying to move her weak arms, Marelda replied in a harsh whisper. "Something terrible."

"What? What is he become?" the mage asked urgently.

The princess' eyes began to clear so that the darkness of the night replaced the fire that had engulfed her. "Something that can't be real," Marelda insisted. "Something from nightmares."

Dolan awoke in the cabin as the sunlight hit his face. The slave yawned, stretched, and looked up at the bed above and next to him. When he sat up the fact that the princess wasn't there was confirmed. He turned toward the table at the sound of her voice.

"Did you sleep well?" Marelda simply said as she sipped her morning tea and studied her books.

"Yes, and I feel amazing," Dolan added as he stood up. Further movement proved to be free from the stiffness and aches he'd experienced lately. He pulled on his boots while he watched the princess with a smile.

Marelda turned her green eyes toward her thief. "What are you smiling about?"

The slave chuckled as he stood up and brushed his hair back with his hands. "I feel great and I have you and that weird mug of something really don't want to know about to thank for that," he said, the smile widening into a grin. "What does my Lady wish for breakfast?" Dolan continued as he headed toward the shelves where their supplies were kept.

"There's no time," the princess stated as she drained off the last of her tea.

"No time?" Dolan repeated as he took an apple. "Why not?"

"We have to go now," Marelda said as she stood up.

"But you said we had three days," Dolan reminded her as he polished the apple on his shirt.

"You slept for over a full day, and," the princess paused as she closed her books, "I miscalculated the time. It opens within a few hours."

"Damn!" The slave looked at his apple then held it up. "Can I at least eat this on the way?"

"If you can get dressed and memorize this map at the same time," Marelda directed as she handed him the copy she'd made that morning from the book, "you're welcome to eat."

"Not a problem," Dolan said as he glanced at the map and headed toward his vest and jacket. He stuffed the apple into his mouth, gripping it by his teeth as he swung into his clothes and followed the princess. At the doorway she sent him back to fetch his dagger and backpack. He had just hoisted the pack onto one shoulder and was hooking his dagger and its sheath onto his belt when the tiny cabin disappeared. With a cough he spat out the apple.

Marelda laughed as she glanced back over her shoulder. "Move it along now, boy! We've got a lot to do today!" The princess slowed down just enough to let her slave catch up as he wiped the apple on his vest to remove the small amount of dirt it had collected from the fall. When he opened his mouth to ask a question she reached back and pushed the apple into his mouth. "You said you wanted to eat it."

Dolan lifted his lantern higher as he edged his way into the cave. *Of course I get to go first*, he scolded himself. He looked at the map and frowned. *Am I even in the right place?* The hole in the sky had been almost the same, if one ignored the fact it was midday and not night, and the princess had chanted the same words, though this time she said it would merely stabilize the gate. It had been opened, and the thief had felt his skin crawl as they went through and the feeling they were being watched washed over him; it was just like before. Now, alone inside the cave, the eeriness increased.

Silently he counted to himself as he advanced. The assignment was to go two hundred paces inside, then watch as the princess caught up to him. The map had been uncertain, as had been his mistress when she tried to explain her errors and why she wasn't sure anymore of how long the gate would remain open. If they were lucky the wizard wouldn't be near the crown, and he could just take it and leave while the princess closed down the gate. Marelda had not sounded like she believed in luck today.

One-ninety-five, Dolan thought as he stopped at a wide opening. One step inside showed him it was an enormous cavern, at least as large as the castles in the other magical realms. The thief stepped in further and looked around. The walls glistened with light from his lantern as the gold, silver, and gemstones reflected back the flame inside. "Lady and Lord," the slave whispered as he looked around at the riches just seconds from his hands.

In a corner directly across from the cavern entrance a pedestal stood. Sitting on it was a golden crown covered with clear, red, and green gems. Dolan took one step forward, his eyes twinkling, when a bolt of fire shot across his path. Freezing in place, the slave looked up at the largest creature he'd ever seen in his entire life, a creature of nightmares and a monster from stories parents of all classes told their children. With a scream the thief turned and fled down the corridor toward the cave exit.

The princess jumped and readied her sword as the screaming hit her ears. It continued, increasing in loudness as she walked carefully into the cave. At a turn she cried out as her slave bolted toward her. She grabbed his arm as he tried to flee past her. A quick survey and a hasty sniff made her shove him outside as she let her backpack fall to the ground so she could remove her jacket with one hand. "Get face down on the ground!" she ordered.

Dolan covered his head as he was beaten with her leather jacket. "Mistress, please! I didn't mean to disobey!" he began as she tripped him, forcing him to the ground.

"You're on fire!" Marelda countered.

The slave froze at the words, then screamed as his nostrils filled with the scent of what he imagined was his burning flesh.

"Take off your jacket!" Marelda yelled as she knelt down and scooped up handfuls of dirt. As soon as his smoking jacket left his body she covered it with the dry earth. One glance assured her that nothing else was on fire. "Dolan, just be quiet now."

"I'm on fire, I'm on fire," he was repeating as he hit himself with his hands, his head turning wildly from side to side in an effort to see where the flames were spreading. He stopped cold after she slapped him, his mouth falling open in shock.

"It was just your jacket," Marelda said slowly and softly as she held him by his shoulders.

"My jacket? Just my jacket?" Dolan repeated.

"Yes," the princess replied as she breathed a sigh of relief. She went back to the burnt and torn jacket and dusted some of the dirt off.

"It set me on fire," Dolan said as he approached, one wary eye on the cave.

Marelda picked up the remains of his jacket and smelled it. "I don't think so," she said as she stood up.

"Oh, yes it did," Dolan replied.

"This smells like oil, the oil from your lantern," Marelda informed him. From one of the sleeves a metal ring fell. "And that looks like what's left of said lantern."

The slave blinked a couple of times as he considered the jacket, the tarnished metal ring, and the cave. "Maybe, but that thing in there is going to do a lot worse to us."

"You saw the wizard?" Marelda asked as she dropped the jacket. "Tell me, what form is he in?"

Dolan pulled away angrily. "You said he could become a bear, or a unicorn, or a lion! You never told me he'd be a demon!"

The princess frowned but simply repeated her question.

"I'm not going in there, and I don't care if you beat me within an inch of my life!" the slave announced as he backed up a few steps. "In fact, kill me now quickly if I've pleased you at all, 'cause not going back."

"What's in there?" Marelda demanded as she grabbed him by his wrists, her hands twisting his cuffs so that they cut into his body at the edges.

"A dragon!" Dolan screamed back. He fell backward onto the ground as the princess released him. "It's a damned dragon! The worst thing I've seen in my entire life!"

Marelda turned back toward the cave. "A dragon," she repeated. "Interesting choice," she muttered as confidently as she could muster.

"Interesting choice?" Dolan gasped as he stood up quickly. "It's a demon!" The slave turned back toward the glowing gate, falling as his cuffs shot bolts of pain into him.

"It isn't a demon, just a wizard who's made an interesting choice," Marelda said, as she held up one hand and called on the runes of the slave cuffs. She waited until the slave was back at her feet, his face creased in anguish, to lower her hand, so the pain stopped in his wrists to be replaced with her fingernails digging into one of his earlobes.

"Mistress, please. Let's just leave," Dolan begged as he was forced to his feet. "You have two; can't you do something with two?"

"No, of course not." Marelda tempered the harsh tone of her words with the knowledge running through her mind and the look of pure terror in her slave's dark eyes. "But now that we know what he is, we can better fight him," she tried to assure him.

Dolan screamed as the tree next to the cave burst into flames. Above was the form of a dragon, darker than any night, smoke billowing from his jaws and flames issuing forth.

Marelda bolted for the cave, pulling her thief behind her. Inside, she pushed him against the wall as the flames hit the mouth. "Damn! He must have another way out," she cursed herself for miscalculating again. "Move deeper inside!" she croaked as she pushed her slave forward with one hand as she retrieved her backpack with the other. As she glanced behind them the place where her pack had been was covered with flames.

Once beyond a curve in the cave they stopped to lean against the dry walls. "How much further to the place where you saw the dragon?" Marelda asked as she looked behind them.

The slave shook his head in disbelief at the question. "We can't go in there!"

"How much further?" the princess demanded as she gripped his hair in one fist.

Dolan bit his lip as he was hauled to his feet by his hair. "I'm thinking! It's," he paused and looked before them and to the curve the princess blocked, "about one hundred and ten paces."

Marelda let her grasp relax into a petting motion as she watched the dragon's breath shoot toward them but stop a few paces short of the curve. "I think his range is only about eighty," she figured out loud. "And how many paces did it take you to get to where the dragon was?"

"At one-ninety-five I was looking into this cavern, just packed with riches," Dolan said as he placed his hands on top of hers as she held him fast by his hair. "My Lady, please, I'm not going to run."

Marelda cocked her eyebrows. "I suppose you realize that there's really no place to run?"

The slave nodded as best he could, then sighed thankfully when released. He slumped down to the floor of the corridor, wincing each time the hot air created by the monster's fire raced past them. "So, do you have any magic that will take care of this?" he ventured cautiously.

"I might," the princess replied as she slid to the ground as well, placing her backpack before her. She took out her book, the one she'd had with her when the quest was begun, and began looking in the index. After a second she turned to the section on dragons. "He's a black dragon, yes?" she asked as she held the book so her thief could see it.

Dolan pulled his hands down from his eyes and looked at the image. "Yeah, it looks pretty much like that. I can't believe I'm sitting here talking about a dragon," he added in a harsh whisper.

Marelda took a deep breath as she moved the book back onto her lap. "Would you rather be with the jeweler, or his friends?" she suggested with a tight chuckle.

The slave tilted his head as he considered the alternatives. "That's a difficult question to answer at this point. Um, do, ah, dragons like to torture their victims before they kill them?"

"Not real dragons, and I suspect not this one either. They generally kill anyone who tries to take their treasure; they aren't noted for conversations," Marelda offered weakly.

"Oh, then that decides it. I'd rather be here about to be burnt to death," Dolan replied, then coughed as another wave of smoky air rushed over them.

The princess looked over the pages detailing black dragons, flipping to pages about the last of the wizards who'd taken the sacred royal emblems. Her options were limited by her experience, her knowledge and the life energy she'd collected. "We need to be very smart about this, Dolan," she said as she stood up.

The slave got up as well, groaning as he straightened out his back. "Since you rejected my best idea earlier, I'll simply follow your lead, my Lady."

"I have a plan forming," Marelda began as she led the way back toward the entrance. Suddenly both thief and princess had to grab onto the walls as the mountain shook. The corridor filled with dust, blinding them momentarily. After the shaking had ended and the dust had settled, the princess patted her slave's hand as he rested it on her shoulder as though to steady her.

"I have a very, very bad feeling," Dolan muttered as he followed the princess back down the tunnel in the darkness. After a few minutes he heard her strike a match and then saw her light her own lantern. The ground beneath them was hard and reflected the light upward, not the loose sandy rock he'd stepped on earlier. A few feet from the entrance they both stopped to stare at the fallen rocks completely blocking the cave.

"This isn't good," Marelda simply said. She examined the boulders more closely, then shook her head as she returned to where her slave was standing watching the tunnel in the other direction. "Bad news is that it is covered and it would take too much of my magic to clear," she announced.

"Is there any good news?" Dolan asked hopefully.

"Sure, unless he changes form, he can't reach us," Marelda pointed out.

"So we just wait until he goes to sleep or something, dig a hole inside and then get the crown and leave," Dolan theorized with a forced smile on his lips.

Marelda walked around her slave and headed back down the

tunnel. She ignored his questions until they were just outside the dragon's range and she could see the entrance to the cavern. "It's a great idea," she agreed as he repeated his plan. "But we don't have that much time. I'm not sure when that gate will close, but we can't be in here when it does."

"Why not?" the slave asked warily. When the princess refused to explain, Dolan threw up his hands and walked back and forth a few steps before stopping directly in front of her. "Please tell me, Mistress. What do I have to do, get down on my knees here and beg? Fine I'm doing it," he said as he sunk to both knees, "but please tell me what is going on. I can't be a good slave, let alone a good thief, unless I know what is going on. Please, Marelda," he begged, using her name for the first time.

Dolan bit his lip as she slapped him. He wiped the blood from the corner of his mouth and held up one hand. "I'm sorry, Mistress," he replied slowly.

Marelda threw back her head with a groan of frustration. "No, I'm sorry for snapping. This is just a lot harder than I had planned for."

"I just want to help," Dolan declared softly, then added as he looked directly into her eyes, "I just want to live."

The princess nodded. "Then this is what we're going to do. You run for the crown, because once you have it, you'll be safe — he won't risk harming it just to kill you. No matter what happens, you get that crown and you get it outside the gate into Sigrid's hands. Understood?"

Dolan nodded as he looked at his knees on the rougher floor of the cave in this part. "And you?"

"I'll distract him with a little fire of my own."

The slave stood up with a frown. "Will fire hurt him?"

"Sure, haven't you ever heard the saying 'fight fire with fire'?" Marelda stated as she glanced down the tunnel toward the cavern.

"Bycale!" the princess yelled out the wizard's name as she entered the cave. She seemed ill-prepared as she walked around the cavern near the piles of treasure, her sword drawn, her backpack gone, with only her clothing as a weak armor. "Bycale! I know you're here! I can smell the stench of sulfur!"

Marelda turned as a shadow on the wall moved and grew larger as the dragon approached. Out of the corner of her eyes she noted her thief's progress through the treasure strewn about the cavern, moving in a curved path toward the pedestal with the crown. *Just do this long enough for him to get that crown*, she reminded herself. "Come out, Bycale, and taste my steel!"

"Don't you mean fire?" The dragon's voice made the cavern rattle as he appeared above the largest pile of gold, silver, and gems.

"I mean steel!" Marelda corrected as she waved her sword in his direction.

The dragon laughed, sending the treasure tumbling down and the princess scurrying out of the way. "The steel is worthless, even more worthless than any flame your pathetic sex magic can create!"

Marelda stepped back in surprise at his words. Setting her face in a determined frown, she insulted him back. "Well, at least I did not sell my soul for my magic! The smell and your form betray that you are merely the slave of a lower master!"

With rage the dragon used one of his smaller front arms to knock more treasure down toward the princess. He looked around and threatened, "Boy, your mistress lied to you! I do so enjoy tormenting those who trespass and try to steal from me! If you leave now, empty-handed of course, I may let you live!"

Dolan crouched down behind a large silver plate. He didn't say anything but watched closely until the monster's attention was drawn to the princess once more. The crown was only a yard from him, but the dragon's fire could easily roast him if the creature just spotted him. After a few moments of the dragon not looking toward him, the thief sprinted for the pedestal.

Marelda stood perfectly still as the dragon turned his head down to her level. She'd thrown a tiny fire ball at him, but it had done nothing but make him laugh. The dragon considered her with his solid red eyes and licked his jagged teeth, his sulfurous breath made her nauseous.

"That tickled, it did," the wizard chuckled. "But you've wasted your time, little one. Fire can't hurt me."

"I know," Marelda replied. As the dragon opened his mouth, thinking to consume her, she thrust out both hands chanting at the top of her lungs.

The wizard screamed as the green spears of ice flew into his mouth, lodging themselves in his throat and coating it with a thick layer of ice. The dragon whipped his body around as he tried to close his mouth, his tail knocking the pile of treasure near the pedestal around and tossing the thief and the crown to the ground.

Marelda jumped out of the way as she continued chanting and shooting. The ice was now only daggers that sometimes pierced but more often broke on the black scales. The ice built up as she focused on his jaws, trying to keep the ice there as thick as possible.

Dolan scrambled down the pile and grabbed the crown on the tip of his blade so he could lift his arm and let the crown slide down onto his elbow. The crown was larger than he had expected and far heavier as well. The thief hurried to his feet, careful to jump over the monster's wildly swinging tail.

As the slave made his way over the pile of treasure toward the exit, he watched as the princess slid to her knees, her hands still sending tiny shards toward the demon, who was screaming and clawing at his mouth. Dolan stood up as he saw the exit a few feet away. He turned back to the scene below him and yelled as the dragon lifted one foot to crush the prone princess. The cries of concern turned to screams of pain and fear as a shower of green ice, black scales, and red blood pelted him. After the debris stopped falling, the thief half ran and half fell down the muck-covered treasure heap toward the princess. "Mistress!"

Dolan dropped the crown at his feet as he knelt over the pale, limp form of the princess. "Don't be dead, please," he begged as he lifted her head onto his lap. "You're the only one I've ever given a damn about, so don't go and prove I'm not allowed to have good feelings about anyone." Around him the air was filled with smoke and the stink of a thousand horrid things. The slave grabbed the crown and rested it on the princess's stomach, then lifted her up in his arms. As he stood he noticed a fairly clear path between the treasure piles toward the exit.

Once outside the cave he recognized the wooded area that surrounded the gate on both worlds. Hurrying as best he could, the slave made his way back to the other entrance. The boulders there were just as huge as they had appeared to be from the inside. He turned toward the gate, then fell to his knees at the sight of empty sky. "It's closed," he whispered as he laid the princess on the grass. "But we're still alive," he pointed out to himself and her as he looked around for signs of the universe crumbling around them.

The princess didn't move. Dolan placed his head on her chest but heard no heartbeat. He unbuttoned her jacket, her vest and her shirt and listened again. "You're alive," he exclaimed as he heard the faint but steady beat. As the princess moaned he sat back, covering her quickly with her clothes. "Mistress? Can you hear me? This is Dolan, your slave and thief. Remember me? You have to wake up, please, I'm begging you, down on my knees and all that stuff you like," he added as tears fell from his eyes. His throat still burned, and his chest was struggling from the stench of the dragon.

Marelda blinked her eyes several times as she tried to focus. The sunlight caused her great pain, so she laboriously lifted one hand to shield her eyes. "The crown?" she croaked.

"Yes, it's right here," Dolan said as he took her other hand and placed it over the last sacred object. "You killed a dragon," he whispered as he pushed his sweat-dampened hair back with his hands. "A dragon, Lady and Lord, I've survived a dragon too."

Marelda muttered a few impolite terms as she turned toward him. She looked at his belt and reached for the buckle.

Dolan opened his mouth as the princess unbuckled his belt and then started to unlace his pants. "The gate is closed, shouldn't we deal with that," he offered weakly as her hand caressed his cock through his underwear.

Marelda's green eyes swung upward. "I need your help with this, boy."

The slave felt his face flush as he rose up onto his knees so she could pull his clothing down. When she repeated her first sentence he took his cock in hand and began stroking it slowly. Her scent started to fill his nose, erasing the wicked smell of the dragon from his mind and urging his body to respond faster.

He had performed a few times for the jeweler and several times for the man's wife and her friends but now he felt pride as he worked himself into a frenzy. The princess used him to help feed her magic, not merely to entertain herself or to humiliate him. A new feeling washed over him as the princess took him inside her mouth and sucked out his orgasm: pride. With a mumbled "thank you," Dolan withdrew his hands and just let her take all she wanted from him.

"This is not what I was expecting!" a new voice made the slave and the princess pull apart and look up. An old man dressed in fine robes was staring at them with disgust in every wrinkle.

The plump blonde mage chuckled as she stepped around and offered her pupil her hand. "Took a lot out of you, but I see you have the crown," she commented as she lifted both princess and crown up from the ground.

"Cover yourself up, boy!" the old man ordered.

"What are you doing here?" Marelda asked as she looked from her mage to Alroy, the chief advisor of her parents, and back again. "I don't see the gate," she explained weakly.

"I'll explain it all once we have you back at camp," Sigrid promised.

"Camp?" Marelda repeated.

"Yes, I've been traveling for several days now trying to find you," Alroy stated as he watched the slave pull up his pants, eyeing the princess closely. "I'm to bring you home in triumph," the advisor added.

Dolan watched silently as the two aristocrats led the princess away. He looked down at the ground, then bent to pick up his dagger. Catching the senior mage looking back at him, the slave trotted off after them. Just beyond the woods an army of colorful tents was waiting for them. He followed the princess toward the largest but was blocked from entering by a guard out front. "No slaves inside the royal tent without Her Majesty's order," the guard informed him.

"Great," the thief muttered as he backed up, his hands raised in submission until he stood a few feet away. Sitting down on the ground he narrowed his eyes toward the tent. *I guess it's back to the same old thing,* he cursed as he watched several slaves being herded back from the woods, their arms loaded with logs and their feet attached together with chains.

"Hey!" he yelled as he stood up upon seeing another guard approach with what appeared to be his backpack, the princess's backpack, and her sword. Several slaves followed after this guard with their arms full of treasure. The guard by the royal tent simply told him to sit down and be quiet. Dolan shut his mouth with effort as he returned to sit. The slaves and the guard disappeared behind the royal tent, then reappeared to go back toward the dragon's cave. The procession continued until the sun had set.

The guard simply offered the bowl of stew and the chunk of brown bread to the slave, who'd been sitting staring at the royal tent all afternoon. When the slave took the bowl the guard wrinkled up his nose. "You smell like something awful!"

Dolan narrowed his eyes and took a sniff of his sleeve as he lowered the bowl. "Yeah, well having dragon spilled all over you tends to be smelly business, Sir," he added with a glance back toward the royal tent.

"We got all the gold and stuff out of there," the guard told him.

Dolan glanced up at the unexpected information. Most free people, especially those in any position of power, just ignored slaves. "Sir, do you know if Her Majesty's backpack and sword have been returned to her?"

"If they were in the cave they were just added to the pile," the guard replied.

"Sir, there was also a backpack with some clothes and stuff for me," Dolan explained. "Do you think I could get it and get cleaned up? I don't want to offend anyone else," the slave quickly added in his most humble and subservient tone. "I haven't much to offer you in exchange, but," he left the suggestion dangle as he licked his lips.

The guard shifted his weight as though looking around then mumbled, "I'll go see what I can do for you."

"Thank you, Sir," Dolan offered quickly. He watched the guard head in the direction of the royal tent then go around behind it where the parade of treasure had disappeared. The thief shivered in the cooling night air. *Now all I need is a coat,* he decided as he wolfed down the hot stew and looked longingly at the various fires throughout the camp. Even the lowest slaves who'd been lugging wood and the treasure were chained in groups near the fires eating. The thief felt more alone than he had in his whole life, a feeling that he'd never imagined he'd fall victim to or care about again.

"Well, I know she won't be needing you after she has me," a light male voice said from behind the tent flap Dolan had been led to so he could wash up and change his clothes. The guards hadn't even required any payment for his backpack, simply handed it to him then brought him here.

"You're just gonna be a quickie," another male voice replied.

"You both are so incredibly full of yourselves," a female voice chided them.

"Oh, I hope it's not just myself I get filled by," the first male voice countered. All three erupted into laughter.

Dolan entered the tent and found two male slaves and one

female slave. They were dressed in fine clothes though each one had their chests bared to display nipple rings, confirming their class as sexual slaves. Each was wearing make-up on their faces and had elegantly decorated silver cuffs on wrists and ankles. They all three put their fingers to their noses and pinched them closed.

"Lady and Lord, what a stench!" the slave whose voice he'd heard first exclaimed as he tossed back his long blond hair.

"Workers outside!" the woman ordered as she turned away.

"I'm not a worker," Dolan said suddenly, feeling very angry and embarrassed at the same time. "I was sent here to clean up and change," he stated as he held out his backpack. Luckily the backpack had been protected in the tunnel and spared the drowning in ice and gore he himself had received.

The second male slave now let his hand fall to his dark brown mustache as he looked the smelly creature up and down slowly. "You're the one who traveled with her?" he half asked and half guessed.

At Dolan's nod the blond male waved his hands in front of his face. "Thank you, then, for taking my place. I couldn't have stood such a life," he added as he shook his head and picked up a mirror.

"You're from the castle?" Dolan asked as he stood numbly and watched the three put on finishing touches of makeup and perfume.

"The princess' favorites," the brunet male suggested.

"In your dreams," the woman stated as she rolled her eyes. "You can have the place then, just stay away from my stuff," she cautioned Dolan as she closed her makeup case.

"Yeah, don't touch any of our stuff," the blond male added as he shut his as well.

The thief was silent as he watched the three walk past him, each one making a point of holding their noses as they did so, to the guards waiting outside. "Damn!" Dolan cursed as he threw his backpack down. After a few moments to calm himself he started to strip in preparation for using the bathtub in one corner of the tent. They were just sluts, but he was a thief she'd chosen for a purpose, and he had served her well, so she wouldn't forget, him he consoled himself as he sat in the warm water.

Marelda pushed her half-finished dinner away from her. She placed one hand over her stomach trying to calm the churning inside. The bath and the clean clothes had helped the external physical side effects, but she was still drained by the combat.

"She needs to have her strength renewed," Sigrid repeated to the chief advisor as he stood and watched anxiously.

"Those were all her favorite foods that the cook says he can make in camp," Alroy countered. "I suppose you have a better idea?" he sniffed.

"I've taken care of it," Sigrid replied. Just then one of the guards parted the flap and stuck his head in. "Bring them in," the mage commanded with a grin.

"What's going on here?" Marelda asked as the tent flap was held open by the guard and three of the castle's sex slaves entered. The three moved softly and quickly to kneel then prostrate themselves as close to her feet as possible.

"Oh, now I see," the chief advisor began as he stepped forward with a smile, only to find himself spun around toward the tent flap.

"They need some privacy, and you're too old for this type of service anyway," Sigrid suggested as she steered the older man toward the tent flap.

"This is your fault, this entire magic thing," Alroy countered in disapproval as he glanced back at the slaves. "I mean, a good fuck is one thing but for a woman of her status to draw that from those things..."

"She's just doing what she needs," Sigrid corrected him. The mage pushed the old advisor out of the tent then looked back at her pupil. "Take however much you need, my dear," she instructed in a low serious voice.

Marelda sat still as the slaves lay before her. The blond, the one of the slaves that she'd used the least number of times at home, glanced up, flirting with his pale lashes. "It's Dif, correct?" she asked.

"You honor me, Mistress, by remembering my name," the blond replied softly as he lifted himself up a bit more onto his hands and knees.

Marelda smiled, then looked at the other two. "You're Lica, and you are Jaff."

"You honor me, Mistress, by remembering my name," they both replied using the practiced phrases.

"So, are you all prepared?" the princess asked.

"Yes, Mistress," all three eagerly confirmed.

"Good," Marelda sighed. She leaned back in her chair and

ordered the three to their feet. "Then show me," she further instructed. As they stripped off all their clothing then posed themselves in several ways to show off their smooth-shaven and squeaky-clean bodies, the princess's grin widened. *This is what I miss about the castle,* she admitted to herself.

Dolan dried himself off for the third time and smelled his arms. It was no use; he couldn't smell anything. He wrapped the towel around himself and hurried to the tent flap. Pulling it aside, he saw the guard who had brought him dinner and his backpack and then walked him to this tent looking at him. "Sir, this is going to sound strange, but do I smell any better?" the slave forced himself to ask.

The guard chuckled as he took a big whiff. He nodded. "Aye, just like soap and water. Not like those three who left. Could smell their perfume a mile off," the guard added with a deep laugh.

"Sir, did they serve Her Majesty back at the castle?" Dolan asked softly.

The guard cocked one eyebrow. "Ain't my business what she or anyone else of royal blood does in private," he insisted.

"Of course, Sir, I apologize for asking. Thank you, Sir," Dolan replied with a sharp bow of his head. He ducked back inside. Near the tub he discarded the towel so he could put on a nicer set of clothing. He'd thrown out the ones he'd been wearing and now packed the mended ones onto the bottom of his backpack with the soap and cleansing supplies on top. The odd underwear was shiny and red and slipped over his thighs and hips like a fluid to hug him but not bind him. Next the soft black leather pants went up easily, though it took him several attempts to make the underwear lay flat underneath. The short red boots had no laces, so he merely slipped his feet in them once the matching red socks were on. The shirt matched the shoes but was a soft linen instead of the liquid-like material of the underwear.

With a glance around he snatched one of the mirrors and checked his face. "Bet you all still have to cut it down," he commented, comparing his smooth cheeks with the short but full beards the other two male slaves had. He pulled on the vest that matched the pants and admired his reflection. Then he frowned as he recalled how much finer the other three had been dressed. *Of course, I'm not just a bedmate. I'm a thief, her companion, her man-at-arms,* Dolan repeated silently until he was holding his head high with pride. He hid the mirror quickly under the towel as the tent flap was shoved open by a guard.

Two guards entered, carrying the blond slave boy while another followed with the blond's fine clothing. The three guards laid the slave on one of the three mattresses on the floor, dumping his clothing on top of him. One of the guards paused to look over Dolan as they exited. "She ain't called for you yet, boy," he teased.

Dolan waited until the tent flap closed behind the three guards to approach the blond. The man was pale, and his body had numerous bruises on it that looked like teeth marks and possibly the dug-in crescents from fingernails. The thief recalled how the three perverted guards back at the castle of the sorceress had been lying in their own blood because the princess needed energy for her magic. A quick touch on the man's neck assured Dolan that the slave was alive, at least.

Returning to the tub the thief took the mirror and considered his own image. A few days ago he could have sworn he'd been looking much the same as the blond, but he'd had no mirror to confirm that. Now, though, his cheeks were full and tanned, his hair curling as it dried. "Better you than me," he muttered with a glance back at the blond as he tried to decide how loose the lacing on his shirt should be.

Marelda watched the slave Lica closely as the guards helped Jaff leave. At least he'd had enough strength left to put on his shirt before being escorted out. The princess noted that Lica, though she stood perfectly still wearing only the slip she'd been ordered to put on after inspection, was glancing at her nervously. "Lica," Marelda spoke clearly as she held out her hand. "Come here, girl."

The female slave walked with her body held in an elegant pose, then knelt and took the offered hand. Her eyes betrayed the fear witnessing her companions' use had inspired as she glanced up and kissed the princess' hand.

Marelda turned her palm and caressed the slave's smooth face and her short hair. "Are you crying?" the princess whispered.

"With joy, Mistress," the girl said weakly.

"Lica," Marelda said, taking the slave's chin in her hand and lifting her head up. "I can't take from you what I took from them, obviously," she added with a smile. "No, I just want to enjoy your skills. If I recall correctly, my brother tells me that you give a fine massage as well as fine orgasms."

Lica smiled sincerely, her eyes twinkling as she moved closer, gently pushing between the princess' legs and parting the robe she'd been dressed in since the slaves had entered the royal tent. "His Majesty is most kind in his praise. I wish only to please you, Mistress," the slave whispered as she lowered her head.

Marelda closed her eyes as the skilled tongue and lips moved quickly up and down each of her thighs. A very liberal sexual education had been hers, and the staff at the Vanhilmer castle was trained to accommodate any of the royal family or the free staff members at a moment's notice but the palace sluts were especially trained for pleasure. The past month of traveling and fighting evil had been an adventure, to be sure, but now as she relaxed and just enjoyed the slave girl's skills, Marelda felt herself yearn for her own bed.

Soon the princess had her hands wrapped in the short hair of the slave girl as her orgasm approached. Somewhere in the back of her mind she felt less fulfilled as the spasms washed over her again and again, her soft cries matched by the slave's gasps.

The princess pushed the slave away gently as her third orgasm faded before the girl could hurry toward another. "That was very nice, Lica. Too bad Joshua couldn't just concentrate on you," she added as she considered the plain upstairs maid her youngest sibling had run off with.

The slave whimpered as she bowed her head — likely she knew exactly what had been going on at the castle; slaves always did, no matter how much you attempted to prevent their learning about things. "I tried, truly I did, Mistress," she began to wail.

Marelda leaned forward and caressed the girl's short hair again. "It wasn't a. accusation. I just have a great deal on my mind." The princess stood up and pulled her robe around her. *What's wrong with me? I use the staff all the time at home.* The princess looked at her bracelet with a sigh. "Lica, go to your tent and tell Dolan to report to me immediately," she ordered.

"Dolan?" the slave girl repeated as she rose to her feet. She picked up her skirt and slipped into her shoes without bothering to pull on her stockings. "Is that the dark slave who traveled with you, Mistress?"

"Yes, he'll need to be cleaned up first, I'm sure," Marelda replied. She looked at the basket of exotic fruit that her parents' chief advisor had tried to tempt her with as the slave girl hurried into her underpants and wrapped her skirt around her; she'd leave as bare-breasted as she had arrived. "Lica," the princess said to attract the slave's attention. She tossed her one of the round orange fruits. "Thank you for a good time."

Lica blushed and bowed, then clenching the fruit between her breasts, she hurried from the tent.

Dolan examined the brunet slut's face as he lay on his mattress asking questions in a tired voice. The thief stood by the tent flap, his backpack over one shoulder, and refused once more to comment as the slave questioned him on the princess's apparently rougher requirements. He was about to tell the other off when the female slave entered.

The woman tossed a bright piece of fruit into the air then caught it with a giggle. She stopped and paled a bit at the sight of the still unconscious blond. Then she turned to the new slave and motioned toward the tent flap. "Her Majesty has sent for you, if you're Dolan, that is," she informed him.

"Yup, that's me," he replied as he straightened up. He watched as the female slave easily and sadistically warded off the brunet's attempt to grab at the fruit. It was clear that her use had been far more pleasurable than that of the other two. Without a word the thief exited the tent.

"She's called for you?" the guard asked.

"Yes, Sir, so I am informed," Dolan replied, allowing himself a grin.

"Aye, so that minx informed me," the guard confirmed. "I'll take you then, boy," he further offered.

As they walked, the slave making sure he was at least one step behind the guard, Dolan noticed the old man who'd given him such disconcerting looks standing at the flap of a tent not far from the royal one. The senior mage was waiting for him at the princess' tent and told the guard to leave him. The slave looked nervously as the buxom tutor placed one arm around him. "You've done very well, slave. I'll admit I wasn't sure you'd last long. Now you just do as you're told and you'll be fine," she suggested strongly before vanishing in a puff of smoke.

"Damn, I am never going to get used to that," Dolan shuddered. He smoothed back his hair, double-checked his tiny beard and mustache, then took a deep breath before entering. The tent seemed devoid of anyone, though it was richly decorated with furniture and even rugs on the ground. The princess's backpack and her sword in its sheath were the only signs that he had come to the right place. Taking another step inside so the flap could close, the slave cleared his throat softly. "My Lady? Mistress? Your Majesty?" he called.

Marelda stepped out from behind a elaborately designed dressing screen wearing riding pants, a white shirt with billowing sleeves, and boots that looked much like her old ones, though it was doubtful they'd been cleaned so well so quickly. "Oh, you're all dressed up," she said as she pulled on a vest.

"This isn't appropriate?" Dolan asked as he looked down at himself.

"Oh, no, it's fine," Marelda replied.

"I have the ones you mended for me in here," Dolan said as he swung the backpack to his front. "The other ones were all disgusting, so I threw them out, but I can go get them and wash them," he offered. "I didn't have time to clean the riding boots, so I hoped these fancy boots would do."

"I understand; all my clothing was tossed out too. I'd toss the riding boots too; I don't think much gets out dragon's blood," Marelda guessed. She pulled on a leather coat, this one much longer than her other one. "I thought we would go for a walk. Talk about some things," she told him as she threw him another leather jacket, this one black like the pants he wore.

"Yes, my Lady," Dolan replied as he put on the coat, then placed his backpack on the table next to her own when she indicated he should do so. He followed her outside and noted that every eye in camp turned toward them as they walked through it. At each campfire, the guards and even slaves muttered their respects or simply stood up silently.

The edge of the camp was just beyond the area where the tiny cabin had been, but the princess continued walking until they were several yards away. "I prefer to talk out here away from prying eyes and spying ears," Marelda explained as she stopped in front of a fallen tree trunk.

Dolan glanced back at the camp, wondering who she could mean. At the edge of the camp he saw the old man, Alroy, standing and looking at them. "You mean like him?" he asked as he crouched down in the grass so he could face her as she lowered herself to the log.

Marelda narrowed her eyes, then flicked her fingers toward her parents' chief advisor. She smiled as the brisk breeze she created knocked his hood back from his head and sent him stumbling backwards. "He's nosy, to say the least," the princess agreed. "But I'm more concerned about agents from other realms."

"No problems with rivalry in the royal family, my Lady?" the thief asked softly. Such stories of court intrigue had been gossip among all classes of folk, and it was common knowledge that the Vanhilmer family was large for a aristocratic one.

Marelda chuckled at the suggestion. "No, not my sister and brothers. They couldn't care less about politics. That's a very good thing," she added as she turned her gaze to her boots. Silently she thought about everything her mother, her father, Sigrid, and her common tutors had told her.

Dolan just shrugged as he adjusted his position. The new coat was warmer than the previous jacket had been and definitely a luxury item. He held on to the insides of the pockets as he waited for her to continue. That would have been difficult for him to do weeks ago, but now he felt patience and an odd unexpected confidence as he looked at her. The longer she remained silent, though, the more his mind wandered to the three pleasure slaves back in the tent.

"Do you know what I did with Lica and the two boys before sending for you?" the princess suddenly asked as she looked up and met his eyes.

The suddenness of the question knocked the slave back onto his ass with a grunt. His owner simply watched as he shifted his legs underneath him more securely. "Ah," Dolan began, then coughed as he tried to organize his thoughts more clearly and politely. "They, ah, didn't tell me, Mistress."

Marelda tilted her head to one side as she pouted. "Of course not. They are too well trained for that, at least," she added with a glance back at the camp where the old advisor had resumed his watching. "Alroy is very good at keeping things in order back home."

Dolan looked back, then returned to carefully watch the princess as he spoke. "I assume you enjoyed them as is your right, Mistress."

"My right?" Marelda repeated as she leaned forward. "Yes, I did replenish my strength from the two boys and then a had a quick one with the girl. But," and she paused and used one finger to emphasize her next statement, "I didn't ask for them. Sigrid sent them to me. Much against Alroy's wishes, I might add."

Dolan frowned a bit as he shook his head slightly. "Why would he disapprove? I'm just a simple slave from a small city. All this talk about castles and wizards and magic is pretty much over my head, my Lady. But I thought that palace sluts were yours to use as and when you wished."

"The second statement is correct but ignores the fact that as heir I have certain responsibilities and a certain air I must maintain." Marelda stood up. "I know you aren't like them. That's one of the reasons I guess you were chosen."

The slave stood up and followed as the princess headed off again. Soon they had doubled back and were standing inside the dragon's cave. The once treasure-filled room now echoed with their footsteps. "Wow, they took it all," Dolan whispered as he stopped just a few feet inside.

The princess walked a few paces further, then turned to face him suddenly. "So now I have fulfilled the prophecy, in part. There are still so many things to do. Figuring out what to do with you isn't the least of them," she added with a concerned frown.

Dolan swallowed, then placed his hands behind his back and rocked back once on his heels. "Let me guess, you need a human sacrifice now, huh?" he said, trying to make the question sound light. He swallowed again as the princess simply looked at him in seriousness.

"If I told you 'yes,' would you run?" Marelda asked flatly.

"What would be the point?" Dolan replied as he held out his arms, thrusting his hands so the cuffs were visible underneath the edge of the coat. "You already reminded me of my place earlier today, my Lady. I'm not stupid; I don't need a repeat performance. I figure right now I'm living on borrowed time as it is anyway."

"No, you're not stupid," the princess agreed as she approached him. She stopped and looked him straight in the eye until he lowered his head, then smiled as a feeling of power and trust grew in her. "Come outside with me, slave," she ordered huskily.

Dolan followed the princess back out into the rocky terrain to a nearby glen now covered with new lush grass. At her word he removed his boots and coat then went to kneel on the ground. Off to each side was a wooden stake pounded into the ground with a set of manacles attached to it. "I was joking about the human sacrifice," he forced himself to chuckle.

"Take off the rest of your clothes, then lie down with your hands at the stakes," Marelda instructed. She kept her face neutral, though her body clenched in anticipation as he did as he was bid with only a few glances around him as though calculating his chances for escape. Once he was in place she snapped the manacles on him. Teasingly she played with his hair and face, then stood up so she straddled him, her neatly shined boots on either side of his body.

Dolan lifted his head up to follow her hands as she lifted them up. When she began to chant he pressed his head back to the ground in fear. Her scent surrounded him, and he felt the now familiar arousal pulling apart his fears. He watched as she took off her clothes and continued chanting, her eyes focused down on him and his growing erection. The green light streamed from her fingers onto his body, causing it to clench and shudder, not in pain but in confusion and excitement.

Marelda looked up and spied her tutor watching her with a deep frown. Sigrid, however, stayed where she was as the princess continued the spell to break her enchantment on the slave. *I need to know if he'll offer everything to me freely*, she thought silently. As though hearing and understanding, the mage disappeared.

The slave shook his head a bit as his feelings changed. His eyes focused anew on the princess's nude body as she chanted. Her form no longer seemed so elegant, so otherworldly, yet she was beautiful and powerful, and his own body responded by pulling at the stakes toward her as his breathing increased. His skin flushed as she lowered herself to his chest and the musky scent from her mound wafted up to him.

"How do you feel?" Marelda asked as she braced for the results of her spell. He could reject her now, not that that would stop her, but she found his wanting her actually mattered and might fuel her magicks with greater power.

"I want you," Dolan whispered as he sat up as best he could. The princess, unprepared for this response, slid down to his waist. The slave pulled on the stakes as he lunged forward and kissed her passionately. "Train me to be your palace slut," he begged as he turned his lips to her shoulders.

Marelda's eyes widened as she allowed herself to relax into his struggling body. "You want to be like the other three?" she whispered as he worked his way up her neck with fevered kisses.

"Anything you need, anything you want," Dolan replied as he pulled on the stakes. His arms and hands ached to touch her as she lifted herself back and then settled back down, one of her hands caressing his eager member. His eyes popped open as he felt his cock being pulled between her thighs into the heat and moisture he'd known rarely with servants and peasant girls. "Yes, Mistress!" he cried out as he fell back onto the ground.

Marelda moved her hands from underneath them, surprised that his sudden movement hadn't broken their contact. The pain she'd been expecting dissipated into a dull pressure similar to the one she felt when aroused. She lifted herself a little, then settled back down, allowing her body to grow accustomed to the new sensation of being filled. Then she experimented at tightening her muscles and found that sensation better as it moved her clit as well. Leaning down toward him increased the pleasant rubbing she was most familiar with. This was an exceedingly rare encounter for an aristocratic woman to take with a male slave, but it would be necessary later. Smiling at how he struggled and gasped under her, she stopped all movement and looked down at him as she placed her hands on his chest. Even without chanting there was a flow of light between them.

Dolan opened his eyes after a few minutes to blink at his owner as she sat passively on him. "Mistress, please, please," he pleaded over and over. Now his mind did not question his reactions as it had before; he merely knew that he needed her, wanted her, and would do anything to have her. In his lust-filled eyes her image grew and filled his view until nothing existed beyond her embrace. He cried out, "Yes, yes," as she began moving up and down, back and forth in a slow dance.

"Keep pace with me. Work for me, boy!" Marelda ordered as she leaned down to rest against his chest. As his hips moved now to accommodate her and his hands tried to touch her she flicked his nipple rings with her tongue and fingers.

A thousand or more times Dolan had found himself on his back or stomach being used by the jeweler and his friends. A dozen times, not often in the years he'd been running, he himself had quickly availed himself of loose women in exchange for a bit of food. Too many times to count, he had begged the princess to use him and had been taken and left weak. Now he felt afire as his nipples ached and his balls tightened.

Marelda gasped as she sat up with the first violent jolt of her clit and the first clench of her channel around his shaft. Somewhere she began the chant she'd memorized, but as the deep wave of pleasure struck her the words exploded from her mind. The world turned as she tried to focus on the spell or the stars overhead. Her body took over all training as she pounded up and down several times with a scream.

Dolan's scream mingled with the princess's as he felt his own groin contract and then explode. The rush of pleasure canceled out the pain in his nipples as the rings were twisted violently in his owner's hands.

Marelda slid off of her slave and lay down on the ground next to him. She touched his chest, sighing as he groaned at her caress of his sore nipples. After a few quiet moments she leaned up and traced his lips with one finger. The tiny flickers of now white light there made her smile deepen. "You were the one, it seems, after all," she muttered, more to herself than him.

Dolan sighed as he thought about the three pleasure slaves. Their fine clothes, the obvious special care they received, their smug attitudes, none of that was worth one tenth of what he now saw in his future. "Mistress?" he asked as he moved enough to accommodate her resting more comfortably on his chest.

"Hmmmm?" Marelda replied as she focused on the aftershocks of her orgasm and the white light of her magic as she wiggled her fingers.

"Will there be more training like this for me at your castle?" Dolan asked with a grin.

Marelda's face settled back into a concerned expression at his words. She had removed the spells connecting her pleasure to his, forcing his desire, and yet he was clearly enjoying himself. She felt a strange sensation in her body as she leaned down and untied his hands. When he caressed her and began kissing her again, she smiled and sighed. "Yes, some things will have to be done back home," she agreed, "but we can do other things out here as well."

Chapter Seven:
Rebirth

The thief stood still in the empty entryway for several moments. He looked around at the silken tapestries that hung on the walls, each of them showing a scene from Vanhilmer history, the bright red hair of most of the main characters resembling the princess's strongly.

"I almost forgot you," the chief steward said as he returned to the entryway. He wiped his hands on the towels at his waist and walked around the thief. "Not bad clothing, for traveling anyway," he stated as he touched the red shirt.

Dolan snapped his arm back and glared at the steward. "Where's my mistress?"

"Oh, the princess is busy, busy, busy," the steward stated with an exaggerated grin. "Everyone here is buzzing with her praises. The glory days of this palace will soon return."

Dolan turned his head as the steward kept circling him. "So do I just stand here in the entryway until she returns?"

The steward chuckled and used his fingertips to fan out his beard. On his wrists were two golden cuffs which shone in the light from the elaborate chandelier hanging from the ceiling overhead. "Come with me, boy; I'll find a place for you in the palace. We can always use more hands, especially with the parties that are sure to be thrown now."

The thief paused a moment, looking down the hallway where the princess had been swept by the strange old man, her tutor, and a crowd of red-headed aristocrats near her own age. *She'll find me when she wants, when she needs me, she will,* he told himself firmly. He adjusted the pack on his back and nodded at the steward. "Lead the way, sir."

"Call me Daemon," the steward added as he led the way down the narrowest of the hallways leading from the entryway. "Things are very formal around here, but between us slaves, I prefer a bit of brotherhood — and sisterhood too; wouldn't want to offend the girls."

Dolan raised his dark eyebrows and chuckled as he walked as close to the steward as the hallway allowed. If this man were any indication, the attitudes of the slaves in this place would be something he could get used to, as long as he didn't run into too many more stuck-up sluts.

His new quarters were far larger than any he had survived in when owned by the jeweler. The room was narrow, not more than six feet wide and six feet long, but with very high ceilings. A bunk bed occupied the far side of the room while a wooden closet which reminded him of the hotel stood near the open doorframe. No door, of course; the steward explained that no one got locked in at night; the dungeon was for punishments, and if anyone had half a brain they wouldn't want to visit there.

"What did you do before the princess bought you?" the steward asked as the thief unpacked his bag and set his worn clothing on the top bed.

"I was a gem cutter and a jewelry maker," Dolan replied. "Lately I've just been my Lady's thief and personal servant."

The steward frowned, then laughed and clapped his hands. "That's very funny. Thief indeed." The steward's face deepened when he noted the dagger the new slave removed from his belt and set on the bed. "No weapons allowed in here, boy, unless you're to be a guard."

Dolan picked up the dagger and studied it carefully as he spoke. "The Princess Marelda gave this to me and told me to keep it with me at all times. I won't give it up without her direct order. You'll have to take it from me if you want," he added with lowered eyebrows and a frown.

The steward paled, then waved his hands. "Then you best keep it on you, boy. But be careful not to let it lie around where others might get their hands on it. We're a contented bunch, but it is best to be safe, right?"

Dolan nodded, a bit sad that even here there was obvious fear in the slaves, and slipped the dagger back into his belt. With a tight smile he followed the steward back out into the communal area of the slave quarters.

The slave's quarters were just inside the palace. The series of rooms were arranged in a three-quarters circle around a central hub. This hub had only one door leading outside, and it was guarded by a large hulk of a man chained to the heavy wooden door. Into the kitchen and palace were several other open passageways. The hub consisted of an open area with two long tables and benches where the steward said meals were taken, often on a staggered schedule so that someone would be free to serve the family at any moment. To one side, near the women's rooms, was a curtained-off area for their bathing, and matching it was one for the men. Dolan noted with surprise that the shower heads were divided by thin walls, as were the toilets, thus affording a bit of privacy he never thought possible in mere slave quarters.

"You'll bathe every day when you rise, and again if you are called to serve at the evening meal or to entertain one of the royal family or their guests," the steward explained as he showed the thief how to work the equipment. "These, of course," he said, holding up one of the hoses attached next to the shower heads, "are to prepare completely for their pleasure. Use this every day as well. For myself it has been years since I've been honored with such duty, but I feel so much better just knowing I could."

Dolan's stomach tightened as his mind registered what the hoses were for. He tried to smile at the steward, who somehow seemed actually sad he wasn't being called to such service, but found his eyes wandering over the slave quarters looking for any way to escape. Of course there was little chance of that, considering the guards and porter, even if one did not consider his enchanted cuffs. Then again, maybe Marelda would mark him as her own and he wouldn't have to suffer other use.

As they left the hub they bumped into a young male slave carrying a set of towels toward them. The boy was about the same age Dolan had been when he had run away, the sparse beard on his chin and cheeks barely showing. "Sorry, Daemon," the boy squeaked as he picked up the towels.

"Kyle," the steward said, then clicked his tongue but chuckled as the boy blushed. "This here is Dolan, your new roommate."

The thief stiffened as he eyed the boy. Kyle held out one hand as he held the towels close to his chest with the other. "You can have the bottom bunk if you want," the boy stated.

"My stuff is already on the top," Dolan replied as he touched the outstretched hand. He almost pulled back when the boy's fingers wrapped over his palm and shook it several times. Slaves back at the jeweler's had never touched each other, in kindness or in violence, unless so ordered.

"Fine," Kyle beamed. "Got to go; I have a lot of cleaning to do."

"He's a good boy," the steward stated as the boy hobbled away.

"What's wrong with his leg?" Dolan asked.

"Wasn't born in this house," the steward simply replied. "The Lady and Lord are most kind folks. I'd say in the image of the Divine Couple, they are."

The thief noted the tension in the steward's voice, deciding he'd ask the boy himself what really happened to his legs when they were alone in their room. They had looked straight and strong. With a second glance at the retreating figure of his new roommate, Dolan just nodded, then followed the steward into the room the boy had rushed from.

The kitchen was enormous, certainly bigger than the entire house and workshop of the jeweler. Another door with another guard led to the outside, just as in the hub. Slaves of both sexes hurried about, and the lack of crying and beatings, and indeed the presence of a few smiles and giggles, confused the thief's mind as the slaves rushed about doing their work.

"There'll be a feast tonight," the steward explained. "We have all the cooks we need, boy, but I suspect we could use an extra hand in serving. You ever do anything like that?"

"Yes, I have," Dolan replied with a grim expression.

"Very good," the steward stated. He stepped forward into the center of the room, the new slave following, and called out a name as loud as he could. Everyone paused in their work until a tall slave dressed entirely in black stepped forth. "Mylick," the steward addressed the slave, "this is Dolan; the Princess Marelda brought him back with her. He'll help you at the feast this evening."

The chief butler sniffed as he walked around the new slave. "He doesn't look like much of a butler, wine server, or even clean-up crew."

Dolan narrowed his eyes, clasped his hands behind his back and rocked on his heels with a low chuckle.

The chief butler shook his head. "You have no sense of propriety," he whispered and sniffed again.

"Mylick is more into the formalities around here," the steward replied.

"Send him to the fields; he smells," the butler stated with a wave of his hand.

"Fine with me, pretty pants," Dolan spat back.

The steward stepped between both slaves as the butler advanced. "He's not going to the fields or the stable. The princess brought him in the front door, she did. She'll give us instructions when she has time. But for now, he serves table so she can see he is well-watched and not being idle. Idle folks don't eat around here," he added to the new slave.

"I didn't start this," Dolan simply replied as he backed up, one hand sweeping up his vest so the dagger showed. Dolan knew how to scrap to survive in slave quarters, this fancy bastard didn't scare him in the least.

The chief butler gasped, then nodded quickly. "Well, then, we shall find a good place for the princess's acquisition."

Dolan followed the chief butler for the next few hours, learning by example how dishes were served and what courses were served in what order. Though the snotty butler never complimented his attempts, the thief noted that the other serving slaves gave him smiles as he mimicked their moves.

Marelda looked at her elder sister Annabel with an amused smile as she was shown through the palace and all the redecorating she had been allowed to keep, some of the art and a few rearrangements of the furnishings, after their parents had returned. She nodded as Annabel explained how she thought a new coat of paint in a particular shade of green in the slave quarters would increase productivity.

"It is so good to have you home," Annabel suddenly stated as she hugged her younger sister.

Marelda blinked a few times and returned the caresses tentatively. "I did it for the family, for the realm, for the world. It was my duty."

"Of course," Annabel replied as she continued her hug. Then she stepped back with an unfamiliar look on her face, one of seriousness and concern. "Will those things really get the entire realm back?"

"Well, they'll help start the process, we'll need to make it all work," Marelda explained. She frowned when her sister looked around the slave quarters as though concerned about who was listening, then moved close to her and grabbed her by the arm. "What is it?" the heir asked.

"Josh is in the barn with his — maid," Annabel said in a whisper.

"I know, and Daemon knows, and Sigrid knows, of course. Josh asked me to tell you that he wants you to come and see them."

"What did mother and father say about this?" Marelda asked as she too glanced around the slave quarters.

"They threatened to sell her — they could; free people are nothing compared to a royal decree, and send Josh after Benjamin into the monastery," Annabel replied. "Then they realized that since you are returning in triumph, they could put the decision into your hands."

Marelda nodded, recalling her mother's snort of contempt when she asked after her brothers. "Let's sneak through the kitchens, then, and go see him. I want to make a good decision if I have to make one."

The staff fell silent and stood perfectly still as the princesses walked through the kitchen, the heir glanced around her but did not spy her thief anywhere. Daemon hurried to them then ordered the guard to open the door. He looked around the room then clapped his hands, ordering them all back to work.

The princesses went immediately to the barnyard and into the main stable. Marelda waited with the frightened stable boy as her sister went to fetch the youngest prince. "Don't tell anyone about this," she ordered, pressing her dagger to his neck when the prince and the round, very pregnant maid entered the stall where she waited.

"No, Your Highness; never, my Lady," the stable boy promised as she drew back her dagger.

Marelda nodded her head toward the door, patted the stable boy on his head, then sent him scurrying outside. She looked at her brother and his companion as they both knelt in the hay before her. "Stand up, Josh; that's no way for a prince to behave."

"It is when he faces his Lady and Liege," he replied, refusing to rise and clasping the frightened maid's trembling hands in his own.

Marelda blew her breath up onto her bangs tiredly then spoke. "What is your petition, then, since you insist on behaving like a vassal?"

"I wish permission to marry this woman you see here," Josh stated and dared look up into the heir's eyes.

"Is she pregnant with your child?"

"Yes," the prince replied.

Marelda crouched before the terrified maid and tilted her head up by her chin. "Was it out of love you conceived my brother's child, or under the orders of your young lord?"

The slave looked at the prince with tenderness, then back down at the princess's feet. "Love, my Lady," she whispered.

Marelda stood up and looked at her sister. "I believe them," Annabel replied simply. "I mean, she's nice looking for a maid, though I think it is a big mistake to offend your former betrothed," she added loudly in the prince's ear.

"Back off, missy bad taste," Josh retorted as he started to stand up.

"I've made a decision," Marelda announced. Her siblings and the maid looked to her anxiously. "When I ascend the throne, you may marry her; however," she hastened to add when the prince hugged his soon-to-be bride, "you will forfeit half of your inheritance for going against the expressed wishes of our current Lady and Lord. Pray that we can settle this matter with your betrothed or you will lose far more than that."

Josh nodded. "I hear and obey," he stated with a bow then pulled the girl up into his arms. "Of course, once you get the entire realm back, my inheritance, even at half, will be damn big."

"It will take more than a mere ceremony to restore things," Marelda stated as she clapped his shoulder on her way out. "I'll need all of your help — all of your help," she added when they paused by the exit to the kitchens.

"At your service," the two royal siblings replied with serious faces as the maid merely bowed her head.

Marelda waved her brother and his girl away so they would not be seen by any kitchen staff as the two princesses headed for the kitchen. She placed an arm around her sister's pale shoulders. "Can you make certain that Benjamin will be here for the coronation?"

Annabel batted her eyes in surprise. "You trust me to do that?"

"You, my sister, will be the second-highest-ranking woman in the world after we reunite everyone. What, you thought I was going to appoint you as palace interior decorator?" Marelda stated with one raised eyebrow.

"Well, I think I have a talent for that," Annabel began.

"Annabel," Marelda interrupted to restate, "I need all of my siblings here in order to regain the realm. Each of you has a very important duty to perform."

"You know so much," Annabel replied as she opened the kitchen door and stepped back into the palace. "You know how to rule, how to be practical; I'm afraid I just don't."

"Nonsense," Marelda replied with a squeeze on her sister's shoulder.

The staff once more paused in their tasks to watch the princesses enter. The steward noted the heir and scurried across the room. "May I assist you, my Lady?" he asked, bowing low, one hand sweeping the floor.

"Have you seen the slave I bought back with me?" Marelda asked as she motioned for him to rise. "He has black curly hair, a very short beard but nothing on his cheeks, a bit sunburned, in rather plain clothing by our standards."

"Yes, my Lady," the steward replied. "He has been placed in a room and given duties as table server for the feast tonight."

"I don't..." Marelda began when the chief advisor, Alroy, rushed into the kitchen.

"Your Majesty, your parents are calling for you. We must hurry," the advisor instructed.

Marelda sighed and hung her head. "Make sure he serves the royal table," she muttered to the chief steward before following the chief advisor out of the kitchen and back through the slave quarters.

"You really shouldn't be in the kitchens," Alroy began to preach as they walked.

"We're walking through the slave quarters, discussing internal matters relating to the staff; they are part of the staff," Marelda pointed out.

The chief advisor stopped by a boy kneeling on the floor scrubbing it next to them and pulled the slave to his feet by his hair with a few sharp words. "On your feet, boy! Show more respect for your owner and your betters." Alroy's seemingly weak body had a lot more strength as he held the slave and turned with a frown toward the heir. "You have every right to be here to take what is yours, but the kitchen is so, so ..."

"Work-centered, filled with slaves," Marelda offered with a grimace as the boy went limp in the advisor's grasp. She motioned one finger and the slave was released so he could kneel directly at her feet. "What's your name?"

"Kyle, my Lady," the boy replied with a tremble in his voice, his eyes only looking at her boots.

"Get back to work, Kyle," the princess ordered gently as she stepped past him and pulled the chief advisor after her.

The slave boy glanced up after the princess and winced as he rubbed the back of his head where his hair had been grasped before returning to his scrub brush and bucket. He knees were starting to hurt from the stone floor, but one glance at the chief advisor made him double his efforts.

Dolan tossed his bedding onto the floor and lifted up the mattress. He glared down at his crippled roommate, who stood glancing worriedly out of their room. "Where is my stuff, Kyle?" Dolan demanded as he jumped down to the floor.

"Daemon had me take it to the chief overseer for use by the field hands," the boy croaked.

"That's my stuff," Dolan stated as he stepped forward. He knew how to fight for what was his, and what the princess had bought him was a treasure by his standards. Even though the boy was crippled he'd fight if pushed.

"You'll need to talk to Daemon about it, I can't do anything," the boy pleaded. "Your new clothes are on the right hand side of the closet," Kyle offered as he opened the doors to show.

Dolan glanced at the closet, controlled his anger, and nodded; they looked better than the ones he'd had back at the jeweler's, nicer even than his traveling clothes. *If this is what I'm supposed to wear, I mean, I have the dagger, these nicer clothes, and the others were just mended, right? You're scaring the kid, knock it off.* "Good," he replied, then sat back onto the lower bunk bed with his arms supporting his body. "So, Kyle, how about we get to know each other a bit?"

The boy smiled and nodded. "I'd like that. I haven't had a roommate in months."

"Really? Why's that?" Dolan asked as lightly as he could, knowing that easing into the real questions he had would increase the chances of getting truthful answers. "Last roommates I had were a bunch of us waiting in a cage to be sold at auction. Not really a pleasant experience I'd like to repeat," he added.

"Oh," Kyle replied, then looked out the door again. "That's what happened to my last roommate too. So," Kyle tried to smile as he asked the first pointed question, "why'd you get sold off?"

Dolan rolled his eyes and sat up straight. *Give an answer to get an answer.* He pulled open his shirt and displayed the brands on his chest. "I was caught after running away. They do these nasty brands and beat you raw, then sell you at public auction. But," he said closing his shirt again, "the five years of freedom was worth it. At least that's what I told myself at the time."

Kyle stepped forward and undid his own shirt. "Me too," he confessed, showing his own brands off.

Dolan blinked. That was not what he had been expecting to see here in the palace, especially on some crippled kid who looked younger than him. "Must have been hard with your limp," Dolan guessed softly as his mind thought the revelation through. He couldn't imagine even trying to run away with such a handicap; suicide would have been his choice in such a situation.

"I was fine before I ran," Kyle stated.

"You know, the chief steward wouldn't tell me what happened to you," Dolan said after a few silent seconds. "I'm just curious, really. I know my former master was a beast, which is why I ran. I wouldn't run now, though; this place seems much better."

The boy glared at the thief suddenly, then looked down at the floor. "I ran from here about three years ago. The free staff here don't take kindly to runaways."

Dolan caught his roommate's eyes after looking at his feet, which he now noted weren't covered in sandals like every other slave he'd seen in the palace — in fact, they looked odd. "Don't try to run away from here if you aren't sure you won't be caught, ever," Kyle cautioned seriously.

After several silent minutes, the crippled boy went to the bunk beds. "I'll do your bed back up for you."

Dolan stood up and grasped the other slave's arm. "Why would you do that?" *Tell me what happened to you, why?* he silently pleaded; his time with the heir had made him too cautious to voice the words.

"You got to get cleaned up and fed and dressed and all for tonight's big happenings," Kyle explained. "I stay in the kitchens out of sight, so I got plenty of time. Besides, you don't want to get on the wrong side of anyone here. Trust me on that."

Dolan eyed the other suspiciously, then released him. "I do my own clean-up and pay for my own mistakes, understand?"

Kyle shrugged and turned to the doorway. "Your skin. I'll save you a place out in the dining space then," he added as he left.

The thief sighed and picked up the sheets, blankets and pillow from the floor. He climbed the ladder and tucked everything back into place. From up there he surveyed the tiny room. It seemed so small compared to the hotel and the campsites that had been his home for the past month, yet when placed next to the auction block cages, his frightened nights on the run, or the crowded jeweler's slave pen, it looked enormous. The thought of the hotel room and how he'd been punished for questioning the blacksmith made him wince. It had taken his feet a couple of days to recover; Kyle's never had. Obviously this is where the heir learned to punish disobedient slaves, and that thought made him grow cold inside.

He got down and went to the closet. Inside, on what his roommate had told him was his side, were a set of black clothes identical to the chief butler's except for the black hair band that he assumed he was to wear, as the other servers had when he had practiced with them. The practice or non-formal garb of dull yellow hung next to the black, as did an extra hanger he assumed was for the black and red he currently wore.

The bell informed him of dinner time for the servers and the main cooks. He left his new quarters and walked to the saved place next to his roommate. When the chief steward joined them, all stood up and bowed their heads as he mumbled a few words in thanksgiving to their owners and to the Divine Couple for their bounty.

As he sat down, Dolan realized that though this was not exactly what he expected, it wasn't bad. The food was at least as good as what he had prepared during their journey, and there was no fighting over portions as during his childhood.

After the meal the chief butler tapped him on the shoulder and waved toward the bathing area. "You'll need to wash up thoroughly, boy," Mylick instructed. "I'll instruct you how to do so and then how to wear the uniform," he added with a sniff.

Dolan narrowed his eyes, a fearful knot growing in his stomach as he noted the butler's tongue flick over his lips. "I can do it myself, friend. I assume I wear the black for tonight?"

The chief butler opened his mouth, then closed it when the chief steward entered his view. "Yes. Report to the kitchen when you're finished, and hurry; the feast won't wait on you."

"I didn't think it would," Dolan muttered after the chief butler turned on his heel and headed back toward the kitchen.

"Watch out for him," the chief steward offered as he handed the new slave a small box. "Some stuff you'll need for the shower."

Dolan mumbled a thank you and headed toward the bathing area. Inside most stalls were occupied by the servers he recognized and some cooks he didn't. The naked bodies were mostly bruise-free, a rarity for any slave in his years of experience. A chuckle and even jokes could be heard, another rarity.

He waited until one of the stalls was empty, then entered. He removed his clothes and hung them on the peg outside the stall proper as he had seen all the others do. The tile felt warm and wet from the previous user.

The water felt good against his skin after years of lakes and streams. Inside the box, which was made of some type of metal, there was a large bar of soap, a vial of liquid that smelled a lot like what the princess had poured into his hair, a comb, and a razor. He glanced down at his body and shrugged as he noticed that, true to her word, none of his body hair had grown back. He fingered the razor and looked around himself. At the jeweler's a slave was killed for handling such an item, but here they were handed out.

He set the box on the floor and took out the soap. His skin tingled as it lathered up, covering him with a sheen of white. Next his scalp tingled from the medicated shampoo; he doubted that disease was much a worry when the slaves were expected to bathe at least once a day.

A deep moan from the stall on his left made him stare at the shadow of its occupant. The shadow was bent forward, the hose extending to his ass and apparently entering him. The shadow arched a bit more and wiggled his ass, his moans continuing. Dolan backed up into the other thin wall, but similar, weaker sounds issued from that side as well.

The thief touched the hose and remember numerous purgings by the jeweler. The thought of doing it to himself brought a queasiness to his stomach.

"Having a problem?" The chief butler's voice behind him made the thief turn around. Mylick stepped into the stall, his naked body much firmer than his everyday uniform allowed one to guess.

"There's no problem," Dolan said as he backed up against the solid wall to which the shower head and hose were attached.

The chief butler growled as he touched the brands on his chest.

"What a piece of work. You'll embarrass us all tonight. You need to learn your place, boy and I'm clearly the one who must teach you."

Dolan tried to slip free from the other's hands as the chief butler pounced, but the other was much stronger than he looked. Dolan found himself in the frighteningly familiar position of his head slammed against the floor tiles as his legs were pushed apart. A tight smile broke his lips as the butler tried to press his hot, hard cock into him.

"Damn!" the butler cried as a shot of lightning struck his cock and made it shrink in pain. He shoved the thief against the wall and ran from the stall. The chief butler had proven that the princess's spell still worked, and Dolan was grateful for it.

Dolan touched his head and found slippery wetness on his fingers; a look at its red color on his finger confirmed his immediate thoughts. He bit his lips as he rewashed his hair with the medicated shampoo, which burned the cut. His eyes looked at the hose as the red of the water settled into clear again.

"He'll tell them that you didn't clean up properly," another male voice said. This slave was one of the other servers who Dolan had practiced with earlier. "It's not that hard; if you relax, it can be, well, um," the server tried to explain but ended up blushing and hurrying away.

Dolan nodded as he considered the warning. He took the hose and noted the end was rounded and thin, not quite as large as the objects the princess had placed inside of him, and certainly smaller than his master or his friends and their devices of torture. Bending over, however, made his head spin and threatened to drive him into unconsciousness. So he sat on the tiles and bent his knees up as he had done when the princess had placed her mark inside him. He used water to moisten his asshole and then his fingers to loosen it. Oddly, he received no shocks from this brief penetration, but then he wasn't a stranger, and surely the princess knew he would be required to do this in the palace.

Once the hose was placed a few inches inside of him, he took a moment to try to control his breathing. After being used daily by the princess in some matter, either dildo or fingers, the three days of their escort back to the palace had left him feeling empty and lonely, he realized. He reached up and pushed the button beneath its connection to the wall.

A moan escaped his throat but he clamped his lips and ass

tight as a warm liquid bubbled inside of him. The pressure built up until a gasp burst from his lips. Automatically the liquid stopped. He looked around and wondered what he should do next. Suddenly a sucking feeling was pulling the liquid from inside him. He tossed his head to one side as his mind stirred up images from the past. Finally all sucking stopped and the hose turned cold. He pulled it out and stood up on wobbling legs. A thin stream of mostly clear liquid dripped down between his legs. One more sudsing with the soap and he was finished. This entire setup seemed odd to him, more complicated than any ordinary shower. Perhaps it was created with magic, that wouldn't surprise him at all in this place.

He took a towel from the rack across from the stall and wrapped it around his waist. Carrying his clothes in one hand and making sure the towel stayed in place he hurried out of the bathing area and into his room. The crippled boy was sitting on the lower bunk bed and didn't move when the thief entered.

Dolan opened the closet and laid the red and black outfit on the bottom. He removed the hanger with the black garments and took out a matching pair of black sandals. "You just going to sit there?" he asked the boy.

"No; I should get going," Kyle replied as he stood up. He glanced at the thief's brands, then scurried from their room.

Dolan finished drying off his body and rubbing his hair before discarding the towel into a bin in one corner which had a few other towels in it. He took the comb from the box and ran it through his hair until it moved smoothly.

The black uniform turned out to be different from the chief butler's. The pants were actually tight-fitting leggings which laced up over his groin; the lack of undergarb left nothing to the imagination once these were pulled up. The tunic hung down in front and back enough to cover him to mid-thigh, but was cut open so that his nipple rings were visible, as were the brands marking him as runaway and a thief, and his arms were bare. At first Dolan wondered if this were a joke, but the figure of two other like-dressed servers confirmed that it was indeed the uniform.

He slipped into the sandals and laced them before wrapping the hair band across his forehead and over his ears so that his curls were pushed back from his face. Inside the closet was a mirror which covered the inside of the doors. If he stood on the opposite wall, he could almost see his entire body.

"I look like a whore," he said to no one. "A runaway whore." He nodded and chuckled as his first suspicions of who the princess was seemed a bit rectified by his words. After a moment to collect his thoughts, he followed the chief steward's advice and tucked his dagger into his leggings, under the tunic. A bit of re-shaping and it was well hidden and not too dangerous to himself, he hoped.

Marelda adjusted the diadem on her head and shifted positions in her seat at her mother's right hand. Each dinner guest came forward slowly to be introduced to the Lady and Lord of Vanhilmer, and each had to be acknowledged as either vassal or friend — enemy was not used as a term, but clearly some of the ambassadors were set against a reunited world government.

Annabel twirled one of her curls and smiled grimly at her sister when their eyes met. "Some of their clothing?" she whispered as an ambassador in a dull gray gown stepped forward and offered his head in fealty.

Marelda rolled her eyes as much in boredom of the entire event as in comment on her sister's words. Her bracelet glowed slightly, the dark hot glow which signaled trouble, when a tall, lanky man with white hair approached the royal table. "Stay where you are, Duke Eddington," she announced as she stood up. The Lady and Lord looked at their heir in concern. "Guards, search the good Duke," Marelda ordered.

Immediately the Duke drew the hidden sword and jumped toward the Lady. The court gasped as the princess's dagger stopped the attacker in his tracks and pinned his neck to the floor.

"How messy," Mylick commented as a group of low-level kitchen slaves hurried into the dining hall with bucket and rags to clean up the body.

Leaning against the doorframe, his arms crossed over his stomach, Dolan grinned. Even in this palace, with those fancy clothes and that tiara on, his owner was still a fighter. As she looked up toward the kitchen, the thief shifted and nodded, sure her grim grin was meant for him.

The chief butler sniffed and drew the new slave's attention toward him. "Since you traveled with her, you may serve her this evening. But know that as the heir all eyes will be on her. Those brands you earned are obscene; don't add to the embarrassment by behaving as a country bumpkin."

"I'll try, but it will be very difficult," Dolan replied sarcastically. He threw one last look toward the elegant dining room, then followed the rest of the army of waiters back to the kitchen.

As he carried the gold plate covered by a gold lid in exactly the same way as the other servers before and behind him in the marching order, Dolan's eyes darted around looking closely at the guests. There were two ranks according to their relationship to the royal family, but their clothing showed that there was also an economic ranking. Those in the richest clothing were on the "friends and allies" side, while the less-richly-dressed sat among the vassal states. Both groups were far more richly dressed than Dolan had ever seen. The would-be assassin had been among the vassal states.

He walked by the end of the royal table, passing the mage-tutor, Sigrid, who winked at him, then his own mistress who seemed to look passed him out into the gathered group. He kept his eyes respectfully lowered as he passed the Lady and Lord but glanced up to see them looking closer at each server, frowning and nodding, as he moved past them. The eldest princess and one who he assumed was a prince were next and then the chief advisor. It wasn't until he was standing behind her seat and had reached over on her left to set the plate before her that he relaxed a bit. He jumped when her hand suddenly landed on his.

"I've been looking for you, Dolan," Marelda whispered, her eyes only glancing up at him briefly before looking back at the guests. "Are you doing well here?"

"Yes, Mistress. Not quite what I was expecting, but I'm well," he added, bowing his head lower so only she could hear his reply. "That was a great move earlier," he stated when her hand remained on his.

Marelda allowed herself to smile. "I'm glad you were impressed. Now you have to taste my food. Watch Mylick for the example," she added softly.

The chief butler stepped forward and took the smallest spoon in the Lady's setting. He tasted each item on the plate, a small taste pausing between each bite while everyone watched. Then he took the goblet and sipped it slowly, swishing the liquid around in his mouth. With a silent nod he wiped the goblet clean with the towel he had in his belt and set it back on the table. Mylick then looked at the servers and nodded for them to begin.

The thief followed the example, as did all the other servers, but he noted that almost every free eye in the hall was looking at him, while the others were ignored. The food tasted better than anything he'd ever had in his entire life, and he hoped they'd get the leftovers when this dinner was finished. He nodded, adding a smile when he finished tasting the wine. Dolan straightened up, tucked the towel back in his waistband, and took up a position behind her seat as the other servers did. The chief butler, who was standing behind the Lady's chair and thus to his left, gave him a withered smile but was silent.

As the meal continued, the thief found his ears assaulted by the murmur of foolish gossip and obvious flattery that flowed from one table to another. Whenever he refilled the princess's goblet or offered her the towel at his waist to wipe her hands, he had to press his lips firmly together to keep from laughing out loud at her sighs and rolling eyes. Whatever he feared she might turn into once she returned home, it seemed farther away with each passing second.

His legs were killing him and the small of his back ached from simply standing at attention by the time the dessert was served. The lower-level servers carried the large chocolate torte, shaped into the form of a pig with a candied apple in its mouth, to the center of the room, where a table had been set. Dolan shook his head, not believing what he saw when the chief butler cut it open and tiny jelly rolls fell out into the silver platters the servers held. A titter of giggles escaped from his lips so he quickly covered his mouth with one hand.

He stopped himself and knelt next to the princess's chair when she motioned to him with her hand. "I'm sorry, Mistress," he whispered. "Forgive me please."

Marelda took hold of his hair, pulling him closer. "Why? It's one of the dumbest things I've ever seen," she admitted. "However, there are certain things expected here. I've just scolded you, so look ashamed," she ordered him with a grin and a wink as she released his hair.

Dolan swallowed his chuckles and bowed his head low as he rose back up to his feet and stepped back one step. After a few moments of acting the dejected slave he straightened back up and watched as the dessert was served.

At the end of the meal, a juggler and a singer entertained the guests as only the servers at the royal table and a few for the others remained to serve wine. Dolan shifted on his feet just a bit and was rewarded with a glare from the chief butler.

Finally, the servers were dismissed, and they all walked in single file back to the kitchen while the royal family said good evening to their guests. "How could you embarrass me so much?" Mylick demanded as he grabbed the thief's arm as soon as they entered the kitchen.

Dolan pulled free and put his fists up in a defensive stance.

"How dare you?" the chief butler retorted. He snapped his fingers, and two guards who had been stationed at the doorway to the dining room to make sure no poisons or weapons were sneaked inside grabbed the thief. "I have a great deal of authority in this place. You've already crossed me once today. This is the last straw," Mylick declared as he backhanded the slave.

Dolan gasped and tasted blood in his mouth. His dark eyes flashed and a growl rose in his throat. Never in his entire miserable life had another slave ever hit him unless they were fighting over food or clothing. They were both slaves; how dare one assume he had any authority to punish him? His body sprang, and the surprised guards let him slip through their hands. They managed to pull him back before his hands had a firm hold around the chief butler's throat.

Daemon, the chief steward, hurried and pulled Mylick from the thief as the butler paused his assault to take a breath. "Stop it right now! Both of you!" The old steward stepped between the two slaves and glared from one to another. He looked at Dolan closely, then held out his hand. "Give it to me, boy! Right now my orders to protect this house override any other orders!"

The chief butler turned white as the dagger hidden under the thief's tunic was handed over. "You let him carry that in there?" he demanded of the guards.

"I'm under orders to carry it at all times," Dolan insisted.

"I don't recall saying that." Marelda's voice made all three slaves turn toward the dining room entrance. She stood there looking them over. "What's going on here, Daemon?"

The steward stepped forward, offering the dagger on his open palms. "Your Majesty. These two were about to come to blows, so I stepped in to intercede," he explained, tossing an angry glance toward the two servers.

"Your Majesty, he embarrassed your family this evening, and I was simply dealing out discipline." Mylick stopped speaking when the princess held up her hand.

"I didn't ask you," Marelda stated. She turned to her thief and held the dagger out to him. "You are to wear the clothing that I bought you from now on and to carry this dagger regardless," she hurried before the chief steward could speak, "of your duties here. Am I understood?"

"I," Dolan emphasized that first word of his reply, "understand, Mistress. I have only that which I wore here, however, my Lady."

Marelda frowned and looked to the chief steward. "What was done with the others, Daemon?"

"A thousand apologies, Your Majesty," the old man replied with a bow. "I assumed that since they were torn and patched you would not wish him to continue wearing them."

"Where are they now?" Marelda restated as she held up one hand to make him pause in his speech.

"Part of the outer work collection, Your Majesty," Daemon said softly.

Marelda rolled her eyes and placed one hand on her forehead as she sighed. *Great, as soon as I walk in the door, everything gets out of control.* "Have the outfit he was brought in washed and brought to my bedroom first thing tomorrow morning," she instructed the chief steward.

Dolan stepped forward as she motioned to him. "You're with me tonight, boy," she told him. The thief threw the chief butler a smug smile as he followed the princess out of the kitchen. When she held out one hand he offered her his arm only to have it twisted behind his back.

"Mistress, I'm sorry I lied back there. It wasn't intentional, I misunderstood about the dagger," he stated as he was marched out of the dining room to one of the many hallways. He swallowed when she didn't stop moving and refused to comment. His feet moved at her pace, eager to make sure the pain in his arm and shoulder were minimized as he was herded upstairs to an elegant wooden door.

Dolan stayed on the floor where the princess tossed him after they entered the room. His wrists tingled from the metal cuffs' threatening him, so he shifted position to kneel, wrists crossed and offered up to her as he bowed his head. This punishment position had been drilled into him at an early age and was frighteningly second-nature. The tingling in the cuffs stopped, but he held position until her low laughter made him glance up.

Marelda had taken the opportunity to change into a simple shirt that hung down to her knees. "Get up, Dolan," she said when he didn't move further.

The slave narrowed his eyes as he looked over at the princess, then slowly stood up and lowered his hands until they rested at his sides. His breath caught in his throat as she stepped close and pressed her palms lightly against the brands on his chest.

"Did your outfit distract you tonight?" Marelda whispered as she let her eyes drift up his body until they locked onto his gaze.

"Only when I wondered what you thought of it and what you might do to me because I was wearing it," he whispered back. He began to lean toward her but paused when she stepped back, holding her hand out. He took the dagger from his leggings and laid it on her palm.

"This outfit," Marelda began to explain, "as you may have noticed about a great deal of the slaves' clothing around here, is meant to show off the body. I assume you were told that all the slaves here must be prepared to serve any of the family at any time," she said as she played with the dagger by pressing the tip gently against the tip of one of her fingers and twirling it with the other hand.

Dolan nodded as he remembered his shower. "I am prepared, Mistress."

"Let's see," Marelda stated as she now set the dagger at the front center of his shirt. She cut the material all the way to the bottom of the hem, then, using the blade, making sure it scratched his skin as it moved, pushed each side of it to his shoulders.

Dolan shrugged and sent the shirt falling to the floor. He moaned as the knife now cut the tight leggings from his left leg. His eyes closed as the blade next traveled up the right leg, cutting the material to his waist. The air encircled his bare body as the remnants of the clothing fell to the floor between his legs. His dark eyes shot open as the blade next lifted his smooth balls.

Marelda smiled as she watched his cock, already firm, grow to its full length in seconds as she weighed his balls on the knife. "When I first saw you naked up in that hotel room I was disappointed because you didn't respond as I was used to. You're a lot more like the slaves here now," she told him softly.

"Is that what you want? You want just another pleasure slave?" Dolan asked as he looked down at himself and the knife. He sighed as the dagger was tossed to the floor and was replaced with her warm palm.

Marelda decided to ignore his question as she stated, "Someone tried to fuck you right before dinner. Who was it?"

Dolan blinked in surprise then closed his eyes as he spoke, "It was Mylick, the chief butler. He came after me in the showers." She didn't speak but simply caressed his balls and cock, so he continued to explain. "Apparently he expects certain services from the slaves under his authority. I fought him off as best I could, but he's a lot bigger and stronger than he looks plus the floor was slippery and wet," he added with a grin that turned into a moan as one of her fingers caressed the area between his balls and anus.

Marelda continued her fondling for a few moments then released him, smiling slightly as he pleaded with a groan. "Would you be willing to repeat this in front of my parents and siblings? There should be an investigation. We can't have our slaves thinking that they can just go around screwing each other whenever they want," she stated as she turned from him.

"Of course not," Dolan agreed as he regained his composure and crossed his hands behind his back, trying to relax. "I'd be happy to repeat it to anyone you wish, my Lady."

Marelda turned back toward him, her hair falling over one shoulder as she tilted her head to look at him. "You're beautiful," she said suddenly.

Dolan blinked several times, then looked down at his feet. "Thank you, Mistress," he muttered softly, confused at the compliment. The same compulsion he'd felt that night after their final battle was flowing through him. No doubt, no self-reflection, just simple desire and joy.

"But are you prepared?" she asked as she walked behind him. "Bend over and show me," she ordered.

The thief paused, recalling how many times he'd had to display himself at the jeweler's and even before being put on the auction block, then bent forward at the waist, moving his legs apart and taking one ass cheek in each hand so he could spread himself wide. He tensed a bit as he felt her move. A moan escaped his throat as a stream of warm air was blown into his asshole causing it to open slightly in response.

"Let go," Marelda commanded as her hands replaced his. She kneaded his firm buttocks and traced the ownership brand on the one side and the cutting on the other. "So round and firm," she huskily said.

She kneaded them in opposite circles, her thumbs placed close to his hole so that each outward turn pulled him open. He was pink, and his flesh shuddered as she blew more breath onto it. She repeated the process several times until he opened and closed easily in anticipation even when she stopped her direct attention.

Dolan's hands sweated as he pressed them into his thighs for support. "Oh," he gasped as he felt her body lean over his, her mound pressed against his ass, her breasts lying against his shoulder blades and her hair falling over one of his shoulders; only the thin fabric of her shirt separated them. He turned his head as she wrapped her arms over his so he could kiss her skin and breathe in the scent of her hair, now tinged with soap and perfume that had been unavailable outside the castle. Her true scent, though, flooded over him as he struggled to maintain control over his own body, which wanted to grab her and hold her closer to him.

The slave's hands clenched his own flesh as he was allowed to continue kissing and licking any part of her arms he could reach, even rubbing his face in her soft auburn curls. "Command me," he said softly.

Marelda took his chin in one hand as she slid to his side. His pupils were wide and his breath jagged as he returned her gaze. "You're very different now," she stated as she released him. A smile crept over her face as he sighed and lowered his head. "Do you remember what you said to me the first time you spoke to me?"

Dolan licked his lips and looked up from his position. Slowly he straightened up, his cock full and his ass yearning still and crossed his arms over his chest trying to look as uninterested in her body as he could. "I'm afraid I don't. I only remember being very angry at you for buying me," he replied, his eyes watching her closely.

Marelda nodded, her voice gentle as she spoke. "I suspect you were just plain angry at being recaptured and bought. You said," she returned to her question, "'Do you have any orders?' Very similar to your request now."

Dolan shook his head as he stepped toward her, his arms hanging at his side, his nails digging into his thighs to help him maintain control. "The feelings are entirely different now. I assure you of that," he added with a toss of his head.

The princess watched his black curls bounce several times then settle behind his shoulders. She reached out, touching his face with her fingers as she swept them up to his forehead, where she grasped the hair band. As her second hand joined the first in slipping it off his hair, he pulled her close to him. "I thought you needed orders?"

"Tell me to stop, Mistress, and I will," he whispered as he caressed her back, gathering her shirt up in his hands.

Marelda chuckled as she tossed the hair band onto the floor. "I need it straight tonight. Like what we did out in the woods, but without the bondage. I need it for the ceremony tomorrow," she said lightly.

Dolan pulled back a little but kept his hands on her upper arms as he looked into her eyes. "Really? I didn't feel drained of anything out there, but I'm here to serve, Mistress," he replied with one cocked eye and a bit of sarcasm in his voice.

Marelda took his hands in hers and led him back to her bed. "That's not the only reason," she admitted.

"I'm glad," the slave responded as he lifted her up from the floor just enough to set her on his hips so he could enter her easily as he laid her down on the bed. She was wet and open, so he slid inside quickly without resistance. Dolan stopped once they were joined and looked at her face. "This isn't right, is it, Mistress?" he asked as his hands pressed into the bed, afraid of touching her.

"Not exactly," Marelda admitted, "I need you on your back."

"See, I knew I'd be on my back once you got me home," the slave chuckled as his first impressions were fulfilled in a minor decree.

"On your back, or I'll tie you down again," Marelda teased as she pushed his head back playfully. With a bit of effort and a lot of cooperation they rolled over so she was on top. She sighed as she slid further around him and chuckled when he moaned his pleasure as well. Her hands found his and brought them up to her thighs. "Caress me there and here," she indicated by taking one of his fingers and touching it to her clit.

Dolan closed his eyes as he let his hands do their work. He rocked up and down in time to her thrusts, in time to her chanting. He felt his entire body vibrate with hers as a hot sweat broke out on his skin. The tingling began as her breath quickened, making his muscles tense so his fingers fall from her clit to rest on her thighs. Just like the other times when she had used him to increase her own magical energy, the tingling faded from his head and feet and began to travel and focus at his groin. He opened his eyes so he could watch the light green aura forming around her as he felt himself shake and gasp with his orgasm. He noticed the aura was brighter, almost white now as his eyes closed.

Marelda took his hands in hers as she screamed and slammed down onto his hips one final time. Her head jerked several times as she convulsed. The heat, instead of dissipating rapidly as she had been told was common for women after orgasm, built in her groin and shot up her limbs until sparks were flying from her fingertips.

It took several minutes for her spasms to end so she could climb off his limp form. Marelda looked down at her slave, lying there still and paler than he had ever been. She knelt by his face and touched it, gasping at his icy skin. "Dolan?" she asked as she lifted his head up onto her lap. "Dolan? Can you hear me? Answer me, boy." She pulled the nearby quilt over him and tucked it around his body. Every inch of his body was colder than snow. Her bracelet was dark and cold as well.

Marelda stood up and looked around her room until her eyes focused on the fire burning brightly. She pulled him into her arms and staggered to the fireplace, where she laid him on the rug before it. "Dolan! Now you listen to me! This wasn't supposed to kill you, just make you sleep for about eight hours straight! So you start moving or something so I know you're all right."

"Oh, Lady and Lord!" Marelda cried when his skin stayed just as cool to her touch. She pulled him onto her lap and laid his head on her shoulder, cradling him in her arms like a child. "Sigrid!" she screamed.

The plump blonde sorceress appeared immediately. She looked at the couple in front of the fireplace with a frown and pulled her robe closer to her as she approached. "What's happened?"

"I did as you instructed, and he's dead!" Marelda yelled, her eyes wide with terror and tears rolling down her cheeks.

Sigrid shrugged. "He has given you the strength you need for tomorrow; he's served his purpose," she calmly stated.

"Silence!" Marelda yelled. "He wasn't supposed to die. Was he? Did you lie to me?" Her mouth fell open as her tutor looked away. She struggled as the lies she'd believed crumbled in her mind. "I won't let him die."

Sigrid watched silently for a few seconds as the princess laid her slave down on the floor and took the quilt from him. She stood over him and began to move her arms. "Don't do this! You need that energy for tomorrow. It is everything, it is your destiny."

Marelda glared at her tutor. "Then you bring him back. Now!" The princess took one step for every one the tutor made until they had exchanged places. "I've read a little more than what you think I have. You know how to do this. Don't try to fool me," she cautioned.

The tutor tilted her head and smiled. "I guess your talent is greater than I thought, then," she admitted. She removed her robe and nightgown so she was naked. Slowly, chanting loud enough for the princess to hear, she began to circle the slave.

Marelda watched every step, every gesture and listened closely to every word. She had to bite her lip to prevent herself from mumbling along but she knew that even doing that little would draw the sexual energy from her and jeopardize the rituals tomorrow. After three times around Sigrid stopped and knelt at his head while Marelda crossed herself for luck.

The tutor lowered her lips to the slave's and kissed him once. At the touch of her lips his chest expanded and a flush flashed over his flesh. Sigrid jumped up and grabbed her clothing as the slave sat up, his dark eyes blinking.

Marelda approached cautiously as her tutor vanished from the room. "Dolan? Can you hear me?"

The slave turned toward her voice, but his face was twisted in fear. "Mistress? I can't see you! What's wrong?"

Marelda took his trembling hands in her own as she knelt on the floor. "It will go away after a nap. It's just a side effect of the ritual," she tried to reassure them both. "Let me lead you to bed."

Most of the fear disappeared from his face as the thief stood up. "I get to sleep in your bed, with you, not on the floor?" he asked as he let one of his hands slip down her arm.

"I think you're feeling much better," Marelda replied with a chuckle as she pulled him to the bed and helped him lay down. When she had joined him she brushed his hands from her body. "You need sleep, boy."

"I don't feel tired," Dolan assured her. "Other than my eyes I feel fine. Just fine," he stated as he fondled her nearest breast. He grinned as she pinned his hands over his head.

"I'll kick you out onto the floor if you can't behave," Marelda told him.

The slave sighed. "Yes, Mistress. I'll be a good little slave and keep my hands to myself — well, I mean I won't touch anything without permission," he promised. He blinked at the direction of her movement as she released him and settled into bed, making sure she touched him but only barely. "Did you get what you needed?" he asked after a few silent moments.

"Yes, I believe I did," Marelda replied. She pulled the blanket close to her body and forced her eyes to shut. Her body was still shaky from the ordeal and the fact that she had developed undeniable feelings for him.

Dolan threw his arms up over his face as sunlight hit his eyes. "I can see; I can definitely see," he stated.

"I told you it would come back," Marelda replied as she tied the curtains back. She slipped into her robe but remained by the window. Outside, a light, clear snow showed the rolling hills around the castle at their best. "How do you feel otherwise?" she asked when her slave placed his arms around her.

"Wonderful," Dolan whispered as he nuzzled her neck and began licking her skin from ear to shoulder tip.

"No time for that," Marelda warned as she pulled away. She nodded toward a hallway. "Go take a shower; I'll bring your clothes in to you in a moment."

"Is that an order?" the slave asked with large pleading eyes.

"Yes, it is," Marelda stated as she gave him a little push. She smiled as he bowed and backed away slowly for several steps until he bumped into the edge of the bed. His ass was round and firm, the brand and the cutting clear against his pale flesh, as he turned on his heel and jogged off.

The princess went to her full-length mirror and lifted up her hair. "How should I wear this?" she asked her tutor as Sigrid appeared next to her.

"It's more a question of 'must' than 'should,'" Sigrid replied. "Everything must be done correctly today."

"All this ritual, all these steps," Marelda said with a sigh. "I have the robe of unbleached wool hanging in my closet, and the sacred items are in the chapel guarded by three soldiers, so now what do I do with my hair?"

"No shower," Sigrid reminded her. She took the scarlet locks in her hand. "I'll braid them myself so no mistakes are possible."

Marelda watched as her hair was separated and plaited into three braids tied off with strips of unbleached wool. She looked very much like Ariala, the Mother of All, on her own wedding day. "I'm sorry I got angry last night," she said suddenly.

The mage grinned as she set the braids in order, double-checking all the strands. "I didn't realize you were so attached to him. I guess you two have gotten close," she added.

Marelda shrugged as she looked at herself. "We've been through a lot," she simply stated, unwilling to voice the fact that something had competed with her duty for even one moment, let alone enough time to win her heart. "That's probably his clothes," she guessed when a knock came on her door.

"My Lady," Mylick bowed and offered the clothing on his arms as the door opened.

The princess looked at the chief butler for a moment, then opened the door wider. "Come inside; you can help me," she informed him.

The slave nodded his head and entered, his eyes never leaving her bare feet and his arms holding their position with the black and red bundle.

Marelda nodded to her tutor, and Sigrid smiled and took a chair by the window to watch. The princess walked around the chief butler twice, then stopped directly in front of him. "Follow me, Mylick."

The chief butler allowed himself a small smile as he straightened up and followed her down the hallway to her bathroom. He frowned when he entered and saw the new slave staring at him from the shower stall. "Where shall I set these, Your Majesty?" he asked with a sniff of disgust.

"You're going to hold them and help him get dressed," the princess replied as she leaned against a wall, her arms folded across her chest. She nodded when the two slaves turned to her with shocked expressions. "I hear," she addressed the chief butler as he tried to look at ease holding the clothing, "that you have an interest in this boy."

The chief butler cleared his throat and glanced at the princess silently as she approached him. At the tilt of her head and the cock of her eyebrows, both clear family signs that she was on the edge of dangerous anger, he answered, "I'm not sure I understand your question, Your Majesty."

"I know exactly what went on in the showers downstairs in

the slave quarters," Marelda stated. She pointed her finger directly between his eyes as she continued. "Thank the Lady and Lord that all I'm ordering you to do is help him get dressed. If you ever touch him without my permission, Mylick, you'll wish you were in the royal mines digging for precious gems. Am I making myself clear?"

"Yes, Your Majesty," Mylick replied softly. He stood silently as the princess left the bathroom.

Dolan turned off the water and stood in the shower stall watching the chief butler closely. When Mylick refused to look at him, the thief threw back the clear door and grabbed the nearest towel. "Why don't you just wait outside?" he suggested as he began drying off.

"I'm to help you dress," Mylick spat out. "I take orders very seriously, boy. I'll obey, but know this," he added as he stepped a bit closer, "don't interfere with my job around here."

"Or what?" Dolan demanded as he tossed the towel on the floor and flipped his still-wet hair back with an angry toss. "Even if you cut my tongue out or killed me, she'd know. She knows everything that happens to me," he added, holding up his wrists so the metal caught the glint of the overhead sunlight as it streamed through the windows.

Mylick sucked his breath in through his teeth at the sight of the magic runes. "Let's get you dressed then," he simply said.

The chief steward and butler allowed only one slave at a time to stand on a ladder and look in through the windows of the chapel; the rest had to glance through the small opening of the main door. Each muttered and pointed at the last pew where the boy who they'd all assumed was merely a new slave was sitting. Dolan glanced back every now and then when he caught their whispers.

After a brief breakfast in the kitchen he had been escorted to the chapel and shoved into the pew so he was farthest from the altar. He sat there, huddled up as much as he felt wouldn't be obvious as the allies, friends and vassal representatives of the realm entered and sat. To his immediate right was a monk who had smiled at him and nodded silently when he had noted Dolan's wrist cuffs as they poked out of his red linen shirt. The slave had pulled them down immediately.

In terms of clothing, he was poorly dressed, but it was the beard that showed his true status, since facial hair on male slaves and very short hair on female slaves was practically a universal sign of servitude. For a moment he thought of standing up and leaving, but a glance at the guards at the door changed his mind. He jumped, earning another soft smile from the monk, when a trumpet sounded. As they both stood, Dolan thought he spied auburn bangs under the monk's cowl.

The Lady and Lord of Vanhilmer walked in behind a woman and man dressed in robes of the church, signifying that they were the High Priestess and Priest. Behind them entered the chief advisor, a thin man, old and nervous with worry even now, and the tutor of the heir, Sigrid, who looked over the audience quickly.

Dolan frowned as the mage's eyes met his. He touched his lips and felt them tingling; a memory of something seemed to tease him, but nothing formed in his mind. He stood with the rest of the audience but had to glance around the side of the pew in front of him to see his mistress enter.

Marelda's hair hung down in three plaits he hadn't noticed earlier, though surely they had been done while they had been getting ready for this event. The unbleached wool robe clung to her body, showing each curve as the lamp and sunlight struck it, and showing that she wore nothing else, not even sandals on her feet. She turned to the audience and looked over the members carefully, her eyes seeming to focus on each person for a few moments before moving to the next.

"A child of promise, not just of need but of her own free will, of her own desire shall restore the blessed treasure," the High Priestess stated. "With her gift shall she reunite all the land to a natural and peaceful order. This is the prophecy."

The High Priest turned to the altar where the three royal artifacts lay. He picked up the ring and held it out to the princess.

As the ring was slipped onto her finger, the High Priestess asked, "Will your hands protect the land and the faith of our children's children?"

"By the grace of the Lady and Lord, they shall," Marelda replied. A spark of white light shot from her body as the ring settled onto her finger.

Dolan glanced at the monk next to him and found the man fingering his beads and mumbling a prayer. Others in the room were exchanging looks and nodding their heads.

The High Priest now took the necklace from the altar. He held it over the princess's head as she knelt, and the High Priestess asked, "Will your heart care for the land and the faith of our children's children?"

"By the grace of the Lady and Lord, it shall," Marelda replied. A pulse of white light expanded from her body as the white stone touched her chest. Her body twitched slightly, causing her father to take her mother's hand in his own.

The crown now sat on the palms of the High Priest as the princess looked at the High Priestess. "Will your mind guide the land and the faith of our children's children?"

"By the grace of the Lady and Lord, it shall," Marelda stated, a slight shake in her voice. Every hair on her body rose as the crown was placed on her head. With a scream from her soul a burst of shocking bright white light exploded from her and hit everyone in the chapel.

Dolan looked at his body as the light surrounded him. The feeling was familiar to the ones she created in him during the rituals she had performed on their quest. He closed his eyes, letting the warmth seep through him, but unlike before the feeling withdrew. His eyes opened just in time to see the light snap back to the princess.

Marelda gasped as she received the energy back, and with it the knowledge and feelings of everyone in the room. She took the High Priest's offered hands and stood up. Sweat poured from her body, making the robe stick more tightly to her. She turned around slowly and faced the audience once more. Everyone rose to their feet.

The High Priestess stepped forward and addressed the chapel and hallway crowd. "It is fulfilled. Let no one resist destiny. Offer yourself to your Queen, obey her as you would your mothers." Then the High Priest joined his partner, and both bowed to Marelda.

Marelda lifted her hand, which was graced by the sacred ring, and waved it over their heads. "Arise, High Priestess and noble Priest," she said, receiving one glance from the priest before he bowed low and stepped off the altar.

The High Priestess blinked and stepped back so that she stood to the side of the altar. She motioned to the Lady and Lord of Vanhilmer, and they stepped forward to stand before their daughter.

The priestess smiled as she passed her hand over their bowed heads. "Go to the sea, and rest there, as you deserve. Your comfort shall be attended to in your well-deserved retirement. Your grandchildren shall play at your feet as you enjoy the fruits of your labors. The world shall use your names as blessings from this day forth."

Marelda now turned to the old man who had served her parents all these years and watched him take their place before her. "Alroy, you shall accompany my parents, but not as an advisor or servant. As an honored elder and friend, you too shall enjoy the full fruits of your good service."

"You have been our dearest advisor, Sigrid," Marelda began as the mage took the chief advisor's place. "We name you as our chief advisor." The mage smiled as she stepped back and took her place to the right of the queen.

Next the eldest princess advanced and took position before Marelda. "Sister, princess, confidante. Annabel, you shall have the right to choose your own husband. I send you to the seacoast, where your talent shall find blossom in managing trade from our distant lands, assuring that the beauty of our artisans and craft-workers is enjoyed by all." Annabel bowed her head and kissed the queen's ring, then rose, her face shinning with happiness.

The youngest son and his pregnant lover now stepped forward; the former Lady and Lord of Vanhilmer shook their heads. Both prince and maid knelt, their heads bowed as low as those of the vassals. "Joshua, my brother, you have never been content with your life, seeking things which you could not possibly understand. I grant you leniency. You may marry this woman and raise your children. However, you yourself will forfeit one half of your inheritance, and all of it shall revert to the nation upon your death." The youngest prince looked shocked but was silenced when the queen lifted her hand. "Therefore we give you an estate. Manage it well, for it will be your only legacy to your wife and children."

Marelda now motioned for the maid to look up at her. "I give you your full freedom, yours alone, not tied to this man nor to any family so that you may stay or leave as your own will decides. Thus your joining in marriage and life together will truly be a matter of your desire. Go now. Spend your life caring for your children." The woman kissed the royal hands, then was led away in tears by the youngest prince.

Dolan watched the pews empty slowly as the audience stepped forward and received the new queen's blessing and on occasion new titles. He found his sleeve pulled by the monk, who whispered, "Come on now, you're to go as well." The thief followed behind the monk, wondering why either of them would be in this assembly.

Marelda smiled as the monk bowed to her. "Brother, your spirit is pure, and it was you among all my siblings who encouraged me to follow my destiny. Take, then, the office of High Priest, Benjamin."

The monk stood up and looked up at the queen. "I am but a trainee, unworthy of the title, My Queen," he insisted.

Marelda frowned and held her hand out to the former High Priest. She took the amulet he placed in her hand and held it before the monk. "Will you disobey your queen?" she asked.

The audience grew still; Dolan stood watching, suddenly aware that, other than the monk before him, he was alone waiting to approach the queen. All watched as the monk bowed his head and accepted the symbol of rank. A white light shot from the queen to the former High Priest then to the monk. When the new High Priest stood up he seemed taller and stronger, but his predecessor seemed unchanged physically. Without a word he joined the High Priestess by the altar.

Marelda looked down at her slave as he stood staring at her. She motioned him forward until he was in the place each subject had occupied before him. "Kneel," she whispered just loud enough for him to hear.

Dolan's body seemed weak as he sunk to his knees. Without direct command, he lowered himself the floor until he lay flat against the steps to the altar. He lifted his head just enough to brush his lips against her bare feet.

"This slave helped me retrieve the sacred jewels," Marelda announced. "Though he serves me because he must, he also serves me from his own desire. He, too, fulfilled the prophecies."

Dolan bit his lower lip as he pressed his head to her feet. His entire body began to shake as he felt almost a hundred pairs of eyes staring at him.

"Arise, Dolan, my chief slave advisor in charge of palace operations, the new chief steward," Marelda announced. She smiled as the slave stood up and opened his mouth. "Raise your hands," she whispered.

Dolan bit back a cry as the metal cuffs burned, a light glowing from them which caused all in the chapel and those slaves looking through the windows to turn their heads. The pain ended, and he looked at his wrists. Instead of the metal, he saw the magic symbols, now burned into his flesh in the same locations as they had been on the cuffs. He was bound to her more strongly now than he had been before; he was more than a slave but less than a freedman.

Marelda lifted her hands and looked at the audience, who had moved back to the pews in the seconds in which she had performed the last ritual. "I am tired now. We will meet in the morning to form a council which shall serve as my advisory board on our new world, united again by the grace of the Lady and Lord of Creation." She took the thief's hand in hers and pulled him behind as she walked down the aisle to the doors.

They found the other slaves all waiting anxiously for them. Marelda looked back at the gathered slaves. "You who are slaves here in the palace, you will all continue to function as you did before until further notice; is that understood?" she asked.

The former chief steward stepped forward. "Yes, My Queen," he said for them all.

Dolan noted that the slaves all turned from him as he passed except for the cripple, Kyle, who gave him a big smile. The former thief returned the grin and hurried after his owner and queen.

Once inside her suite, Marelda took the crown from her head and set it on a table along with the necklace. "Don't worry," she replied to his concerned glance, "they are attuned to me now. They can't be stolen."

"Then how did they get stolen in the first place?" Dolan asked the question which had nagged him for weeks. "Is there anything I may get for you?" he hastened to add before she could answer.

"Yes, a cold shower," Marelda said. She slipped out of the robe and shook her naked body roughly, sending drops of sweat flying. "Join me, and I'll answer your question," she promised as she walked past the slave toward the bathroom.

Dolan remained silent until she was in the shower, holding the door for him. "I would prefer to just wait out here, My Queen, if you will allow me to do so," he begged.

Marelda frowned and looked at herself. "Did the ceremony make me ugly or something?" she inquired.

"Oh, no!" Dolan replied. "I just, I feel, so worthless compared to you now," he tried to explain. "No, that didn't make much sense," he commented as he ran his hands through his hair. His wrists were encircled by her hands, so he looked up.

"Long ago our world was plagued by war as a dozen nations fought over land and religion," Marelda began. "Two nations, Van and Hilmer, celebrated the marriage they hoped would make them co-rulers on a peaceful earth, a marriage not only of great political powers but of strong magical gifts. That night, as the groom and bride stood by the open window of their chamber, two figures appeared. The figures glowed with a brilliant white light, their hair the color of snow."

"The Lady and the Lord," Dolan whispered. He barely glanced down as she released his hands and laid her palms on his vest.

"Yes, they were the Divine Couple," Marelda confirmed as she slipped the vest from his body. "They presented the bride with the ring of strength, the necklace of compassion, and the crown of wisdom. They blessed the couple, and a light descended on them which burnt their hair the color of the setting sun; their eyes were made like emeralds. Red for the fire god of the husband and green for the goddess trinity of the bride."

"As your own," Dolan exclaimed as his pants were unbelted by the queen's hands.

"The woman put the sacred items on and was carried to the nearest battlefield in her consort's arms," Marelda continued with a smile. "There they declared an end to the war and began preaching the word of the Divine Couple."

Dolan slipped out of his shoes as though in a daze as he focused on her words.

"Soon the word was spread over the entire world and the nations fell at the feet of Vanhilmer. Peace and prosperity ruled. But human greed is never easily defeated, especially when the Van and Hilmer cultures continued underground to spread the message of masculine strength and father right or feminine wisdom and mother grace. Only five generations later a warrior-prince killed his sister, who was to hold the throne. His own magic weak and his sin enormous, his children's children lost almost all the gifts of the Lady and Lord," Marelda added sadly. "Our world was torn asunder by greed again within another generation; the evil sorcerers took advantage of the weakness to steal the only visible signs of the divine power and hid them in darkness, where you know they perverted the magic."

"Where you retrieved them," Dolan added as he stepped out of his pants. He sighed as her hands pushed his shirt to his shoulders.

"Only in the heart of Vanhilmer have we observed the sacred rites and kept the faith. It was prophesied that one of our line should return the world to peace," Marelda whispered as she slipped the shirt from his body. She slid her hands into the waistband of his underpants and loosened them so they fell to his feet. "But now, thanks to your help, we will regain that peace again."

"Just doing my duty," Dolan replied as he took her hands in his.

"Are you still afraid to join me?" Marelda asked as she pulled him toward the shower.

Dolan nodded. "Yes, but then I don't recall ever being unafraid with you, Mistress," he replied.

"We'll have to work on that, then," Marelda said as she pulled him to her. "There is a balance to all things. When the natural course is followed, harmony extends unto all living things," she added softly. The Queen slipped her arms around her chief steward, wiggling against his body as he caressed her in return. Their lips met in mutual kisses as the water wet them. As they had the night before, their bodies joined, but now a purer white light unnoticed by either radiated from them. The sacred crown, necklace and ring all glowed as they had not even that first night centuries ago before they had been placed on human beings.

About the Author

TammyJo Eckhart, a dominant sadist, has been consciously active in the BDSM community since 1993 when she moved to NYC to pursue a master's degree in ancient history at Columbia University. There she became involved in TES (The Eulenspiegel Society) on a semi-regular basis as well as helping found the Columbia University group, Conversio Virium (1994-1997) where she served as Treasurer, Health Service Committee Chair, and finally as  Spokesperson. From 1995-1997, she hosted the Applemunch, a monthly dinner for those interested in BDSM living near Manhattan, NYC. For five years (1998-2003) she was the education coordinator for the Indiana University group, Headspace. Her non-fiction has been published in Laura Antoniou's *Some Women* (1995) and in the journals SandMUtopian Guardian and Prometheus. Her fiction has appeared in anthologies from Circlet Press (*SM Futures* (1995)), Greenery Press (*Dreaming in Color* (2003)), and Blue Moon (*Color of Pain, Shade of Pleasure* (2004)). Four collections of her own femdom erotica are have been published. *Punishment for the Crime* (1996) and *Amazons* (1997) by Masquerade Books, *Justice* (1999) by Greenery Press, and *Eroscapes: Erotica from the mind of TammyJo Eckhart* (2004) by Wells Street Publishing. In her writing and in real life, she has been told that she shatters the common stereotypes of dominant women. She has also selectively trained would-be submissives or slaves and mentored some new tops and dominants. As of the winter of 2006, her "kinky family" is comprised of Tom, her husband since 1992, and Fox, her slave since 1999. Currently she is the featured book reviewer for KinkyBooks.com who occasionally takes her to conventions each year. She has presented workshops and lectures for college groups and regional conventions for several years. Please feel free to visit her website currently at http://www.kiva.net/~teckhart/